METALLIC RED

JENNIFER ANN SHORE

Digital ISBN: 978-1-7326083-4-4

Print ISBN: 978-1-7326083-5-1

*For Dominic, my slick
chrome American prince.
I love you unconditionally
and always congruently.*

1

If I were fully human, my negotiation skills would make me something of a legend, like a diplomat bargaining for the release of POWs, a lawyer campaigning for prison reform, or a drug kingpin working a global supply chain. Instead, I used my talent — honed after reading, watching, listening, and researching anything that could help my case — to go to high school.

From everything I understood about humans, most eighteen-year-olds would be celebrating the freedom earned with age and experience, not campaigning to follow a bell schedule and do homework, but I missed out on those things and so many others.

I didn't have friends, just associates of my family and the businesses who weren't interested in what I watched online or read about in a fiction book. Rather than running around at recess or playing in the mud, I spent most of my childhood sitting silently in meetings or studying on my own.

I had no curfew, no inside jokes, no real meaningful life and experience to speak on, and I craved it, just like I craved blood.

For months, I wore my parents down. At first, I merely posed the idea, and then I talked in hypotheticals. After that, I started leaving school brochures around the house.

My mother tended to indulge my questions and curiosity about being human, and I expected her to take my side or at least to understand why I wanted to explore the human side of myself. I'd spent the past eighteen years being surrounded by vampires or no one at all.

When it came down to it, though, she stayed silent beside my father, who saw no benefit and made it clear. Each time I asked, I tugged at the invisible thread of his patience, attempting to unravel a reaction into something I could leverage, but he remained stoic. Typical vampire.

"My answer will not change, no matter how often you attempt to do so," he said darkly against the natural light of our kitchen.

Once again, I rehashed my argument, all the details of the preparation and benefits of my integration with humans, while he poured blood from a bag into my favorite mug.

"And when is the last time we had any information on or allies with the local young, human population in our area?" I added, digging for anything that might sway the decision in my favor.

He slid the nearly full cup across the counter into my open palm. "Why would I need a teenage ally?"

"Because in some cases, teenagers have the power to sway adults," I said, taking a sip to hide my smirk.

I thought it entertaining, but I appeared to be the only one.

"Your self-interest reveals your naïveté, Mina," my father said evenly. "Do you understand what kind of risk you'd put us in each and every single day? You've done your research and have an argument, I'll admit that, but it's rife with your own selfishness. You do not have the level of discipline required to endure it."

"To endure what?" I asked, staring him down across the kitchen counter.

"Humans."

"Humans," I repeated, fidgeting at his response.

This was the opportunity I patiently waited for, the flaw in his logic that I could pounce on, drawing from my over-full notebook of reasoning. I was ready for it.

"How can you say all of that when I am, in fact, half-human myself?" I asked bitterly.

He remained silent and still, and as I geared up to lay into him, he locked eyes with my mother in a silent conversation.

"Mina." My mother's voice was gentle enough to halt the floodgates before I even opened them. "I can tell you're on the cusp of a very succinct argument, but I think we all know who has the final say in this."

Another nudge toward my victory. "The King?" I asked, so innocently.

I picked up the phone from the dock and pressed the number for Trinity, my uncle's secretary, on the speed dial. She skipped the pleasantries and patched me through to the correct line, and he greeted me with tentative enthusiasm.

Five minutes after I uttered, "Uncle Derrick, I have a proposition for you," I had an agreement.

I hung up the phone.

"Overruled," I practically sang.

Surprisingly, my father showed the slightest hint of emotion on his face. The scowl barely registered as a flicker of anger before it morphed again into his typical neutral mask.

"We'll see about that."

He stormed out, and my mother chased after him without a second glance in my direction.

Whatever campaigning he did to oppose Uncle Derrick's agreement apparently faltered because less than one week later, Trinity falsified documents, arranged registration, updated my wardrobe, and notified me that I was all set to attend high school.

All of that preparation on my part, hers, and the ones she hired eventually led me to a half-filled parking lot, anxiously tapping my steering wheel. Vampires didn't approve of needless movement, but here, locked in my Jeep, I could be as nervous and restless as I wanted to.

Although I had to remind myself to be rigid and collected around other vampires, I watched enough movies to know that I couldn't completely relax around humans, either. I understood the clichés of a new girl starting a new school in her senior year and all the possible personalities I was up against, but I thought I was more prepared than the average teenage protagonist.

Two nights ago, once Trinity confirmed which school I would attend, I broke in. With no need or desire to sleep, my nights were usually spent holed up in my room or on solo adventures. Breaking and entering was a new activity for me. I climbed in through the unlocked library window and borrowed the yearbooks to read through the crowning achievements of those in my grade and memorized names and faces.

If there was a game show dedicated to handing out money for knowing names and details of people they've never met, I would go home with millions — and a valid reason to do some deep self-reflection on my life direction.

As more students arrived and filed in, I inhaled gratuitously, finding the fullness of air in my lungs comforting somehow, like I was whole instead of split between two entirely different kinds of beings. I expelled the air and opened the door, reminding myself to move somewhat clumsily, like most humans did.

With my bag slung over my shoulder, I flicked the car door shut, cringing slightly when it slammed. My Jeep stuck out in the throng of German and Japanese sports cars, but no one paid attention to it, me, or my accidental demonstration of my strength. Still, it served as a reminder that I needed to be very careful.

I fixed my eyes forward and followed the path up to the front doors. I didn't get a chance to do too much looking around at night, and in the day, the property and building were more charming than I expected. The brown bricks contrasted the white columns and green, well-maintained grass, and it gave off a sort of homey yet prestigious vibe — a far cry from the lockers with graffiti, rebellious students smoking cigarettes in the bathrooms, and overall grunginess I saw in nineties movies.

As I crossed the threshold into the building, the volume

of chatter from the cafeteria increased. I peeked in, curious to see why the students congregated there, and the smell of hot grease invaded my senses.

I coughed violently, expelling the rancid air from my lungs, and darted into the main office.

The scent dissipated when I closed the door as quickly and gently as I could, but I had to actively tune out the sound of playing cards slapping against tabletops and the occasional bout of laughter.

"Are you all right?" The scratchy voice belonged to the receptionist, who sat low behind a high, dark wooden desk.

She seemed to be in her forties, judging by the permed curly hairstyle that was popular when she was my age. Her perfume, dotted on her wrist and sprayed across her neck, distracted me from the faint scent of coffee on her breath. She popped a piece of peppermint chewing gum, and the thought of chewing a scented piece of rubber repulsed me just as much as whatever was cooked in the kitchens across the hall.

"Are you all right?" she asked again, waving her hand in front of my face.

I forced myself to blink, composing myself. "Today is my first day. I was told to arrive here to check in and that you'd have my schedule and anything else I needed?"

After fishing out my wallet, I slid my driver's license across the counter, and she studied my name and address.

"Mina Byron," she said, slowly, before keying it into the computer. "I've got you right here. Actually… let me see something."

I wiggled my toes to the tick of the clock. My bright white tennis shoes blended into the white marble flooring.

I smoothed the early signs of wrinkles on the front of my shirt. New clothes always felt a little too stiff against my skin, but I was grateful that I didn't have to wear a uniform. Well, a uniform by human standards, at least — my closet full of new clothes was brighter and more modern than most vampires tended to wear.

Even with an extended lifetime and large sums of money, made mostly from human manipulation, vampires were fickle beings. The notion of hiding in plain sight was taken literally on most occasions, remaining silent in public and wearing lots of black to blend in, but I believed it usually made them stand out.

The woman blew a tiny bubble with her gum and chomped it between her teeth, catching my attention once again.

"Do you need any other information from me?" I asked.

She squinted at the screen. "You just moved here?"

"No," I said simply before I offered up additional context that I knew humans expected and loved. "We've always lived in this region. With my father's work, home-schooling was more practical, but things have settled down enough to where I could attend school in person."

She blew the air out of her mouth in a way that fluffed her bangs away from her forehead.

"Big change for senior year," she quipped, eyes still focused on her computer. "Judging by your coursework, you'd be able to take the GED and skip the rest of the year. I should have done that, but no, I had to stay close to my deadbeat boyfriend."

Her brow furrowed.

"Oh, this is weird."

"What is?" I asked.

She pressed her lips into a thin line, clearly not going to indulge me on whatever she saw. I tried and failed to read the reflection of the screen in the window behind her.

A very real sense of panic crept up at the idea of Trinity's contact somehow messing up my paperwork. I stayed out of the details for whatever she had to do to jump the waitlist and get me into the school, which meant I didn't know how to lie my way out of it.

She scratched her temple with a long acrylic nail.

"They adopted a new scheduling system over the summer before I got hired, and I think there is a mistake," she explained. "You're in every advanced and AP class offered, but you don't have a lunch hour."

The relief was instant and palpable enough to me that I could have hugged her.

"Oh, no, that was intentional," I explained. "I have to fast during the day. It's a special diet for a medical condition. I've had it since I was born."

I said the words quickly, trying to make it sound genuine, as if I hadn't practiced it in the mirror dozens of times while watching makeup tutorials.

The woman gave my appearance a once-over, taking in the contrast of my dark hair to near-translucent skin. "You do look pale."

I tapped my fingernails on the counter.

"Sorry, that was rude of me," she backtracked, glancing at the streaky lines of self tanner on her arm.

Humans apologized for telling the truth, contrasting the directness I was accustomed to with vampires. I found it endearing.

She beelined for the printer, mumbling to herself along the way, as the office door swung open, amplifying the sound of students emptying into the hallway from the cafeteria.

I braced myself for the awful food smell, but an artificial woodsy scent flooded my senses.

"Hey, Deb," the deep, male voice called as he stepped in.

He nearly barreled straight into me, but I sidestepped to avoid all contact.

"Oh, sorry."

I glanced up to see an apologetic frown that belonged to... Charlie Schenley. He had a buzz cut in last year's yearbook photo, so it took me a second to place the human standing before me with overgrown blond hair.

"It's okay," I said, but I wasn't sure him touching me in any fashion would have been anything other than a complete disaster.

Charlie stepped up to the counter and leaned his elbows on the smooth surface. Even in a simple shirt, low-slung jeans, and boots, I was certain he could step into any magazine shoot and hold his own. His limbs and muscles were long and lean, courtesy of hours on the soccer field — midfielder, if I recalled correctly — and he had such a relaxed way about him that I was desperate to emulate.

I became conscious of my own severely perfect posture and forced myself to slouch. I tried a few different arm gestures and positions, but it felt awkward and unnatural. Charlie's head inclined toward me, so I busied myself with the task of picking up my license from where the receptionist discarded it and putting it back into my wallet.

He cleared his throat. "Is Deb around?"

"You're asking me?"

He gestured around the empty office. "Who else would I be asking?"

"Right," I said lamely.

I focused my hearing on the small room at the end of the hall. The machine beeped in rapid succession until a bang erupted. Deb cursed and tore a few pieces of paper.

"I think she's fighting the printer," I guessed.

He bit a smile at the corner of his mouth. "Is she winning?"

Another bang reverberated down the hallway loud enough that even his fully human ears could pick up on it.

"I guess not," he answered his own question.

Deb had the papers I needed, so I stayed rooted to my spot, but I wondered what Charlie needed from her. I wanted to ask what he was waiting on. Would it be rude to pry? He was on a first-name basis with her, so there was familiarity there.

He tossed the hair off his forehead with the flick of his fingers, making me aware that my own hair fell flat on either side of my face.

Deb stomped back toward us with a folder. She gripped a small stack of papers and a folder in her hands. Her entire demeanor changed from agitated to pure delight when Charlie came into her line of sight.

"Hey, Deb," he said simply.

She all but melted as she shoved everything from her hands into mine, never breaking eye contact with Charlie.

"Charlie," she grinned. "This is twice in one week you've come by to see me."

"Coach said that I turned in a spring sports permission slip by mistake," he explained, cutting straight to the point. "Do you have any left for fall?"

She hurried back around her desk and rifled through drawers.

The bell rang over the loudspeaker, completely startling me as I flipped through my class schedule, list of school events, and other flyers. Charlie seemed unfazed by the urgency of the students in the hallway making their way to class, and I wondered if I should be more like them or him. I opened the folder, looking for some guidance but found none.

"Excuse me," I interrupted, catching their attention. "There aren't any directions here."

Deb waved me off. "The map of the school is in the folder."

"No, it's not that," I clarified. "I didn't see any guidance on how the bell system works."

Charlie regarded me as if I were from another planet.

"She was homeschooled," Deb explained to him before turning back to me. "If you look at your class schedule, there's a timetable at the bottom of when the periods begin and end, and the bell rings with about five minutes between to move about and use the restroom if you need to."

"And the one I just heard was…" I checked the paper. "The notice to get to the first period? But that's in one minute, and I have AP Bio on the third floor. I'll never make it in time."

"Deb will write you a pass," Charlie offered, seeming almost bored by the entire exchange.

I wasn't sure that he was the one who got to make decisions like that, but she quickly obliged. She scribbled on a pink piece of paper and sent me off, shifting her focus back to her conversation with Charlie.

After shoving the information into my bag, I tore out of the office, taking the most direct route possible to class. I avoided the stragglers in the hallway, all of whom appeared to have no sense of urgency or punctuality.

I showed up late and frazzled, fully prepared to make a public apology, but Mrs. Scott ushered me in with a smile.

"Mina Byron, I assume?"

"Yes," I confirmed.

"Take any open seat and follow along as best you can for today," she instructed. "See me after class with any questions, and we can talk about your make-up work."

I took a seat at an empty table in the front. Once I settled in and retrieved a notebook and a pen, I realized I made the wrong decision in seating choice. Having my back to a room full of humans made me feel exceptionally vulnerable. I could practically feel their stares drilling into the back of my head. Channeling some learned human nonchalance, I flipped my hair back and focused on absorbing every single second of Mrs. Scott's lecture.

When the bell rang, signaling the end of the session, I approached her tentatively. I didn't need anything clarified, and I was grateful she didn't seem bothered by it. I wasn't sure how teachers would react to my homeschooling cover story, but Mrs. Scott merely sent me off with an assignment on genetics that would replace the first lab they completed the week prior. The requirements and explanation were longer than my paper had to be, and I chuckled a little bit as I located my next class.

AP Calculus, Spanish 4, and AP English followed a similar pattern. The subjects were drastically different, but the demeanor and structure remained the same. I gained a little more confidence every time the bell rang, a loud reminder that I was fulfilling my wish to lean into my human side and passing each little forty-minute test.

I tried to focus on flaws to help fit in. Humans listen to music too loud, leave their mouths open when they chew, say the wrong thing at the wrong time, and perspire when they're feeling nervous. While not all of those things were possible for me — I rarely ate or listened to music, and I couldn't sweat — I channeled nervousness when I felt calm, stumbled over my words when I knew clearly what I wanted to say, and asked questions instead of spouting the answers.

It was annoying, challenging, and the most fun I'd had in years.

While some students zoned out in lectures, I concentrated on shunning my vampire instincts. It went against the years of careful conditioning to fit into the mold of vampirism, and if I was honest with myself, it was more taxing than I expected. By the time I made it to the library for my independent study, I was ready for a break. The quiet block of time to let my mind race without thinking of how to respond and engage with the humans was much needed.

When I approached the librarian to explain my existence, she was too preoccupied scrolling through a dating site to do anything other than point me toward the back tables.

I walked past the tall rows of bookshelves and clusters of desktop computers to sit across from Eloise Clark. She smiled at, the same one from her yearbook photo, and I forced the motion back to her. I was more accustomed to vampires bowing or shaking the hand of an influential human. Either would be odd for a normal, human high school girl to do.

She refocused on her magazine, lazily flipping through the pages. The others around us texted on their phones or read on e-readers. I made a mental note to have Trinity purchase those things for me.

I rifled through my bag and pulled out my English assignment, the first six chapters of *Jane Eyre,* a classic I'd already read more times than I could count. I tuned out the world around me, and in the margins, I began translating the first few lines to Spanish then Italian, loving how the formal style of English used in the 1800s translated so fluidly. I didn't have to pretend to be enthralled.

While trying to recall the correct verb conjugation of "cluster," Eloise's stomach growled, and I jerked up in surprise.

"Sorry," she whispered. "I left my lunch on the bus."

My body reacted very differently when I needed sustenance, so I found humor in her cheeks turning pink. If only she knew about the full-body convulsions, the descending of my fangs, and if I was really desperate, the burning of my eyes. A little stomach grumble was nothing.

Her gaze dropped back to her magazine, and I stared at her, collecting all the details I missed at first glance. The shade-too-yellow highlights that were likely meticulously applied from a box. The smudged nail polish and slightly uneven filing of an at-home manicure. Her bag bore a brand name but was a little worn, and the pattern came out at least three years ago.

I wasn't the only one trying to fit in, and I wasn't sure who was doing a better job of it. Feeling a little softness toward her, I pulled a chocolate bar, the only human food I consistently liked to eat, from the front pocket of my bag and offered it to her.

"You sure?" Her voice was low, but I caught the surprise in it.

My inner alarm sounded. As I debated the appropriateness of the gesture, gratitude rolled across her features. She swallowed, and I didn't miss the eagerness in her expression.

"Go ahead," I encouraged softly

She peeled the wrapper and devoured the chocolate, practically drooling. I stopped myself from inhaling the sweet scent of chocolate I loved so much because of our proximity. It was better to be overcautious in my situation, to not risk breathing in the exquisite scent of human skin or listening to the sound of blood pumping in their chests.

Eloise sighed with happiness, and I forced my attention back to my book, repeating the same lines over and over in my head to distract myself. I shouldn't have thought about the skin or the blood. I needed to focus on what Mrs. Reed was saying to Jane, Eliza, John, and Georgiana. Eventually, by stubborn determination of will, I did. I lost myself in their words and my little trilingual project.

From somewhere inside my mind, I registered Eloise

swallowing the last bit of chocolate. I doubted it would be enough calories to keep her hunger in check for an extended period of time, but the combination of sugar and fat would provide temporary relief.

She smoothed the wrapper down across the wooden table top, and the sound scratched in my ears.

"Shit," Eloise gasped.

Her finger raised to her eye level, and she examined the small splinter embedded into her skin. I knew what she was going to do before she did it, but instead of figuring out some way to stop it, I completely froze.

Eloise brought her hand to her mouth and gripped the splinter between her teeth. In a smooth motion, she flicked her hand forward and blew the splinter on the floor. If I wasn't terrified, I'd be slightly repulsed at her actions.

She cursed again as a small dot of blood appeared on her hand.

I forced my mouth shut, catching the cry in my throat. A tremor ran down my left leg. I gripped my chair, only loosening my grip when the wood began to crack. I didn't trust myself to move, to rush off to the bathroom, to do anything other than sit and force the stillness.

The next thirty minutes were pure torture, even when the small dot clotted. I closed my eyes and tried my best to think of anything other than the delicious, metallic scent of blood.

When the bell rang, I was relieved to open my eyes and discover that everyone around me was too caught up in their own selves to see the half-human, half-vampire teetering on the brink of insanity.

2

The Code of Conduct, set forth by the kings and queens of the regions in the United States of America, explicitly prohibited revealing oneself as a vampire to humans unless there was an intent to turn them into vampires.

I have always been aware of this rule, of course, as all vampires are, but Uncle Derrick reminded me of it three times during our negotiation. He made me promise that if I felt out of control, even for a second, while attending human school that I would bolt. Whatever fallout my exit would cause, he would deal with excuses or coverups, but I just had to flee at even the inkling of revealing my true nature.

All of the preparation, hope, and excitement I had for getting close to humans was nearly undone by a chocolate bar and a tiny sliver of wood.

"Stay human, stay human, stay human," I whispered to myself.

I hustled out of the library and was even more careful

about avoiding human contact in the crowded hallway. The errant elbows and innocent bumps, all normal human gestures, were grenades with catastrophic consequences for me.

My lips barely moved, but repeating the mantra helped. I once read a study about the power of the mind, how positive thinking can help heal the body, and I was serving as my own living, semi-breathing lab rat.

In a fleeting moment, I recalled my father's warnings about my own selfishness and the risk I posed by putting myself in this situation. I shook it off, needing to focus on defying my own nature and proving my own strength.

As long as I made it to the next classroom, and then to the gymnasium for my last class, I could speed home to a blood bag.

I wound the corner into my next class, Health, and beelined for a seat in the back by an open window. The fresh oxygen provided the tiniest bit of relief. I counted each breath, in and out, slowly, bringing gradual reprieve to my trembling muscles and aching gums.

By the time the bell rang, I managed to relax slightly against the cool metal of the chair. I pressed my palms against my thighs and exhaled through my mouth.

"Move," a high voice snapped above me.

I glanced up at Brooklyn Winters, the class president and yearbook editor. The photos I saw didn't do her ferocity justice.

She leered at me, trying to intimidate me out of the seat. Her dark brown hair was cut in an ultra-modern blunt bob, emphasizing the severity of her bone structure. She crossed her arms across her chest and waited for me to obey her demand.

My brain scrambled for how to best react to the situation. Refusing her meant I'd make an enemy of a powerful person in the high school social construct. Obliging her meant I could lose the lifeline helping me hold myself together.

"Winters, take a seat," Mr. Berry ordered in a bored tone.

He closed the door behind him, stepped up to the podium in front of the class, and flipped open his laptop.

"I'd love to, but she's in it," Brooklyn pouted and tilted her head in my direction.

She seemed to be very accustomed to getting things just the way she wanted them.

Mr. Berry rolled his eyes, and I liked him already.

"Take a vacant seat," he said, emphasizing the latter half of the sentence, and gestured to the open rows.

Brooklyn huffed like a petulant child and stomped toward the front of the classroom. Every pair of eyes in the room flittered between the two of us, waiting for some smug response or reaction from me.

"So, you must be Mina Byron," Mr. Berry said as he tapped the touchpad on his laptop.

I nodded.

He raised his eyebrows in a mocking glare. "Is there anything you'd like to add to your introduction, or can I begin?"

"I'm all set, thank you." Despite my inner turmoil, my voice came across as clear and confident.

"Okay then, let's get started." Mr. Berry leaned forward

on his elbows. "Now that we've finished our unit on sexual reproduction, we were going to do the classic couple up and take care of an egg experiment, but Dean Pritchert stopped that after the senior prank last year left him with an egged house."

"Hell yeah," Tanner Cannon called out, high-fiving a few guys around him.

Tanner Cannon. Soccer player. Defender, maybe. I tried to remember where he stood in the team photo last year or what his jersey number was, but the black and white image in my mind was a little fuzzy.

"So what's the plan for this year then?" Eloise asked.

I couldn't help but glare at her from my vantage point. She, sugared up and curious about classwork, had no idea what I went through because of her. I stifled my resentment as best I could. Festering ill will for something completely out of her control probably wasn't healthy.

"Some outdated lessons on check writing or personal finance?" Brooklyn offered. "You know there are apps for that. And credit cards someone else pays for."

Mr. Berry drummed his hands. "Well, for starters, we shut up and listen when the teacher is speaking."

I swallowed a chuckle.

"This year, we will be pairing up, sans egg, and working through the standard realities and challenges of a married couple, including setting a budget, creating a schedule, and managing household tasks."

He dumped a stack of papers on the desk in front of him, and Nick Adelman — debate club and National Honor Society — begrudgingly passed them out. I flipped through the packet as Mr. Berry explained more details on what to expect. There would be mini-projects along the way, ending with a final, co-written paper.

It seemed straightforward enough, just like all of the assignments that had been doled out in classes, but this would be the first one I would need to work on with someone else. I glanced around, surprised to see the others were just as agitated and eager to see who they would be partnered with as I was.

For them, it was all about social status and work distribution, but I just hoped whoever I was partnered with wouldn't violate my personal space. I noticed Tanner had a habit of resting his hand on the shoulder of the person he was speaking to, and human females tended to be a little handsy with their friends. I'd built up an imaginary three-foot perimeter around myself, a safe distance to not set me off or catch me by surprise, and I crossed my fingers that I wouldn't be paired with someone who insists on greeting after-school sessions with hugs or something.

I took in the room and nearly recoiled as I noticed Charlie Schenley, the guy from the main office in the morning. He sat at my right, lazily dragging his finger across the page as Mr. Berry read aloud, only stopping to mark due dates with his pencil. My eyes followed the lines on his arm and how his muscles adjusted to the movement of his hands.

With his head tilted down, his unruly hair fell forward. My fingers itched to touch the ends, to push it back off his forehead like he did earlier. I rested my chin on my palm and took the slightest of inhales, absorbing the scent of the fresh green grass on his sneakers and the spearmint gum between his teeth.

Mr. Berry cleared his throat, a natural movement while flipping to the fourth page of the packet, which snapped me out of my trance.

I was just far enough out of my seat for it to be unnatural, so I righted myself back toward the front. I'd read about the feeling of breaking out in a cold sweat, and if I could do such a thing, it would have been the time. I glanced over at him again, unable to help myself.

Charlie traced his lip with the eraser on his pencil. Sensing my scrutiny, he looked over at me. His eyes met mine in a familiar way that indicated he knew I'd been sitting next to him the entire time. Had he been watching me? Taking in my reaction? Seeing how off-kilter I was?

I didn't get answers to my questions, but he did offer me a sly smile that went all the way up to his eyes.

Mr. Berry began assigning partners, recapturing my attention. "Marissa, you're with Nick. Eloise, you can pair with..."

Multiple hands shot up in the air.

"Mr. Berry, with all due respect," Brooklyn interrupted, not sounding like she offered any respect at all, actually. "I don't think it's fair that you get to pick my husband for me. I'd like to have a say in who I'm purchasing a home and naming my children with."

Tanner chimed in, "Yeah, no high-maintenance chicks for me, Mr. B."

"Is there a reason why you are discriminating against same-sex couples?" Eloise asked.

"Jesus Christ," he said, exasperated. "Just pick your own partners and have your first assignment in by next Friday."

In vampire culture, no one would have dared to disrespect another like that, but in this setting, Mr. Berry merely crossed the room, sank back into his office chair, and began scrolling on his phone, effectively tuning us out.

One by one, people in the room paired off with their friends or significant others, from what I could pick up on. With no friends or a significant other of my own, I decided to ask Mr. Berry if I could work on the assignment by myself instead of waiting around for one of the stragglers to approach me. I didn't even mind if I missed out on points for not having a partner.

I felt like I needed to seem occupied as the chatter and decision-making of the other students picked up, even though no one bothered to look in my direction, so I dug through my bag.

"Charlie?" Brooklyn called, a false sweetness dripping from the word.

She rolled her hips as she walked back to perch herself on top of his desk.

He sighed. "Brooklyn," Charlie said evenly.

"So are we doing this thing?"

It was a question, but it wasn't.

She leaned back, palms against the surface, and crossed her legs. The confidence within her poured out as she flipped her hair and watched him with wide eyes. She wanted to display her dominance of the situation, and of him, and he wasn't having it.

He dragged his fingers through his overgrown blond ends. "Nah, I'm good."

"Excuse me?"

The bell wasn't due to ring for another ninety seconds, but he stood up, pulling his bag over his shoulder.

"I'm with Mina on this."

Her jaw dropped, and he winked at me before he turned the door handle and left the room.

As trivial as this project was in the span of a human life, Brooklyn seemed devastated by his reaction. She stared at the vacant doorway as the waves of disbelief, hurt, and then embarrassment rolled over her face.

The bell rang, and she jumped off his desk.

"Eloise," she said, impatiently. "Let's go."

Eloise's eyes darted over to me, offering me somewhat of an apologetic look before extending her arm for Brooklyn to loop hers through.

As luck would have it, my final class of the day, Physical Education, was with Brooklyn. She glared at me from across the gymnasium throughout the entire demonstration of proper running and stretching form. For the first time since I stepped foot on school grounds, I couldn't wait to be back among the safety and familiarity of vampires.

3

I gripped the steering wheel so hard that my knuckles were even whiter than usual. I accelerated out of the school parking lot, and with the radio cranked, I tried to focus on the senseless chatter, once again trying not to fall apart.

My arms jerked, and I swerved. I held a hunched, tense posture as I drove twenty above the speed limit on windy roads toward my neighborhood. The woods and rows of houses blurred in my peripheral vision, and I was grateful for the lack of midday traffic. I parked in the driveway, not having the patience to wait for the garage door to open, and dashed inside.

As my shoes met the hardwood floor of the hallway, I let go of everything I held in. The release of tension snapped like a rubber band, and I seized forward and fell to the floor.

My fangs fully descended while my body convulsed. I forced my limbs forward and crawled my way to the fridge, dragging my useless jerking legs along like a scene in a horror firm. I ripped off the handle as I flung the door open.

I brought a blood bag up to my mouth and tore at the plastic casing with my fangs. The familiar rich and salty taste hit my tongue, and I instantly relaxed, sucking the thick liquid in a steady rhythm through the puncture holes.

I drained the first bag with ease. The second one trickled down my throat and filled the emptiness I felt inside my stomach. The third one was my form of dessert, topping off the necessity with pleasure.

Now fully satisfied, I breathed heavily.

"Three bags? That bad of a first day, Mina?" Uncle Derrick asked, gliding into the kitchen.

I cringed at my current sprawled-out state. The empty blood bags were strewn about with droplets sprinkled across the floor. I couldn't decide if I was more embarrassed for being so barbaric or more angry that I wasted those precious drops.

Uncle Derrick took up residence on one of the barstools, looking down at me in silence as I righted myself. I cleaned up the mess swiftly with bleach and dropped the empty bags in our biohazard container underneath the sink.

I checked for blood specks on my clothing and ran my fingers through my hair, deciding that if nothing outwardly looked amiss, I could pretend like everything was normal.

"Can I offer you a glass, Uncle?" I asked politely.

He folded his hands on the countertop. "If there's any left."

I reached for the door and frowned when I realized the handle was still across the room.

"I just came to see how your first day was."

"As my uncle or the King?" Usually the lines were blurred between the two roles, but I wanted clarity on how forthcoming I should be.

"Both," he admitted, accepting the bag and wine glass from me. "I'm genuinely curious about the experience my niece had, but as you are aware, the nobles are interested as well."

I stopped myself from groaning.

The nobles were a group of vampires who helped advise my uncle and run the region through various business dealings and relationship building. They were always extremely curious and a little wary of me, so I tended to keep my distance. That would soon change as part of my concession in the negotiation with my uncle.

As the King of Appalachia, Uncle Derrick has a responsibility to the region to protect vampires and ensure the longevity and success of our kind. As my uncle, he acts like more of a parental figure to me than my biological ones. My parents showed affection for me in their own way, but it sometimes felt like more of an obligation to them than anything else.

From what I understood, it was quite a shock when my father announced that he impregnated a human and intended to turn her after she gave birth. That scenario happened only a handful of times in Appalachia because most vampires are bitten, not born.

I've only met one other person like me, a man named Antonio, who was born thirty years before me. He had fangs, but he preferred human food to blood, and he needed to sleep. I couldn't imagine giving eight hours each night to nothing.

There are only a handful of half-vampire, half-humans because, from what Uncle Derrick has been able to track down, the fetus usually kills the human mother and itself. For whatever reason, luck maybe, I survived, and Uncle Derrick loved me for it.

I spent more time with him at the mansion than I did wherever my parents called home. Growing up, they spent periods of time away, traveling for pleasure or on errands for my uncle. When I turned sixteen, after nearly a year in the southern part of the region, they bought the house and cars and decided it was time to try to act like a normal family.

At first, I was excited to finally have the attention of my parents. I welcomed it because, even as Uncle Derrick's protégé, I felt lonely. He taught me about business, politics, and vampirism. On the rare occasions he traveled overseas, he always brought me back gifts, usually chocolate, while Trinity arranged tutors and kept me as busy as the schedule would permit.

Still, I felt a void in my life, one that I assumed was because of the distant relationship with my parents, but eventually, as I began to sneak out and observe humans, I realized it was because I shunned half of my being. Uncle Derrick always encouraged my curiosity about humans, which is why I knew he would, at the very least, consider indulging me in my desire to spend more time with them.

"So, dear one, tell me all about it," he encouraged, tapping the seat beside him.

After a day of hiding my abilities, I hopped over the

counter with ease, landing gracefully at his side. He pulled at the tube of the blood bag and poured the contents into the glass, then took a sip, waiting for me to begin.

"It was fine," I said. "Boringly, humanly fine. I was on time to every class. I took notes. I have homework."

It wasn't a lie, necessarily, but an omission of the complete truth.

He seemed amused by my response. "First day and you already have assignments?"

"Well, it was my first day, but everyone else started a few weeks ago," I explained. "Don't you remember when you were a human and in high school?"

"Vaguely," he admitted.

He once told me that the more years he spent as a vampire, the fuzzier his human memories became, like an out-of-focus dream that gradually slipped away. I couldn't relate. Dreams required sleep, and as hard as I tried, I couldn't slip into that altered consciousness.

"Explain to me how your day is structured."

I gave him a brief rundown of classes, breaking it down into periods and semesters, along with the extracurricular clubs and activities. He seemed particularly interested in the specific topics covered in class, even going as far as to ask me to walk him through a few of my homework assignments. I dumped out my folders and papers on the counter and watched him flip through the material at lightning speed.

"You're taking Spanish? You were fluent before age ten."

"It doesn't hurt to brush up," I shrugged.

It was either that or choir, and I didn't relish the idea of standing up and singing to entertain groups of humans.

"What is this Health class here?" His eyes raked over the first page of the packet explaining the project that Mr. Berry read in his monotone voice hours ago. "Could these learnings be used to our advantage in our relationship with the human major medical companies?"

I sighed. This was the kind of stuff he wanted to report back to the nobles.

"Not exactly. AP Biology might be more useful in understanding human bodily functions, but this one is more of a guide for a sound and successful life."

"Humans, of course, need to be taught to do that."

He was usually the most understanding, but this belittling irked me.

"Well, vampires do, too," I defended, facing him full on. "How to follow the Code of Conduct, how to remain unnoticed, how to use discretion."

"Clearly, I have failed you," he said, gesturing to the floor where my euphoric blood bath occurred.

Uncle Derrick rarely showed humor, and when he did, it was dry. I couldn't help my small smile from showing.

"Obviously," I agreed.

"So about this first assignment…"

He continued the questions until my parents arrived. My mother joined in, curious enough to ask about the people I interacted with. My father only opened his mouth to greet his brother then stood on the far side of the kitchen.

When the sun began to set, Uncle Derrick suggested we move to the great room.

I sat in one of the chairs in front of the unlit fireplace. If I didn't know any better, the scene before me felt warm and comfortable enough to be human — if only the wine glasses my uncle and parents drank from had actual alcohol in them instead of blood. I had a small serving in a mug, my cup of choice. Maybe it was the human part of me, but it felt more normal to me to have something age appropriate, and I liked the feel of the sturdy ceramic in my hand.

A figure approached the house, causing the four of us to stop our conversation and perk up. One sniff of the air revealed it wasn't human. Vampires had a distinctly metallic scent.

My father stood to open the door and revealed Trinity, Uncle Derrick's secretary. She was tall, blonde, and had a wispy, gentle way about her as she held the ever-present tablet to her chest.

She bowed before addressing him. "Excuse me, your majesty, but the Queen of the Mid-Atlantic awaits your call."

He set down his wine glass and stood up, buttoning his jacket, for style reasons, not practical ones. Fashion was one of Uncle Derrick's many indulgences, even though vampires could weather all seasons completely nude and not be affected. I could handle the elements better than full humans, but it was wildly uncomfortable to have my fangs chatter from the cold.

"Oh, and Mina, would you prefer the seamstress to come here tomorrow early morning or Thursday evening?"

"Probably best to do early mornings," Uncle Derrick answered for me. "She might need some time to recover after school."

"Right, right, human schooling," Trinity said, making a note of it. "Let's do that then. I will send a note to her scheduler now."

She dipped her head again before excusing herself to wait in the car.

I curled my legs up underneath me. "Why do I need a seamstress?"

"For the monthly gathering of nobles in our region," Uncle Derrick pressed. "The one you agreed to attend moving forward as part of our deal."

I put it out of my mind, hoping he'd forget but knowing he wouldn't. He remembered everything.

"I am aware of our agreement," I said honestly. "I just didn't realize I required a seamstress for those."

"Well, you certainly can't wear," he paused, giving me a once over, "whatever this is."

I traced my bare skin through one of the holes in my jeans and conceded to his point.

"Come see me tomorrow evening, Max." Uncle Derrick's tone made it sound like a suggestion, but whatever he wanted was not optional.

My father inclined his head, silently confirming he would oblige.

"Marie, thank you, as always, for the fine hospitality," Uncle Derrick said graciously. "And Mina." He paused, gaze moving back to the door that led to the kitchen. "Mind your strength."

It was code for "Don't let your internal blood store get so depleted that you rip off the refrigerator handle." I appreciated his discretion in front of my parents, so I offered him my best smile before I stood and sprinted up to my room with my schoolbag in hand.

I sat at my desk and tried to take my time with my homework. I wanted to appreciate the motions of solving problems and writing an argument on my new laptop, but I finished it, and my make-up assignments, by midnight.

"Time to get back to the normal routine," I sighed, pulling up YouTube to dive into another session of contouring tutorials.

Out of all the media digested in my lifetime, I'd learned the most about human nature from watching vlogs, which was slightly terrifying to admit to myself. I found the news on standard television too disturbing, even for someone whose skin is as strong as a suit of armor, and while I appreciated movies, I was well aware of their fictional elements.

Noise on the staircase carried up to my room. I could tell it was my mother by her light tread — my father practically stomped on the stone staircase when he walked. She sped up and joined me on the padded bench in front of the window where I liked to sit at night.

It was peaceful, I thought, to look at the moon, especially during the time of night when the sky was as dark as my hair.

She handed me a brand new phone, still in the box, and an e-reader, just like the one I saw in the library. "Derrick had Trinity collect these for you."

"Thank you," I said, sliding a fingernail under the plastic packaging.

"Your father and I got them, too, so we can communicate with you if needed during the day."

My parents never understood the feeling of being torn in half by two different worlds. They tried to empathize with me, and I appreciated it, but even my mother, the more empathetic one of the two, had trouble relating to what it was like these days, so her confession surprised me.

"He agreed to it?"

My father didn't even use the house phone.

"Of course," she said, like it wasn't a big deal. "I also asked Derrick if he wanted Trinity to arrange a phone for him, and he didn't even acknowledge my request with a response."

Many vampires were still wary of technology. My parents had a modern house with a television, set up with my assistance, but there were thousands of vampires living simpler lives from another era in rural areas.

I went along with my father once on an assignment and was baffled by the homes composed of stone, cement, and exposed plywood. It was back when my parents tended to disappear for long periods of time, but for whatever reason, Uncle Derrick asked him to do rounds in the region to ensure the Code of Conduct was followed, that vampires weren't at risk.

On the drive back from that trip, I read through the entire Code and its additions, noting that after I was born, a clause was added to ensure that they would also minimize human harm to best of their ability. It was one of the ways Uncle Derrick had shown solidarity around my existence, his own form of protection, by adding it to the Code and figuring out how to work with the human healthcare system to get access to blood.

The accumulation of centuries-old wealth — as I called

it, blood money — helped.

My mother stood to leave me alone with my thoughts and new technology, but after seeing my expression, she paused.

"Are you all right, Mina?"

I reached for her hand, and she gasped. Vampires were not affectionate creatures, but after seeing humans touch and emote all day, I wanted a little bit of tenderness.

She wiggled out of my grasp, and I turned to hide my frown. In the window, I caught our reflections. I had my father's and Uncle Derrick's ski slope nose, but my long limbs and almond-shaped eyes were hers. The resemblance between us had always been striking, but as I grew up and she stayed outwardly frozen in time, we were now closer in appearance to sisters than mother and daughter.

"What do you remember most about being human?" I asked.

She rarely gave me a glimpse into her own human life, mostly because my father didn't like the subject and he was always around.

With just us, she indulged me. "The pain," she muttered.

"Of turning?"

Her eyes met mine in our reflection. "Of existing."

I chewed on my lip and hoped she would continue.

"The memories of my human life seem out of focus to me, like the dreams I used to have when I would fall asleep."

"Uncle Derrick says that, too," I admitted.

She didn't seem completely surprised that he shared that information with me. "As a human, I did love to sleep, especially those first few weeks after you were born." Her tone was light, nostalgic even. "Your father couldn't be around me when I was healing; the blood drove him crazy. The most vivid memories I have are some of the last ones of you and me together. I tried to keep myself awake long enough for your dad to come and hold you during the night. When I was recovered and healthy by human standards, my life truly began when I turned, and I could focus on you and the years ahead with your father."

This wasn't new information to me, and I became frustrated with the lack of details. "But what about before you met him?" I pressed. "Before I was even a part of the equation?"

She turned away from the window, forcing our eyes to meet in real life, not in glass. "I was just like every other human, caught up in the problems of social status, constantly thinking about the what-ifs. The trivial details all just seem so meaningless compared to everything I have now."

I leaned back into the pillows, trying to digest her words.

"But your experience is so uniquely you, Mina. I was raised human and became a vampire, fully understanding the choice I had and what I was trading in. You've had a foot in each world since you were born, with no say in the matter. I wouldn't wish that on anyone."

From my peripherals, I saw her reach to smooth my hair down. At the last second, she drew her hand back, as if she had an electric shock. Her realization of her own capacity for compassion scared her, and I sensed she wanted to run away from it.

"The seamstress should arrive in a few hours," my mother said, backing out of my room.

She was genuine in sharing her feelings, but I found nothing but emptiness and slight pity at how distant she kept her memories. Vampires mock humans for what they value and worry about, their quest to find meaning and share it with someone, but the summation of it all was what I thought made life worth living.

4

Each day in close proximity to humans got a little easier.

In the week since I started school, I spent so many hours studying their reactions and conversations that I could start anticipating moods and movements, which helped me hold myself together throughout the day. I still didn't inhale fully, but I only needed one recovery blood bag when I arrived home.

The biggest challenge was to lean into my human side, especially slowing myself down in Physical Education. It was easy on yoga and meditation days, but when we were outside on the track, it was against my instincts to let a few people go ahead.

My teachers called on me regularly in class, even when I didn't have my hand raised, and other students began casually greeting me, usually with a smile, in the halls and when I sat down in class.

I made it a point to always sit by a window, but as we moved into the crisper fall temperatures, I was disappointed that most teachers began sealing their windows shut. Ms. Semple, my AP English teacher, ran hot, so she left hers open. I could smell a light dusting of perspiration when she walked down the rows. Aside from loving the coursework, I could always count on a few breaths of fresh air for the duration of class, until the day I walked in to find the desks arranged in pods of four, denoting the shift into group work for the next week, as she had noted in the syllabus.

Finding as close to my usual seat as I could, I hunkered down, skeptically watching the others file in to see who would join me.

"Ms. Semple?" I asked, calling for her attention. "Do you mind?"

I pointed to the window crank, and she waved her hand, giving me permission to go ahead. I fiddled with the lock, nearly breaking it entirely. When the fresh air hit my face, I sat back down.

"Damn, Mina, you must be cold blooded or something," Tanner said, pulling on a hooded sweatshirt with the school's logo and the soccer team's championship years on it.

I forced a laugh and grabbed the copy of *Jane Eyre* from my bag, along with my notebook and a mechanical pencil. I wanted to have more conversations with humans, but I was terrified I'd ask something stupid or obvious and give myself away. I stared at the collection of numbers listed on his chest.

"So you play soccer?" I asked.

Tanner laughed. "Play? More like I live for it."

"Oh." I planned to go down a YouTube rabbit hole of

the fundamentals after school. "Cool," I added. I felt like a fraud when I used human slang.

"We have a game on Thursday night," he mentioned nonchalantly. "You should come watch."

My head snapped sideways, skeptical at the easy-going invitation. I didn't want to seem overeager, so I paused, pretending to mull it over.

He cocked an eyebrow. "You have something better to do?"

"Maybe." I didn't.

"Like what?"

I pursed my lips. "I'll go."

"Sweet," he said. "It's a home game, right after school. If you want to paint my number on your face, it's—"

"Why would I want to paint your phone number on my face?" I demanded.

He laughed again. "You're funny." He turned slightly, showing off the number four on his back.

I felt a little stupid at my misinterpretation, recalling that gesture of support from a few sports-based television shows I usually scrolled past. If I were fully human, I would definitely be blushing, but in my current state, I happily distracted myself with the arrival of Nick Adelman from Health. His girlfriend, Rita, also in the National Honor Society, sat across from me and completed our pod.

They were arguing over something when they approached but stopped when they sat down. Rita offered me a warm smile, and I returned it, tucking my hair behind my ears. I noticed human girls did that sometimes. In fact, they seemed to constantly be flipping, examining, or in some way touching their hair.

"I like your earrings, Mina," Rita complimented, eyeing the red roses on my earlobes.

"Thank you. They were... my great-grandmother's."

That was technically true. They belonged to a vampire named Eliza, who turned the man who turned Uncle Derrick and my father. Unlike humans, vampires could choose who would become their blood relatives.

"Are those clip-ons?"

I nodded, thumbing the small red stone in the middle of the petals. Eliza bought them in the late 1800s when clip-ons were gaining popularity. I wondered if I should compliment humans to engage with them more. It was a nice feeling, to be appreciated for making even the smallest effort. I scanned her outfit, a long-sleeved, button-down shirt and jeans, figuring out what I could offer praise for in return.

Before I could, Ms. Semple cleared her throat and began listing off the instructions for the group assignment. We had to spend the period discussing and agreeing on three major themes of the book and then writing them down with examples from the text.

"Team huddle," Tanner whispered loudly, swinging his arms out to pull us all toward the center of the desks.

Before his hand met my back, I practically laid down across the surface, just to avoid human contact. He didn't pick up on my momentary panic.

"Let's get this shit knocked out ASAP and then you NHS kids can help me with my stats homework. It's a take-home test, and I'm going to bomb it without your brains."

"How did you, a C+ student, manage to get into AP English?" Nick asked, partially amused.

"Semple's got a thing for me," he said, winking at her as

she walked by. "Okay, three themes from this dead tree." He held up my copy of *Jane Eyre*, and seeing we didn't share his urgency, he added, "Hurry up, smarties."

"Are we allowed to rush through it like this?" I asked.

The other tables seemed deep in argumentative discussions about what to put on the paper.

Tanner swiped my notebook and pencil. "What do you mean are we allowed? It's one assignment our senior year. If now's not the time to brush past this useless garbage, when is?"

Rita rolled her eyes. "First theme, social status. Jane is of lower class her entire life, and it directly impacts how she feels about herself and her relationship with Mr. Rochester. At the end of the book, when she returns to him with money and wisdom, she can be with him as an equal."

Tanner found a blank page and wrote down her points in chicken scratch, along with mine and Nick's — gender inequality and family, respectively — and we completed our assignment with more than a half an hour to spare.

We all wrote our names across the top, signifying our agreement on all points. Rita dotted the I in her name with a heart, so I followed suit with my own.

"It's interesting how humanity as a whole hasn't really changed that much," I mused. "If you think about it, the problems humans had when this was written centuries ago still apply today." I stopped, and the dots connected in my mind. "I wonder if that's the point of this entire exercise."

"Definitely," Rita agreed. "Like in the book, when Bertha Mason—"

"Enough of this," Tanner interjected, pushing the notebook aside and dropping *Statistics & Probability* in the center of our quad.

Nick sighed. "Okay, what do you need?"

The three of us helped him correct his wrong answers and find the right solutions to the unanswered ones. Working together gave me a sense of unity, like I temporarily belonged with these humans, solving problems, talking, and joking around.

I was a little disappointed when the bell rang, and I headed toward the library with a frown on my face.

"Mina, wait up!" Rita said, jogging to catch up with my strides. "Do you have lunch next? I'm headed to the gym. We can walk together for part of the way."

This was another thing humans did that I found interesting. They walked in packs like werewolves, and some girls even went to the bathroom in pairs. I hadn't come up with a reason to follow anyone in to see what that was about yet.

Rita and I made small talk as we walked. Mostly I stumbled my way through my explanation of my independent study, and she seemed jealous that I got it into my schedule.

We parted ways with a wave, and I spent the period in silent reflection, giving myself a little bit of praise for my first successful group interaction. It felt like I was getting the hang of this human thing.

I glanced at Eloise, who was enthralled in a textbook across the table, and pulled out a notebook to jot down a list of possible things to discuss the hundred-or-so steps it would take us to get from the library to Mr. Berry's room.

If I worked up the courage to talk to her, I decided that I

would compliment her, just like Rita had. When the bell rang for the next class, I was about to ask about her lipstick when she stepped up to me.

"I've been meaning to ask you about that chocolate bar you gave me," Eloise said flatly.

I closed my mouth, internally beginning to panic. Did it make her sick? Was it not good? Was that a weird thing for me to do?

She grinned. "It was honestly like the best thing I've ever eaten in my life, but I couldn't understand the wrapper. What kind was it? Did you get it from one of the stores in the Strip District?"

"Oh," I breathed. "My uncle got it for me. From Paris, I think?"

"I wish I had a jet-setting uncle who collected me chocolate from around the world," she said dreamily, leading the way out of the library.

"Well, he travels sometimes for work," I explained. "He knows it's my favorite human food, so he brings it back for me wherever he goes."

I cringed at my own use of "human food," but she didn't seem fazed by it.

"I don't think chocolate can be someone's favorite food," she teased.

"Why not?" I was genuinely curious and prepared to come up with another answer if I was ever asked that question.

"I guess, like, most people say like, 'I love Italian' or something."

I wrinkled my nose.

"You don't like pasta?" She seemed floored by this. "What kind of person doesn't like pasta?"

As we entered the classroom and sat in our seats, Brooklyn watched us with interest.

"I'm, uh, allergic to garlic," I explained. "So that kind of ruins the entire Italian culinary experience for me."

It was the most cliché thing about vampires, to be put-off by garlic, but I was actually the only vampire I knew who was impacted by its presence. It made a lot more sense after my mom told me she hit up the unlimited salad and breadsticks twice a week at Olive Garden while she was pregnant with me. I'd had enough to last my extended lifetime.

"That sucks," she said.

I shrugged my shoulders, not knowing what else to say. It wasn't that big of a deal for me.

When Mr. Berry wheeled in a cart with a large, flat screen television on it, the room quieted down. I sensed the heart rate of my classmates speeding up in excitement, and there were some under-the-breath cheers. He cued up the film, which turned out to be the first part in an educational series about managing finances.

The voice of a very monotone narrator filled the room, and everyone settled in. He flipped off the lights. I spent so much time alone in the dark watching a flashing screen, and I found the humor in repeating the habit again in daylight but with twenty-some humans. I had never been to a movie theater, and suddenly, I wished I had a big, round carton of buttery popcorn and a box of candy, just like how it is portrayed in shows and films.

I reached down to my bag, wondering if I had another chocolate bar stuffed in one of the pockets.

"Hey," Charlie whispered, leaning down to meet me.

That deep voice and that one word caught my attention.

I glanced around. Half the room watched the movie with glazed-over eyes while others chatted in hushed tones. A few bold classmates were texting and using social media apps.

"Hi," I returned, giving up on my quest for sweets and focusing solely on the flecks of gray in his blue eyes. The colors were muted in the darkened room, but I was close enough to see them with the flicker of lights coming from the screen.

"When are you free after school this week?"

I forced a blink, only to quickly recall that our first assignment was due on Friday.

"Your soccer game is Thursday, right?"

"It is," he confirmed, looking at me. "You're coming to watch?"

I shrugged. "I was invited to."

He smiled and ran his tongue along his bottom lip. "I mean, it's kind of an open invitation, anyone can come watch."

"Tanner made it seem like he was personally inviting me."

"Tanner?"

He glanced over at Tanner, who was bobbing his head along to whatever was playing in his earphones and drummed on his desk with two pencils.

Charlie tweaked his neck slightly, a sign of discomfort in

the awkward position we held. I could have stayed like this indefinitely, but I shifted slightly to rest my elbow on the desk. I leaned in his direction, and he mirrored the motion.

"So you like soccer?" Charlie asked.

I really didn't know much about it. Vampires weren't much for organized sports, but they were irresponsible gamblers in card games and horse races.

"I could," I answered honestly.

He seemed amused. "You could?"

I'd know more about how I felt about the sport after I studied it at home.

"I'll report back," I promised.

"Please do."

A chair screeched against the floor, and Brooklyn's neck craned in our direction, her eyes narrow slits. I checked to make sure that Mr. Berry was still preoccupied with his newspaper.

"So, back to my original question," Charlie pressed. "What about tonight? Are you free to discuss budgeting for our marvelous future together?"

My phone buzzed, the low, soft sound pulling my attention away from Charlie. Swiping it from the side pocket of my bag, I tapped the screen to see an unread message from Trinity, informing me that my dress was hanging in my closet after being altered and steamed by the seamstress.

She tended to have suspiciously impeccable timing, but I did appreciate the reminder of the torture session I was required to attend that evening.

"I can't," I sighed. "I have a... thing."

"A thing?"

"A party."

"On a Tuesday?"

"Yes," I answered him and sent a quick message of gratitude back to Trinity.

When I glanced back at him, Charlie's puzzled expression tipped me off that this entire exchange was not a normal, human one, so I scrambled for a lie. I twirled my phone between my fingers effortlessly, and he watched the motion.

"Well, it's just a little get-together at my uncle's house for his, uh, birthday."

"So, should we both sign the card, letting him know of our nuptials, or are you going to handle this on your own?"

I balked at him, and he immediately smiled.

"You're teasing me," I said, flatly.

"Um, excuse me, Mr. Berry?" Brooklyn's voice, a little shrill, jolted everyone in the room, including our teacher. "Could you please tell the class to quiet down here? Some of us are trying to pay attention."

I turned my head forward. The narrator talked through the difference between a 401k and a Roth IRA. I tried to focus, but I still felt a connection with Charlie, like we weren't finished with our conversation yet.

He inched closer to me, and I stiffened, unsure what his next move would be.

With quick reflexes, by human standards, he took my phone from my lap. Against my better judgment, I let him. A few harmless text messages and my YouTube search history were nothing to worry about, but he was respectful of my privacy.

He pulled up a new contact, entering his own name as HUSBAND and saving it before firing off a quick text to himself so that he'd have my number. He handed my phone back to me with a smile, and I pulled up the message he sent himself.

I cannot wait to see you tomorrow evening, in which I am definitely free and will bring some leftover birthday cake, and we can plan our future together. Love you xoxoxo.

The casual nature of our entire exchange threw me off, but I was also exhilarated by it. He was flirting with me, and the realization astounded me. I didn't know how to return that sentiment, but I at least wanted to cement our plans, so I sent him a real message from me.

Time and place for tomorrow?

My tone was way too formal and direct, very vampire, so in my next response, I decided I would try to be more relaxed.

His thumbs moved across his phone screen. *Does 5 work? My house?*

I typed up my message and paused, wondering if it was the right balance of nonchalance in case he was just joking around with me. He was staring at his phone and chewing his thumbnail, eagerly waiting for my response to his questions, and I decided to open myself up.

It's a date.

He gave me a slow and sexy grin.

I wasn't kidding about the cake, though.

5

Most vampires don't know how to drive. A combination of a distrust in human invention and the readily available funds to pay someone else to drive for them resulted in a congestion of black cars and limousines at my uncle's estate.

My mother, a licensed human driver at sixteen, had a lead foot when she became a vampire at age twenty-five, and it stayed with her. She punched the gas as she veered off the long, paved driveway and cut across the lawn.

"I now understand why you always insist on taking my car," I muttered from the backseat.

Her tiny sports car wouldn't have handled the wet grass and hills as well as my Jeep did.

In the time of my grandfather William — the vampire who turned my father and Uncle Derrick — the property and the hundreds of acres surrounding it were apple orchards. In their first few months of vampirism, my father and Uncle Derrick took long walks through the orchards at night away from humans. It was where they hatched their plans for the future and tried to adjust to their new lives.

When it became clear that William, then the King of Appalachia, wasn't going to be around for much longer, they once again walked along the neat rows of trees, finding clarity while clouded in the sweet aroma of apples.

While the idea of living forever — or in a vampire's case, existing forever — was appealing, it simply wasn't true. Usually, vampires hung around for about one hundred and fifty years, not that much longer than humans these days, thanks to their modern medicine, but there were rumors of a three-hundred-year-old vampire hiding out in London somewhere.

They suspected William was declining for a few years, but it became clear when they saw him running fast enough to remain airborne as they arrived to visit him one afternoon. When humans die, they're usually at their most frail, in bed and surrounded by their loved ones. When vampires die, they get a surge of energy and ability, as if they're using up the last of whatever makes them exist.

I, being a mix of the two, had no idea what was ahead for me. I tried not to think about it too much, but it was hard not to, considering that if I were a full human, I would have certainly been thrown from the car with my mother's reckless driving.

"Almost there," my mother said, her voice light and airy.

If I squinted, I could see the faint lights of homes on the outskirts of the property. One of the major changes my uncle made after my grandfather died was to assimilate us more into the human world for monetary gain. Within two years, the beautiful, untouched orchards had been bull-dozed into a real estate development, but my uncle carved out a slice of land to build his home. He was always trying to get us to move permanently into the gaudy mansion, but we settled in one of his developments closer to downtown and, conveniently, my school.

My mother slammed on the brakes, and we fishtailed to a stop next to a few of my uncle's cars, all with fancy names I didn't care to recognize. I hopped from my seat to the pavement, smoothing out my dress as I followed my parents in through the back entrance.

I inhaled, trying to guess how many vampires were inside by their scents, but I lost count in the slight differences after a dozen or so. We passed a number of storage rooms, including the industrial refrigeration room with a year's worth of blood.

We stepped into the meeting room, and Trinity directed us to our seats. Those seated around the table stood, offering us all bows in greeting and repeated the motion when Uncle Derrick arrived, taking the seat at the head of the table.

"Welcome, all. I trust that since we've all gathered last, your work and efforts have been fruitful."

There were murmurs of "yes, your majesty" around me.

"Before we ask Thomas to begin the updates on our region, I'd like to take a moment to acknowledge an event of great importance." He stopped to pause and address me directly. "Mina, who you all might recognize by her unique scent or the likeness of myself, my brother, and Marie, is prepared to take her rightful place at this table and all the responsibility that comes with it."

He said these words as a reminder to me and everyone in the room. Judging by the looks of interest and the scowls I received while following my parents in, not everyone was thrilled by my presence.

"Let us all raise our glasses," he continued, leading the charge to hold the blood at eye level. "Mina, who has recently turned eighteen in both vampire and human years, is prepared to undergo the sacred ritual at the next lunar eclipse, as is tradition in the Byron family, to indicate the tie of responsibility to the future of our kind as my sole heir."

The final concession I made in the negotiation to go to high school verbally slapped me across the face. It was inevitable, anyway, that I would step up to the responsibility, but I used it for my advantage. Under the watchful eyes of a room full of vampires, I kept my composure.

I tightened my grip on my mug, a thoughtful gesture by Uncle Derrick to have set out for me, but it now made me feel somewhat childish.

"To Mina," he said, beaming with pride, and the chorus of the rest of the voices followed suit. "One of us."

Glass shattered to my left, and the soft swish of every head in the room was near-instant.

A woman, red-haired and elegant, with the exception of the twisted expression of disgust across her features, stood up to address the room.

"Margaret," my uncle said coolly. "I can only assume there is something you would like to say."

"With respect, your majesty, we have strict laws in place to protect ourselves against humans."

Interesting choice of words, her thinking that fragile

humans could compete with the lethality of vampires. The forty-ish vampires in the room could do as much destruction to a town as a human-made bomb.

She raised her chin and continued. "When we founded this noble circle upon the passing of William, we made very careful additions to the Code of Conduct to ensure—"

"I am aware of what you are referencing, and my niece is not in violation, nor am I."

I pictured the very worn document in my head, currently kept in the library on the second floor of the mansion and locked away in a case. She referenced one of the most sacred lines, listed right below the language about the nature of secrecy: "No human shall threaten our existence."

She saw me as a threat.

My vision tunneled at the realization. Me, the lonely and quiet half-human, half-vampire who didn't belong anywhere or with anyone, scared her. I had no power, no allies, no desires to bring harm or any type of change that would impact her, and yet she felt she needed to speak out. The concept floored me.

The rant continued, so I refocused on her words.

"And now we let this abomination into our most precious circle?" Margaret finished.

There was no way to truly kill a vampire. A stake through the heart would be impossible, as vampire skin was impenetrable to everything but a vampire's own fangs. Hypothetically, if someone could subdue them and withhold blood, they'd grow weak and possibly insane, but they'd still continue on living until the natural course of their existence came to an end.

The fictionalized version of vampirism was a running joke between vampires, with many of the rumors and folklore thought up at gatherings like this one. For the first time, I wished that one of them was true — that silver could weaken a vampire, for example. Being half-human, I wasn't as strong or as fast as the others in this room, and it worried me. If this one woman was furious and concerned enough to speak so boldly, what were the others not vocalizing?

"Is there any other complaint you wish to bring forward?" Uncle Derrick's authoritative presence walking toward her didn't reassure me.

"No, your majesty."

"Then I will remind you of another crucial part of the Code of Conduct that you must have forgotten this evening," he said, his tone harsh but fair. "And that is that all vampires will be treated with respect and dignity, even in times of war and uncertainty, neither of which we are in at the moment."

She flinched as he dragged a pointer finger down her cheek and forced her to gaze in my direction. "Mina is not an abomination. She is my niece, my heir, and you will speak to her as an extension of me. Is that understood?"

"Yes, your majesty."

"Good," he said, with a note of finality, and took his place back at the head of the table.

"Thomas, unless you have anything to add to your wife's interjection, please get started with the financial updates."

He rattled off company names and information about the human stock market, which I tried to follow as best I could. I would have to add financials to the list of my research tonight, right alongside soccer. When he finished the specific monetary updates, those around the table shared news and musings from their own interests and interactions with other vampires and the occasional influential human.

Everyone paid particular attention to my father's updates, which not only gave reassurance of our current blood supply, but also relayed his intent to buy up human food manufacturing facilities around the region, with the hopes of creating a synthetic blood alternative to humans. The *True Blood* theme song started in my head.

As I watched each vampire around the table speak in turn, I tried to get a sense of the dynamics and personalities in each, but it was nearly impossible. Vampires are notoriously difficult to read, largely due to their ability to sit motionless indefinitely. Even the woman who was so animated in speaking out against me met my scrutiny with a vacant expression.

Part of the reason I loved going to school so much was that humans were always shifting around in their seats or giving something away with their body language. Eloise kept mostly to herself, but her entire demeanor could change in the moments she became frustrated, unlike Brooklyn and Tanner, who both seemed to simply vocalize every single thought that surfaced in their minds. For Charlie, it was his mouth. He was constantly biting his lip, smirking, pressing his lips together, or smiling.

"Trinity," I called, remembering Charlie's snarky demand for cake, as the rest of the vampires moved toward the great room for a social hour now that the serious business concluded. "Can you help me with something?"

I explained what I needed, and she rapid-fire clicked on her tablet, adhering to my flavor and style specifications.

"I'll have the ingredients, utensils, and bakeware delivered to your home within the next two hours," she promised.

I thanked her and felt very grateful that my mother insisted on buying a human-built home that contained all the necessary appliances. I was oddly excited about putting them to use for the first time. I added baking tutorials to my soccer and financial research.

A little over a week of leaning into my human side, and my calendar was already filling up.

The smile on my face dissipated as I rounded a corner in the maze of hallways, where Thomas and Margaret stood. The quickest way to the great room was through the doors they were blocking.

"Thomas, Margaret," I said, evenly, and was met with no reply.

They didn't move as I closed the distance between us, and I had to stop, stuck in a stare down with two older, stronger vampires. It was too late for me to turn back to where I came from. It would come off as cowardly.

"Well?" I waited for whatever they wanted to say to be said.

Margaret stepped forward, nearly nose to nose, and hissed. "You don't belong here."

Uncle Derrick always reminded me to remain calm, to stay level-headed, and I tried my best. "Is that so?"

"You're not a vampire. You're scum, a lowly half-human

with fangs. It's an atrocity to even be associated with humans, let alone have one we're supposed to bow to."

Watching her become slightly unhinged made me eerily calm, pushing me back into my vampire tendencies.

I sidestepped to her husband, a tall, burly figure wrapped in layers of black fabric. "What is that in your cup?" I asked him.

He glanced between the two of us. Seeing no objection from his wife, he humored me with an eyebrow raised. "Blood."

"That's right," I confirmed. "Human blood that fuels your existence, making it possible for you to stand here and insult me."

Margaret laughed. "You think that I am misguided, that I am resentful to rely on humans, but what you fail to understand is that humans are not above us, that we are not bottom-feeders going after scraps that they donate. We're predators, and they're our prey, and you are both, a plague that shouldn't exist.

"Just because you have abandoned all of your human ideals doesn't mean that you can erase the fact that you were once human, living and breathing. I don't need blood in crystal glassware to remind me of my connection to that which doesn't make me anything less."

Her fangs descended. "Humans are nothing but—"

"That's enough," Uncle Derrick's voice boomed from behind us.

"Your majesty, I was just—"

"Leaving," he finished for her. "I advise you and your husband to bid your goodbyes for the evening and spend the next month changing your course of action."

His fairness and patience was too forgiving sometimes, in my opinion.

Without another word, they both bowed and made their exit.

I stared at the intricate stone at my feet, needing a second to compose myself from the heated exchange.

"Mina," Uncle Derrick said softly. "I understand the need to address the inaccuracies they're spewing, but at some point, to engage with them comes off as defensive, and a sparring match does nothing but give her more ammunition."

"You knew she felt this way?"

"Yes."

"And you didn't see fit to warn me?"

He smiled. "Mina, if I warned you about everything wrong with the world, both human and vampire, we wouldn't have time for anything else."

"What a shame that would be," I agreed.

"I encourage you to focus on holding up your end of our agreement, which includes discovering as much about your human side as you can. Let me wear the burden of concern for the rest."

He took a small sip from his glass and coughed from deep within his lungs.

"Are you all right?" I asked, genuinely concerned by his hacking sounds.

I couldn't think of a time I'd seen him or another vampire do something so human.

"I am taking care of it all," he promised, as blood appeared at the corners of his mouth. "Do not worry."

His reassurance had the opposite effect on me.

6

I hoped Charlie liked vanilla cake.

After I burned the chocolate one, messed up something in the consistency of the red velvet, and disgusted my father with the scent of grating carrots for its namesake cake, vanilla was all that was left. I layered on thick frosting and covered the top in six different kinds of sprinkles, hoping it would cancel out any other wrongdoing.

Holding the glass cake stand in one hand and my notebook in the other, I twisted my leg upward and rang the doorbell with the back of my sneaker, a footwear choice that Uncle Derrick called an "atrocity" when Trinity and I were sorting through racks of clothes at the mansion.

I stepped back, admiring the clean, red brick lines of Charlie's home. It was in a nice neighborhood, with neat rows of nearly identical houses and well-maintained yards and kids rollerblading outside. I sniffed in the floral scent from the oversized pots near my feet. The American dream, minus the half-vampire on the doorstep.

Charlie opened the door. I made the mistake of not immediately cutting off my inhale and gulped down the scent of his body wash and shampoo as he flipped a wet piece of hair back off his forehead.

"You showered?" I asked.

He smiled, leaning with both arms into the doorframe. After a long night with rigid vampires and my usual self-distancing from humans at school, his relaxed demeanor jolted me.

"Coach always has us do a long run before game day," he explained.

"Ah, right."

A beat of silence settled between us, and the corner of his mouth ticked. I shifted the cake in my hands, needing something else to focus on.

"Let me help you," he offered.

His hands moved toward mine, and a big, flashing alarm went off in my head. He was too close. Equal parts of me loved and hated it, but I stayed rational. I stepped back and yanked the glass to my chest in a flash, and he swayed forward.

"Point me to the kitchen?" I asked, ignoring his look of confusion and amusement.

"Sure," he said, gesturing me in.

I walked slowly, admiring the pictures from family vacations, soccer tournaments, and birthday parties hanging in silver frames. Judging from the photos and doll clothing strewn across the couch, Charlie had an adorable little sister. I eyed the comfortable pillows and blankets stacked on the ottoman in the corner and the rings on the wooden coffee table before my attention turned to the kitchen, where a rack of clean dishes sat on the counter.

The stacks of unopened mail, folded newspapers, and markers cluttered the surface of the dining table in the breakfast nook, and Charlie, following my eye line, moved to shuffle things around. I didn't know how to tell him everything was perfect as is, how much I loved the natural chaos of humans, so I just set the cake proudly in the middle of the table.

He shuffled to a drawer for utensils before opening an overhead cabinet, pulling out yellow plates. The color caught my attention, and I found it so endearing, so human, to have something so bright and so fun just because. Everything in my parents' house, and at Uncle Derrick's mansion, was for a practical purpose.

When Charlie set the plate at the setting in front of me, I traced the outlines of the cartoonish lemons. I didn't realize a smile spread across my face until he chuckled, nodding to the design.

"My sister picked them out," he said by way of explanation.

"I like them. They're… cheerful."

He stared at the movement of my fingertips. "That's what she said when she saw them last January. She said she wanted everything to be bright and happy in the house."

It seemed to be that way to me, but vampires could be portrayed as advocates of utilitarianism. It stilted my perspective. "I suppose winter is a good time for holding onto summer colors."

He cleared this throat. "Well, it was right after my

parents got divorced, and I think Emma was just sick of everything being so dreary inside and outside."

"Oh," I breathed.

Unsure what to say next, I focused on delicately removing the glass dome. He cut out generous slices and dropped them on the plates. I swiped up some of the scattered sprinkles on the table into a napkin and sat down across from him.

His first bite was bigger than the tines of his fork, and he nodded in approval of the taste as he chewed. I fiddled with the smooth metal in my hand and dropped my gaze to my own piece. The goopy icing and spongy consistency of the cake didn't seem all that appetizing to me.

I opened my notebook and pulled out the pencil and instruction packet I shoved between the pages. We had a lot of decisions to make, and being my first project with a partner, I wasn't sure how long it would take. I figured we might as well jump right in.

"I already promised Emma that you and I won't get a divorce," Charlie joked.

The implication that he told his family about me made my head spin, imagining the different scenarios of how he could describe me or our very limited interactions together.

"I mean, I know we're still early in our marriage," he continued. "But we're getting out all the stuff people usually fight about right away."

That piqued my interest. "What do people usually fight about?" I asked, genuinely curious about the daily stresses of humanity.

He shrugged. "Money and planning and the kids and who is not putting 'the time' in and whatever."

I guessed he spoke from his own parents' experience, and I couldn't recall a time when my parents disagreed about anything related to those things. Not worrying about bank accounts, health problems, and having more children took out a lot of drama in a relationship, apparently.

"Since we didn't have a wedding, at the very least it makes sense that we have cake," he added, attempting to lighten the conversation.

The mental picture that flashed of me wearing a wedding dress and holding a bouquet while walking down the aisle was not a possibility for me, but I played along.

"Well, best not to go overboard," I said in mock seriousness. "We have to spend our honeymoon in our bathing suits."

"Oh yeah, we wouldn't want to scar the kind people of Fiji for life," Charlie said.

"Fiji?"

He shrugged.

"How many flights would that take?"

"Three or four maybe. Why? Are you afraid of flying?"

"I don't know," I answered honestly. "I've never been on a plane before."

My father, wary of human inventions enough as it is, preferred having a driver — or my mother — take us wherever we needed to go, which, thinking about it, wasn't really anywhere other than home, Uncle Derrick's, and various hospitals and blood donation centers in the surrounding areas.

He seemed surprised by my answer. "What? Never?"

"I haven't done a lot of things," I admitted. "Including this."

"A date?"

My jaw dropped. "This is a date?"

"You said so, not me."

He was right. Damn me for being so bold over text message because now the lines of what constituted a serious answer were blurred. I didn't want him to get the wrong idea.

"I meant baking a cake," I clarified, withholding every trace of humor.

"Is that why no one at the party wanted a piece? Afraid to risk their lives?"

I picked up my fork. "Something like that."

"Well hopefully you followed instructions enough to not poison me. Part of tonight's agenda is discussing our life insurance policies. I'm not going to choose the premium plan if it encourages you to kill me off."

To prove a point, I took a bite. It was too tentative, so I sunk my teeth down until they hit the metal. The mixed consistency between the icing and cake seemed strange at first, but as I chewed, they came together in an interesting way. My heightened taste buds sought out every ingredient individually, tasting how the flour and eggs had morphed in the oven. The sprinkles added an interesting burst of additional sugar.

Swallowing it as completely as I could, I set down my fork and pushed the plate aside, happy to conclude the taste test.

I glanced up at Charlie, whose own fork hung in midair as he watched me. "Why are you looking at me like that?" I asked, wiping my face just in case a speck of icing found its way to my cheek.

Charlie snapped out of it and shoveled another large bite into his mouth. He reached for his backpack, pulling out the blue folder he tended to doodle on every sixth period. I re-read the instructions for the assignment, and we started working through the prompt.

It took us about two hours. I had to excuse myself once to hide in the bathroom and take a breath, and I spent the entire three minutes staring at the white tile of the shower where Charlie washed himself off before I arrived. I inhaled, pleased that some of the bubbles from his body wash remained in the drain.

When I returned, we went back and forth on what jobs we picked, looking up projected salaries on our phones, and planning our budget around them. Charlie was immensely helpful in pointing out the various human expenses, even though he was unaware of my ignorance. We picked a house and calculated the mortgage, insurance, and other bills.

"So our house is going to cost us nearly half of our monthly paychecks," I confirmed aloud. "Think that's too much?"

"Well, we need to set aside a portion for savings and fun money."

"Fun money?"

Charlie's forehead wrinkled. "You know, like, how we want to spend time outside of all this. What do you normally do on the weekend?"

I already planned to spend Saturday working on my colloquial Mandarin, but my instinct said that wasn't a normal activity for humans, who are usually sleeping in after late-night socializing. I wracked my brain for my other activities — racing trains at full speed next to their tracks, having existential crises, observing humans from afar.

"Spending time with family and watching videos," I answered. "Why? What's your normal routine?"

"Well, usually I'll have a game, so my weekend kind of revolves around that, or I'll have to drive my sister to a friend's house or art class or something. If not, I'll hang out with the guys from the team, watch a documentary, or catch up on the news I missed this week."

"The news?" That seemed a little surprising for what I pictured as something for a human teenage male to be interested in.

He tapped the pile of newspapers next to my notebook with his knuckle. "My dad's the editor of the *Gazette*."

I shuddered, getting an instant *Interview with the Vampire* vibe. Vampires usually avoided reporters as best they could. The last thing we needed was intelligent, curious humans who were paid to dig into companies and people interested in our activities.

"So I guess we can plan on some low-cost entertainment, with subscriptions to some streaming services and the paper. We can put aside some money to get takeout."

"Maybe we can plan to go to the movies sometimes, too," I suggested.

Watching a movie beside him in a movie theater seat would be infinitely better than craning our necks in Health class. I shook the thought away, reminding myself that this was all pretend.

He added that to the list and began tallying up our new costs. "So being married will cost us… actually, we're doing pretty well with our joint incomes."

"Being married is pretty easy then," I teased.

"Only because I'm such a fantastic and thoughtful husband. Working long hours at the law firm and still having time to volunteer and spend time with our kids..."

My easy smile faded at the sound of the garage door. I flipped through my mental catalog of romantic comedies on how to handle the situation. Was it even okay that we were here in his home alone?

"Mina and I are in the kitchen," Charlie called once he heard the sound of her jingling keys.

Charlie's mom crossed through the house and entered the kitchen, dropping her bag on the counter. The only commonality she and Charlie shared looks-wise was their smile, which she directed at me after dropping a kiss on the top of Charlie's head.

"Mina, it's so lovely to meet you," she said sincerely. "I'm Amy, and I would give you a hug, but I need to get cleaned up first."

A brown, sticky residue covered the front of her pink scrubs.

"It's pudding," she explained, glancing at the look of disgust on Charlie's face. "I was helping out in the children's wing today. But if it were poop, like you assumed, just remember that one time at Disney World when you—"

"Mom," Charlie growled.

"Oh, please continue," I pleaded.

"I'll save it for another time," she promised, taking her hair out of her ponytail. "Oh, you brought cake?"

"Her uncle's birthday was yesterday. No one wanted it because Mina's a terrible baker, so I accepted it solely out of pity."

"Hey!" I objected. "You seemed to clean your plate just fine."

"It's actually really good," Charlie admitted.

Charlie cut her off a piece and handed it over. I noticed he reused his cleared plate, and she took it without issue. I couldn't recall a time I ever shared a cup of anything with either of my parents.

She asked me about the recipe and how I piped the frosting on the top. As I was explaining how I'd burned the other flavors, the front door slammed, causing me to jump. Withholding my sense of smell was putting me at a disadvantage of knowing who, or what, was around us.

A human dart soared through the room, landing on Charlie's lap, followed by the man I identified as his dad, even if he was noticeably absent from the photos around the house. His parents exchanged a somewhat easy greeting as Emma leaned over the table to get a look at me.

"Who are you?"

I marveled at her directness.

"I'll go first," she insisted before I even opened my mouth. "I am Emma Rose Schenley. I'm eight years old, and I'm in third grade."

I waited to make sure she was finished. "I am Mina Louise Byron. I'm eighteen years old, and I'm a senior."

"Eighteen?" she exclaimed in Charlie's ear. "She's older than you!"

"Older and wiser," I promised. "But not as good at budgeting."

"Did you say Byron?" Charlie's father asked. "Any relation to Derrick?"

I pressed my lips together to withhold the sigh and nodded. "My uncle."

His eyes lit up.

"You know him?" If he did, there was likely some nefarious reason for it. The idea sank in my stomach. I wanted to keep Charlie completely out of my vampire world and in the human one, purely for selfish reasons.

He had the same build as Charlie, and his hair was a touch darker. Their facial expressions were similar enough that even though he projected a coolness, I could see the excitement under the surface.

"I've been trying to get in touch with him for months, but his assistant keeps giving me the runaround."

Trinity was good at that kind of thing when necessary.

"Are you doing a story on him or something?" Charlie asked, gaze jumping between us. "Wait, Derrick Byron, the real estate developer? He's your uncle?"

"Real estate developer, philanthropist, start-up entrepreneur, and now, apparently, he's getting more involved with the medical field," his father answered for me. "Do you know anything about that? Has he said anything to you?"

I fumbled for a response.

"That's enough," Amy cut in.

"Stop grilling her, dad," Charlie added, coming to my defense as well. "She's my friend, not your source."

He blinked, realizing that he was treating me as such. "Right, well, I should get going, but Mina, if you could just put in a word with him, I would appreciate it."

"Dad," Charlie warned, nodding for him to leave out the side door, which he reluctantly did.

"How about I order you kids pizza?" Amy asked when he backed out of the driveway.

"No pineapple this time," Emma cried. "Please."

"Actually, I better head out as well."

The exchange with Charlie's dad had me feeling a little uneasy, and the scent of garlic wouldn't help anything.

"You sure?" Amy asked. "It's no trouble if you want to stay for dinner. I promise there won't be any further interrogations."

I smiled at her kindness. "Thank you, but my parents are expecting me."

The lie was an easy one, but I doubted my parents would even notice I was gone. I gathered my belongings quickly.

"Come back again soon!" Emma called as Charlie walked me to the door.

"I will," I promised, and this time, I wasn't sure if the answer I gave was a lie.

Charlie opened the door, lingering for a moment. If he was debating on how to say goodbye, I didn't let him decide. In fear of having to sidestep a hug, I practically leaped out onto the front step.

"I'll see you tomorrow, then, Charlie."

"See you."

I waved, lamely, and felt his eyes on me as I walked toward the street.

Once inside the safety of my Jeep, I breathed again, appreciating the sharp scent of leather. I turned the key and rolled down the window, enjoying the fresh air for a moment before a familiar scent pulled my attention over my right shoulder.

From the rear-view mirror, I spotted one of the noble vampires. I couldn't recall his name, even though we were briefly introduced less than twenty-four hours prior. He stared at me curiously and then vanished.

7

Thursday was one of those beautiful fall days where the sun was still hot but the air was cool, and my Physical Education teacher took advantage of it. As long as we were outside and moving, she didn't care what we did. At least, that's what she said before she dropped a box of various sporting equipment on the grass and took off to time herself doing laps on the track.

The humans milled about on the field, stepping on the lines of fresh paint drawn as markers for the soccer game. When the rival bus pulled up and the opposing team crossed the parking lot to their locker room, a few of the females froze in place to watch them walk by, and then a mutual whooping between the two parties occurred. I watched in fascination.

My classmates mostly traveled in packs of two or more. I was one of the few loners, and I was more than okay with it. I preferred jogging around a track by myself, focusing on muting my own ability, over trying to navigate all the unknowns of organized group sports.

After two warm-up laps, I stopped to stretch off to the side. It was a superfluous act for me, but I saw other runners do it. I pulled my arms up to the sky, which felt exceptionally silly and vulnerable, so I dropped them back down almost immediately. I reached behind and pulled my ankle up to my hip, wondering what it felt like for humans to stretch their quadriceps, because it didn't bring me any relief. It just made me feel like a flamingo.

I switched legs and counted to ten, deciding I could be done with stretching for now. I moved to take off again in lane number four when the smell of spearmint hit my nostrils.

"Charlie," I said, not hiding the surprise in seeing him.

He stepped up to the other side of the fence and smiled.

"What are you doing here?"

The answer was obvious, given the fact that I saw the mating calls from the other team earlier — his cleats were strung over his shoulder.

"I saw you running on my way to the locker room," Charlie admitted. "You never told me how fast you were."

"It never came up," I shrugged.

"What else haven't you told me about you?"

I forced myself to blink. "Only a few things."

"Well, seeing as we've already planned our financial lives and schedules together, maybe after the game tonight, we could…"

The distinctive rumble of the engine from a half-million-dollar car zoomed through the parking lot, and the whipping sound of a frisbee zoomed toward the side of my head, distracting me from Charlie's words. I spun quickly, catching the round plastic an inch before it hit me square in the face and throwing it back to where Brooklyn stood, flanked by two of her friends.

"Wow," Charlie breathed, clearly impressed.

The car honked, and I turned to see my uncle step out of the vehicle. I wasn't exactly happy to see him, but I was at least grateful that he remembered to remove his simple, silver crown.

"Do you know him?" Charlie asked.

Uncle Derrick didn't have to call me over. His mere presence beckoned me. It had to be serious if he came all the way to my school to speak to me directly.

"It's my uncle," I answered him, feeling slightly detached yet clinging to the panic rising inside me.

"Why is he here?"

I didn't answer him. I just walked to the entrance and prayed that he wouldn't follow me. From my peripheral vision, I saw Charlie wave in Uncle Derrick's direction.

"Happy belated birthday," he called as he headed toward the locker room.

I cringed at Charlie's thoughtfulness, so kind and human, but to my surprise, Uncle Derrick smiled and waved back.

When I approached, he was back to an outwardly emotionless state of being.

"Is that the Schenley boy?" Uncle Derrick asked.

There was no point in skirting the truth. "Yes."

"And he just wished me a happy birthday?"

"Long story," I dismissed. "What are you doing here, Uncle Derrick? Is everything all right?"

For once, Uncle Derrick didn't get to the point. "You know that girl over there is trying to harm you, right?"

I resisted the urge to roll my eyes. "She's a little catty, but she's mostly fine."

He ignored my flippancy. "Humans, in some ways, are more dangerous than vampires, Mina. They're unpredictable, jealous, fueled by their emotions, and you need to be careful."

"Did you come all the way here to warn me about a human?"

"Not exactly," he admitted. "Well, not that particular human. It's the Schenley boy."

"Charlie?" I laughed. "What does he have to do with anything?"

I stopped, recalling the noble who stood outside the Schenley house the previous night. "Wait, were you having me watched last night? Or was it him?"

Uncle Derrick leaned back against the car, not because he needed to, but because he noticed a few of the students watching us and wanted to appear more relaxed, like less of a threat.

"Neither. His father, Daniel Schenley, is the editor of the *Gazette*. He has been prying into some of my businesses for months, harassing Trinity endlessly to get an interview with me or someone at one of my companies. I've been having him followed, trying to see what he knows about me."

His eyes narrowed.

"So imagine my surprise when a report came back to me yesterday that my own niece was with him."

I tried to keep my voice steady, bored even. "Charlie and

I are partners for a class project. His parents are divorced. His dad doesn't even live there, but he came by to drop off Charlie's younger sister."

"What were your interactions with him?" Uncle Derrick demanded.

"We were introduced, and when he realized who I was, he asked if I could help get you two in touch, but I didn't make any promises," I explained.

He stared at the humans over my shoulder and offered no reaction to my words.

"It's not really that surprising, is it, though?" I asked. "I mean, he's a journalist, and you're buying up real estate and investing in businesses all over town."

His head snapped, and he leaned down to appraise my reaction to the next words he spoke slowly. "His curiosity seems to extend past a normal human one. You understand?"

I understood.

Many humans speculated about our actual, true existence in the world. Those who suspected and also benefited from the enormous cash flow in some way always turned a blind eye. If you were close enough to speculate, you were also smart enough to keep your mouth shut.

Those who weren't outright killed in the circumstance of knowing about us were given a choice to die as a human completely or be reborn as a vampire. The turning process, one I had first witnessed when one of Uncle Derrick's political cronies had confronted him and asked to be turned, was arduous. It usually takes a full twelve hours, about the time from sunrise to sunset, and it's an intense process of draining and replenishing the human's blood supply.

A vampire can drink from a human without complications, but when a human drinks from a vampire, a bond is created, even more so when they're dying from their human life and solely depending on drinking from the vampire to be reborn.

Over the years, Uncle Derrick stealthily turned enough human scientists into vampires to create a research firm to try and uncover the biology of it all. So far, the only tangible piece of news I learned from their projects was that animal blood was absolutely not a suitable replacement for human blood, something about the difference of glucose levels. Last I heard, they were burning through millions without result, so they were taking on projects from the human sector to become profitable.

I wanted to learn more about the human world, to be a part of it, not to blur the two together, and without knowing, Charlie's father started to do so. I was irritated because of my own self-interest, but I was terrified for Charlie. He, Emma, and their yellow plates had enough family drama to last a human lifetime. If his father disappeared or turned up dead… I didn't even want to think about it.

"Uncle Derrick, isn't there an alternative?" I asked. "Maybe he could be useful in some ways as a human ally. Haven't we had cases where there are exceptions?"

"This is not one of those," he asserted, opening the car door as an indicator of finality. "You need to distance yourself from them."

I scrambled for any delay or excuse. "But Charlie and I are teamed up on a school project for the entire semester and—"

"And you expect me to indulge this and risk exposing

us so you can earn a grade that has no true impact on your existence? Trinity will take care of it tomorrow morning." He turned on the car and paused to meet my eyes. "Some days I think you are ready to have the world at your fingertips and other days I swear I am staring at a child."

I gasped, completely stunned at the words. This harshness was new. I didn't prefer it over being coddled. I wanted a happy medium, and I needed to make it clear.

"No," I barked, surprising even myself with my forceful tone.

He glanced up at me through the open window. "No?"

My gums ached, desperate to allow my fangs to expose themselves as part of my anger, and I paused, trying to find the right words.

"I've always been stuck between two worlds," I said, softly. "Maybe, for the first time, I could use it as an advantage." And I didn't want to give Charlie up just yet.

He eyed me curiously. "How?"

"Let me see what I can dig up on this," I insisted. "If I'm going to be spending more time with Charlie, I could find out what he knows, see if his dad has told him anything, and try to get access in some other way."

"Be prepared to present your findings at our next monthly gathering."

I nodded, feeling simultaneously exhilarated and guilty, and returned to the track.

Hours later, the bleachers were packed with students, parents, teachers, and other humans whose categories I couldn't identify. The metal stands merely reverberated the sound, and when combining that with the social implications and close proximity of other humans, it seemed like a horrible experience.

I inhaled the rich, buttery scent of popcorn from the snack bar and tuned out, as best I could, the chatter from hundreds of people. I stood by the fence and used my phone screen as a mirror, ensuring the lipstick I'd applied with great care in the changing room after class stayed in place.

Both teams filed onto the field for warm-ups, laughing with their respective teammates as they went through the motions. Charlie, after running through a few sets of high knees and butt kicks, terms I'd learned in my research, passed a ball back and forth with Tanner. With each release, his eyes flickered over to the stands. Emma jumped up and down to get his attention, which made him laugh and miss the return pass from Tanner.

He jogged over to retrieve it, dodging his teammates who were shuffling between cones, and I couldn't help but admire the easy movement of his muscles. He chipped the ball at Tanner, who let it bounce then controlled it with the inside of his right foot. They picked up their steady, back-and-forth rhythm until they lined up in the middle of the field for the national anthem and the coin toss.

They stripped off their warm-up gear at the bench, getting a last-minute pep talk from their coach, then took the field.

Each player moved with such ease that it made me aware of how rigid my own posture was. I leaned down on the fence, putting my forearms on the metal, and mimicked the stance of someone a few feet away. It felt exceptionally awkward to me, but I thought it appeared somewhat natural.

"Hey, Mina," Eloise said, approaching tentatively.

"Hi," I returned.

She stepped up to the space next to me, violating my imaginary three-foot perimeter. I shifted slightly and stopped inhaling.

I held still, trying to acclimate my body to the proximity, and forced my eyes back to the field. We watched in silence as the crowd roared around us.

"I hate soccer," she admitted.

"What?" I asked. "Then why did you come?"

She picked at her nails. For all the work she put into her outward facade of grandeur, she seemed quite careless in maintaining it when it came to avoiding my question. As if she could read my thoughts, she frowned and dropped her hands onto the fence.

"Beats being at home," she admitted, biting at the side of her mouth.

Another thing we had in common.

"Yeah," I agreed.

Eloise's tight expression met mine, and she sighed. "My mom's new boyfriend is over. He's always over these days, and..." She trailed off.

"You don't have to explain if I was being intrusive."

"No, it's fine. It's just that he's super clingy to her. To us, I guess. I mean, they've been together for, like, two seconds, and he's pretending like he's my dad, asking me one thousand questions about where I've been and where I'm going."

That I couldn't relate to, but I tried. "It must be odd to have someone keeping tabs on your whereabouts," I posed.

"Definitely. Like, steer clear of me with your toxic masculinity, dude. I was fine when you showed up, and I'll be fine when you're gone." The annoyance for this man made her more animated when she spoke. "But when I psychoanalyze him, I feel bad for him. I think he feels threatened by me in some ways."

"So he's trying to control a situation because it's not exactly what he wants?"

She hummed. "You have one of those at home, too?"

More like the combination of my father, my uncle, and the entire vampire community. I couldn't say that, though, so I nodded.

Charlie passed the ball to his teammate, who took a shot, sending the ball right into the goalie's gloved hands. The crowd groaned collectively.

"I heard that Tanner invited you to the game," she said casually.

I raised an eyebrow at her question. She smiled, but it didn't meet her eyes.

"Rita told me." Eloise tugged at the ends of her hair. "Tanner and I had a thing in tenth grade, which means that she feels obligated to notify me every single time he hits on a girl, which is often by the way. No offense."

"No offense taken," I assured her.

"He's not even very good," she said, watching him hang around midfield. "I don't know why he would want anyone to witness this. He's only on the varsity team because there aren't enough defenders."

Our offense was aggressive and controlled most of the

game so far, not giving our defensive players much to do other than shout and run around to set passes back up toward the opponent's goal.

"So he's not good at soccer or statistics. He's a... player with girls, and he regularly shouts out comments in class. Why did you date him?"

It was rude of me to summarize him in those few unflattering traits, but given Eloise's tenacity, I couldn't reconcile them together as a couple.

She seemed taken aback by my question. "You're not actually interested in him are you?"

I paused. "Not in the slightest," I admitted to her visible relief.

The referees blew the whistle for halftime. I fully expected Eloise to wander off and go sit in the stands with her friends, but when she asked me to keep her company in the line for the snack bar, I happily agreed. We chatted comfortably, covering mostly school-related topics, while we watched the second half.

She cheered when we scored two goals, one of which Charlie assisted, and occasionally would say hi to other students when they walked by. Eventually, people began to greet me as well, and while I avoided all physical contact, the atmosphere drew me in.

The noise from the stands, which was once overwhelming, felt like a warm buzz in the background, giving a soundtrack to fuel the fun. The smell of grass, mixed with paint and sweat, felt comfortable and familiar, and the intensity at which Charlie moved, pushing his muscles with impressive speed and control, did something to me I didn't even have words to explain.

When the clock ran out and the whistle blew for the final time, the crowd rushed the field.

"I thought this was only something that happened in the movies," I said to Eloise, practically screaming at her from a foot away.

"It's a rivalry game," she explained.

I didn't know what that meant, but I didn't want to ask.

"You coming?" she asked, already making her way onto the field.

I shook my head and lost her in the crowd. My front-row view to the series of chants and cheers was a good one. The humans were overjoyed and a little chaotic about the positive outcome, which entertained me.

Charlie lifted Emma, who was particularly grossed out by all the sweat and dirt, into his arms. He spun her around, and she screamed with laughter until he stopped. She put her hands on his shoulders and leaned to his ear to speak to him, and he nodded, following the line of her finger that she pointed at me.

Our eyes met, and he grinned. He kissed the side of her head and handed her over to his mom, who offered her congratulations. As he made his way over toward me, hands slapped his back in praise. He offered a nod of gratitude to every admirer.

"Good game," I complimented. "You played well."

He stepped up toward the fence, flashing the skin of his stomach as he wiped the sweat from his face with the edge of his jersey. I took in the red flush of his face from the physical exertion and felt grateful for the metal barrier between us.

My gums ached.

"Thank you," he replied, just like he had to everyone else who congratulated him, but then he shifted, his face alive with a certain brightness that was emphasized by the stadium lights. "I probably would have played better if you were in the stands."

I balked. "I didn't realize that I had such an impact on your performance."

"I kept looking for you in the crowd," he admitted.

"Oh." The crowd around us, encouraged by the coaches and security guards, began to disperse. "Well, I was right here the entire time, impressed by your spatial awareness and body control, along with the rest of your adoring fans."

He smoothed his hair off his forehead. "Someone did her homework last night."

I smiled. "A little bit."

"Mina, you coming to the diner with us?" Eloise called.

She stood in a small group of people. I recognized most of them from my classes, and the humans I didn't know stared at me curiously.

"Say yes," Charlie pleaded. "It's tradition after a big win."

I grimaced, wanting to but knowing I couldn't. Between the day at school and the length of the game, the vials of blood I downed after Physical Education wouldn't sustain me for much longer.

"Last time we went, Tanner ate ten of those cookies with the smiley face on them. Maybe he'll go for a dozen this time. You can't miss it."

He sensed my hesitation and waved Eloise over for reinforcements.

"I'll call your parents and promise them you'll be home early," she offered, eyeing the two of us.

I laughed, wishing that was the reason I couldn't go. There were too many unknowns of seating and distance, and a tremor ran along my right arm.

"Come on, Byron, can't you see you're wanted?" Tanner chimed in. "Do I need to get on my knees and beg?"

Eloise's eyes narrowed at him.

"Oh, please don't," I groaned and turned, focused solely on Charlie. "I want to, but I can't tonight. Another time?"

I wanted to go, not just because of the promise I made to Uncle Derrick hours earlier to do some digging, but I refused to get as close to compromising myself as I did the first day of school. I hoped this wasn't a one-time-only offer.

"Mina, there you are," Brooklyn practically purred, sliding up next to Charlie, who watched her with trepidation as she dug in her purse.

Charlie's coach yelled for him and Tanner to join their teammates for a debrief, and he frowned.

"You sure you can't come with us?"

"I'm sorry," I sighed.

He nodded and jogged toward the locker room, pulling Tanner along with him.

An off-white envelope blocked my vision, and I yanked it from Brooklyn's outstretched hand.

"What's this?"

Brooklyn rolled her eyes. "Open it and find out," she said impatiently.

As slyly as I could, I sniffed. Thankfully, I only picked up on the scents of paper and ink, so I slid my finger under the seal. It was an invitation to a slumber party at her house on Saturday night. I stared at the loopy font.

"What's this?" I asked again, but this time, she explained herself.

"A peace offering." She said the words with a sour look on her face, directly contradicting the intention of her words. "I think we got off on the wrong foot, and if we're going to be in classes and breathing the same air the rest of the year, I figured we should try and be friends."

I glanced at Eloise, and she shrugged, which didn't help or discourage my skepticism.

"It's this Saturday," Brooklyn continued. "You don't have plans, do you?"

Her eyes flickered over to the door to the locker room.

"No, I don't have plans," I admitted.

"Great," she said, a little too enthusiastically. "All the details are there, but make sure you bring your pillow and blanket or whatever you want to sleep with. And don't be late!"

I said goodbye to Eloise, and as I walked to my car, I read over the invitation. I called Trinity, asking her to arrange a few things, and made my way home, fully prepared to overanalyze everything all night long.

8

Friday at school was thankfully eventful, and I spent most of the day Saturday readying myself for the slumber party, trying to discern Brooklyn's motivation behind the invite. I hardly believed that it was a peace offering, given that I still occupied her seat in Health and stayed partnered with Charlie for the project.

Just because I wasn't fully human didn't mean I was completely unaware of a potential back-stab situation. Although, vampires preferred to stab from the front, in clear view, while explaining their moves like a game of chess.

Still, I went through the motions of having Trinity track down all the things required for a sleepover. I would have to pretend to sleep or, at the very least, act as if pulling an all-nighter was difficult. Trinity introduced me to the concept of athleisure, which is apparently more common than traditional pajamas at teenage sleepovers. I didn't question her knowledge or how she came to be in possession of it because a large part of her job was assimilation, but I did feel like I was wearing a costume instead of clothing.

I parked a few houses down from Brooklyn's and, to my relief, saw Eloise walk up the sidewalk while juggling her oversized bag and pillow.

"Eloise," I yelped, calling for her attention.

She crossed over as I retrieved my own overnight bag and bedding from the backseat.

"Hi," she breathed.

Perspiration dotted her face.

"How long have you been walking?" I asked.

"I took the bus and got off at the wrong stop."

We walked up to the door together.

"I would have picked you up."

She pressed a chipped nail into the doorbell, setting off the musical notes that rang through the house. "I don't like to ask for favors."

"It's not a favor when it's for a friend," I argued.

I took a leap because I wasn't actually sure that we were friends, but I wanted to be.

Brooklyn opened the door and stepped aside, staring at us expectantly. Eloise and I exchanged looks of confusion, but Brooklyn kept her mouth closed and put her hand on her hip.

"Was I supposed to bring a gift or something?" I asked.

Trinity never failed me before, but I wondered if she missed some sort of etiquette.

"Everyone's already upstairs in my room," she said, ignoring my question.

We were right on time, according to my phone.

"Okay," Eloise said slowly.

She stepped in and kicked off her shoes, and I followed her. Brooklyn stared at my sneakers as I entered, so I repeated Eloise's movements. Brooklyn's eyebrows pulled together before she slammed the door and led us both up to her room.

I noticed the price tag was still on my pillow, so I ripped it off and slid it into my bag.

Her room was a teenage dream, with white wood furniture, a large flatscreen television mounted on the wall, and a massive bed in the center covered in pink throw pillows. Her walls were lined with framed posters of cityscapes and B-R-O-O-K-L-Y-N spelled out in neon lights.

We settled in, and I had to admit that while girl talk was definitely not my specialty, I was getting better at it with practice. Watching Brooklyn spar back and forth with Marissa and Jamie, the two girls from my gym class, about which celebrities were hotter was like a sport of its own. Rita, Eloise, and I laid on the floor, passing fashion magazines back and forth, occasionally pointing out something exceptionally cool but very expensive.

Eloise rolled over toward me on the thick carpet and shoved a perfume ad in my face. "You need a dress like this for homecoming," she insisted. "That dark green color would be amazing with your skin tone."

Brooklyn scoffed. "Well, it's easy to wear any color when you're the palest person on Earth."

"What's wrong with you?" Eloise asked her.

"Well, it's true."

I handed the magazine back to Eloise, who was still glaring at Brooklyn.

"I had a skin cancer scare when I was fifteen." Lying to humans seemed to be getting easier, and it helped deflect any additional interest or curiosity in certain topics of discussion. "So I'm really careful about not getting a tan."

"If you don't feel like an asshole by now, Brooklyn, that should do it," Eloise said.

"Guess you're not going with us to Cancun for spring break," Marissa muttered, not that unhappily.

"Ugh, homecoming," Rita groaned, snatching the magazine from Eloise to flip through some of the photos. "I haven't even thought about it."

"You're the only one of us who has a guaranteed date, and you aren't prepared at all?" Jamie asked. "Nick hasn't brought it up?"

"It's not like I sit around fantasizing about hairstyles all day. I've been busy with final college applications, NHS, and all my AP classes."

Brooklyn rolled her eyes. "We get it. You're smart, Rita."

"What is… homecoming?" I asked.

Everyone's attention hit me at once.

"Your old school didn't have homecoming?" Rita asked.

"I was homeschooled," I explained, simply, which seemed to bring immediate understanding and pity from the group.

I took the liberty of giving that term to defining my years of self-study, and Trinity forged the forms and tests easily enough. Most vampires didn't bother with school, and the nobles and the King or Queen of each region only had to step in if the individuals were at risk of breaking the Code.

"It's a week-long celebration." Rita jumped to clue me in. "There are spirit days, where each day has a theme and everyone dresses up, and most of the fall sports have games during the week, and then on Saturday, there's a parade down the street in front of the school, followed by a big dance and party at night where everyone gets dressed up."

Jamie sighed. "My parents always remind me that these are the memories that last a lifetime."

"There are definitely some homecoming memories I want to forget," Brooklyn admitted.

Eloise snorted. "Like when you puked your guts out at the afterparty last year?"

"Like when Tanner felt you up in the back of the limo in sophomore year?" Brooklyn shot back.

The group broke out into laughter.

"He's looking good these days, though," Marissa said. "Filling out that soccer jersey nicely." Her remarks immediately earned her pillows thrown at her head by Rita and Eloise.

I was fascinated by the dynamic between the girls, always teasing each other and teetering on being plain rude, but they accepted it.

Maybe I was wrong about Brooklyn. She did take the initiative to invite me to hang out in her circle of friends, so perhaps she was genuine.

"You should ask Tanner to the dance," Brooklyn suggested to Marissa. "Then you and Eloise can compare notes on how his skills have improved."

"Maybe I will," Marissa hummed, just to annoy Eloise.

"So it's like prom, then?" I asked.

"Kind of, but like, the whole school and associated

community is invited to celebrate, not just seniors," Rita explained.

Eloise dug through Brooklyn's drawers of makeup. "So what is your dreamy boyfriend slash future politician up to tonight?"

Rita laughed. "Nick is with Tanner and some of the other guys at Charlie's house."

"Ooh, boy's night," Marissa giggled. "Shall we crash?"

"No way," Brooklyn said. "My mom will be home with dinner soon. Besides, we're doing our own thing."

"Yeah, we don't need them," Eloise agreed.

Brooklyn sat up with a devilish smile on her face. "But let's take cute selfies and post them to show them what they're missing."

They all pulled out their phones, snapping posed photos of themselves and taking videos blowing kisses at the camera. I unlocked my phone, attempting to copy their movements, but I felt awkward and self-indulgent.

Eloise dove back down next to me. I moved at the last second to avoid contact.

"Come on, let's take one together."

She leaned into my frozen form and held up her phone, adjusting to get her preferred angle. I was uncomfortable and my reflection showed it, so I offered the briefest closed-mouth smile, which she caught.

"Perfect," she exclaimed, immediately opening an app to post it. "How are we not following each other already? What's your handle?"

"I don't have a profile," I said to gasps. I needed to stop causing that reaction.

"Why not?" Brooklyn demanded, as if the idea was something so unimaginable.

I shrugged.

"Okay, Homeschool, let's get you into the twenty-first century," Eloise snatched my phone from my hand.

I watched her in quiet amusement as she set up my profile, making me pose for more photos to have a selection of what to choose as my main picture.

"This one," she insisted, highlighting a picture she caught of me mid-laugh. I took the phone from her hand, taken aback by how soft I looked, human even.

She walked me through how to post one of the stills of the two of us, encouraging me to come up with some cute line or type up song lyrics with emojis. She showed me some examples of how she did it on her account. I smiled to myself as I typed up the caption and tagged her and waited for her phone to ping.

"'Eloise made me do it,' very cute, Mina," she said, reading what I wrote before sharing it on her own account.

My phone immediately buzzed with notifications. I tapped and scrolled through the names of new followers, stopping at Charlie's. His profile wasn't as filled out as Eloise's, but there were plenty of action shots from his games and practices.

"My evil plan to make the boys jealous is working," Eloise bragged. "Charlie just commented on our photo."

"Charlie?" Brooklyn snapped. "What'd he say?"

Eloise burst out laughing at her overreaction. "Chill. Just the prayer hands emoji."

"Whatever. This is boring. Let's go see if my mom is home with dinner."

We filed down the steps behind her toward the kitchen, and I decided now was the time to unleash my well-practiced lie.

"Oh, I didn't realize we were having dinner. I ate before I came."

"It said it on the invitation," Brooklyn said simply.

An older, blonder version of Brooklyn stood at the counter, pulling out sealed containers from a to-go bag, and I was happy to not have to make up an excuse to get out of the room if she had walked in with cardboard pizza boxes carrying the scent of garlic.

"Sorry for the delay, girls," Mrs. Winters apologized. "Brooklyn requested a special dinner, and for some reason, I got roped into driving across town when someone has a perfectly good car sitting in the garage…"

I saw where Brooklyn got her attitude from.

She ran a finger under the plastic seal and popped open the lid, and the pungent smell of garlic hit me. I involuntarily hissed and brought my hand up to cover my mouth and nose. Brooklyn's mom, completely unaware, opened more containers of pasta, chicken, and bread, all covered in the herb.

Brooklyn's entire face lit up with my reaction, the smugness palpable.

I stepped backward, right into Eloise, and I sprang off of her when she tried to right me.

"Are you okay?" she asked, concerned.

Without replying, I ran to open the kitchen door, nearly ripping it off its hinges, and dashed into the yard. I bent over, gripping my thighs, and I greedily took in the fresh, cool night air. I suspected her inviting me was a setup. At the very least, I knew I could rely on my instincts, if nothing else.

"Wow," Brooklyn scoffed. "Rude."

"What just happened?" Rita asked.

Eloise strode over to Brooklyn. "She's allergic to garlic, you idiot."

Brooklyn gasped. "I totally forgot."

"Sure you did," Eloise said, totally unconvinced.

"What's that supposed to mean?"

Eloise didn't answer. She was halfway up the stairs when Brooklyn screamed at her. "Come back here!"

I tuned out the murmurs in the kitchen as best I could, listening to Eloise stomp around in Brooklyn's bedroom. I stood up, feeling somewhat back to normal, in time to see Eloise re-enter the kitchen, juggling our bags and bedding.

"Wait, where are you going?" Brooklyn demanded. "What are you doing?"

"I'm done with this," Eloise said simply.

"So you're just leaving then?"

"Mina has done nothing to you except sit in your seat in a stupid class that won't even matter in a few months from now, and you think it's okay to play with someone like this? With something that could kill her?"

I felt a little guilty for that particular lie, but it was honestly the closest thing to the truth that could explain my reaction.

Brooklyn opened and closed her mouth a few times.

"You're becoming a disgusting, unlikeable person," Eloise continued. "The last thing the world needs is another catty woman, bringing all the rest of us down with her. What kind of toxicity is that, Brooklyn? No wonder Charlie doesn't like you."

Even I flinched at that.

Eloise paused. "I'm sorry. That was too harsh, but it's true, and I'm angry with you, and you need a wake-up call." She walked through the open door, nearly dropping everything in her arms when she turned to address Brooklyn's mom who was humming to herself and pretending like none of this was happening around her. "Thank you for having me, as always, Mrs. Winters."

Without another word, she strolled over to me. My car keys jingled in her hand.

"I'm ready for that ride now."

9

After I assured her I did not need medical attention, we drove over to her house, stopping along the way at a store to pick up an assortment of chocolate and snacks. I swiped the credit card that Trinity had arranged for me before Eloise could protest.

"It's the least I could do for what you said back there," I insisted.

"It's what friends do," she said, echoing my words from earlier. "Well, at least, what I do for our friendship. I don't know if I'm friends with Brooklyn any longer. I'm sick of defending her. The last thing the world needs is another female villain, bringing others down."

I didn't disagree with that.

"Is this really because of the seat thing?" I asked as she pointed for me to turn right.

"She feels threatened, I think, by how you just showed up at school one day and demanded attention."

"Is that what I did?"

She laughed. "Now that I think about it, you've literally done the exact opposite, but you know what I mean."

I didn't know. "I just want a normal human high school experience."

"Well, you've got it," she said, pointing to a small, one-story house. "This is us. You can park in the driveway. My mom is on nights and weekends this month."

The house had a square front yard littered with toy guns and a pink bike. I glanced at the busy street and cringed internally, imagining her siblings playing as cars zoomed past. Inside was cramped, and she hushed me to be quiet because her brother and sister were sleeping.

I took in the living room, filled with mismatched furniture, a suffocating amount of knickknacks, old books, and general clutter. An overstuffed laundry basket sat in the middle of the room, with the same pink scrubs I saw Charlie's mom wear.

"They're out," Eloise said, closing a bedroom door quietly behind her.

She sank on the couch and dumped out the bag of snacks on the cushion between us. "And I'm starving. Maybe I should have grabbed a plate of food at Brooklyn's before we left."

I couldn't help but laugh. Eloise opened the chips with her teeth.

"Your mom is a nurse?"

She nodded. "She and Charlie's mom sometimes have the same shifts. It's how she heard about our school. Of course, I couldn't afford to just go, even with the money from the life insurance company from my dad's car accident, so I had to get a bunch of different scholarships."

I picked up a plain milk chocolate bar from the pile.

"So you've known Charlie a while?"

"Since freshman year. We were all new kids then, being transfers from different middle schools around the city. I was so intimidated by everyone for the longest time, with their designer bags and perfect hair, but being friends with Charlie made my life easy."

"Just friends?"

Between bites, she smiled. "So you're into him, huh?"

"Two nights ago you were trying to feel me out about Tanner, and you've already moved on?" I asked, deflecting her question.

"Well, that was before I saw how you and Charlie looked at each other."

"How do we look at each other?"

She paused, staring off for a moment to recall the picture in her mind. "Like you don't want to look at anyone else."

I nibbled on a small piece of chocolate, needing a minute to process that.

"Oh thank god," she said, relieved.

"What?"

"I've never actually seen you eat and kind of assumed you were one of those beautiful, barely-eat-anything types," she admitted. "Although on your first day of school, Brooklyn tried to convince me that you were a vampire."

I nearly choked, going off into a tailspin of what the repercussions would be if she knew the truth.

"She's ridiculous, isn't she?" Eloise continued, putting me at ease. "I can't believe I have put up with her crap for so long."

The pieces clicked. "Is that why Brooklyn greeted us so awkwardly? She wanted to make sure I didn't need to be invited into her house, like the vampires on television?"

"And the joke about being pale," she reminded me.

I laughed nervously, finally getting a first-hand understanding of why my uncle and the other kings and queens invested in publishing houses and media companies.

Every vampire I knew, regardless of how wary they were of humans, had a basic understanding of the myths and folklore surrounding our kind, even though no one had a true understanding of how vampires came to be. There was speculation in evolving as a subspecies thousands of years ago, and according to my own research, there were even hieroglyphics in Ancient Egypt of the undead.

I was truly fascinated by the human depiction of vampires, reading and watching as much material as I could because every story seemed to be more of a reflection of humans rather than vampires. Like in the 1970s, in the height of the Watergate era, *The Night Stalker* series centered on investigative journalism. I couldn't imagine Uncle Derrick as a vampire during that time period, mostly because of the bell bottoms. Decades later, movies like *The Lost Boys* and *Fright Night* capitalized on teenage interests, a pattern that repeated with my generation with *The Vampire Diaries* and *Twilight*.

The only movie to have ever given me an uneasy feeling was the original black and white *Nosferatu*, and if I did some deep psychoanalysis, it was because the vampire, with his rat-like appearance, was the least human of them all, and I loved being human.

"Want to watch a movie or something?" Eloise asked, hunting for the remote.

Hopefully her tastes were more light and modern than what I had been thinking about.

"Sure," I agreed, folding the rest of the chocolate bar wrapper into itself.

"Actually, wait," she stopped, turning toward me again. "There is something I want to ask you."

She looked a little sheepish, and I waited for her to continue.

"Would you teach me to do my makeup like yours?"

I smiled. "It would be a disservice to let all this knowledge from video tutorials go to waste," I joked. "Let's do it."

We moved to the kitchen for better lighting. She washed her face and gathered up her makeup bag contents in the bathroom, and I picked up a newspaper, the same one that Charlie's dad worked at, and noted that the top story discussed a record high of missing persons cases this year.

"My mom keeps trying to use that as an excuse to guilt me into spending time with them," Eloise said, dumping the contents of her makeup bag on the table. "The twins are thirteen years old and already as tall as me. If someone broke into the house to steal us, they'd have the same chance of fighting them off as I would."

"I'm sure she loves it when you put it like that," I added playfully.

She organized her small and well-worn collection of palettes, lipsticks, and brushes, and I frowned, thinking of the drawers full of makeup in my own bedroom. At the very least, I could leave whatever she liked out of what I had in my bag. I set out my own mascara, eyeliner, and lipstick, lining them up with hers.

"Okay, I need you to sit very still," I demanded, bracing myself for any sudden movements.

After I finished, we had another selfie photo session, painted our nails, and watched bad reality television until she fell asleep in the nest of blankets, pillows, and cushions we made on the living room floor. Eloise insisted on sleeping in her makeup, even after she explained to me how bad it would be for her skin, because she said it was too well done to take off.

I laid there, listening to Eloise's long, even breaths and felt more connected to the human part of me than ever before.

If I'd learned anything from the disaster earlier in the evening, it was that humans were just as selfish as vampires when it came to territory and self-preservation, but they were also messy and emotion-driven and fluid, whereas vampires tended to be calculated.

I did a deep dive on social media, realizing that it would have been far easier than breaking into the school to view yearbooks. I felt a little odd taking in all the information now that I knew more about these humans. Scrolling through old pictures and comments gave me insight I wouldn't have otherwise, and part of me wondered if I should wait to experience and learn these things about them through my own interactions.

When Eloise's mom arrived home the next morning, I made a quick intro and told her I had to be back early.

Eloise sleepily waved goodbye, and I smiled the entire drive back to my house.

"How was the sleepover?"

My mother was amused by the entire ordeal, and just like the idea of going to high school, my father quietly seethed. I joined them at the counter, with a mug of blood, and gave a quick rundown of the night, leaving out the garlic incident and the fact that Eloise and I made a quick getaway.

"It was a very human experience," I finished, taking a sip.

"Sounds like it," my mother said. "Reminds me of when I was a teenager."

My attention snapped to her. She rarely related her human experience to mine, no matter how often or creatively I asked.

My father glanced sideways at her. "You participated in these… gatherings?"

"Every Friday, my friends and I hung out at the mall or headed to one of our houses to stay up all night and watch MTV," she recalled, staring at the counter as she spoke. "But you have to remember, I was a teenager in the early nineties. We all didn't have cell phones to take pictures with or apps that could play any video we wanted."

I wanted to laugh at my father's reaction, the blank look in having no ability to relate to our conversation. "What did you two do last night?" I asked, saving him.

"We attended a charity function put on by the university hospital. We've been working on getting a vampire on the board of directors for a while, so we made a large donation on behalf of Byron Enterprises."

"You'll have time to do that and your work in the manu-facturing sector?" I asked my father, recalling the updates from the last monthly gathering.

"Well, it appears that I actually will be the one joining the board," my mother said.

"That's fantastic," I exclaimed, and I meant it.

Before meeting my father, my mother had dreams of working in the medical field, and this would be the closest she could get to the day-to-day as a vampire. I asked them all sorts of questions about the logistics of their approach and what their plan was for once she was officially on the board. We talked through it until a car rolled up the driveway.

"You better go up and get changed, Mina," my mother urged.

"Why? Who is it?"

"The King."

It was an inside joke of ours to refer to Uncle Derrick as the King when we dealt with him in his official capacity. I assumed his visit would center on what we talked about in the school parking lot two days ago, and I wasn't sure how they would react. Frankly, I dreaded the conversation, so I wanted to delay the inevitable.

In a very human-like fashion, I took my time getting ready. I thumbed through the dresses hanging in my walk-in closet before selecting a burgundy dress that Trinity had sent over as part of my human fall wardrobe. The sleeves were wide and the fabric was soft, but the dress was a little shorter than my preference.

Most vampires were surprisingly modest and only exposed large amounts of skin if they needed to blend in with humans in warmer climates. Anything else drew too much attention. I slid on a pair of thick black tights before stepping into my new favorite pair of ankle boots.

I glanced in the mirror, knowing that my hair would look far better with a few curls in it, but in the interest of time, I applied some smoothing spray and ran my fingers through the strands. I was grateful to have the option to cut and apply heat to my hair without the risk of losing it. Hair was one of the few vanity obsessions for vampires because if they cut theirs, it wouldn't grow back.

Being half-human did have at least one perk.

"And there she is now," my mother said as I made my way downstairs.

Uncle Derrick and two vampires stood to greet me, approaching to bow and extend pleasantries.

"Mina, so lovely to see you again," the older of the two said.

I immediately recognized him from outside Charlie's house, the vampire who tipped off Uncle Derrick on my whereabouts.

"Philip, here, has made a tremendous impact on restructuring our priorities in the aerospace and logistics sectors," Uncle Derrick said.

"Thank you, your majesty," he nodded, appreciatively, before turning back to me. "In human terms, you could say I'm the transportation lobbyist."

"And yet you find the time to tail humans, too?" I asked, feigning sweetness.

He and Uncle Derrick exchanged glances, and the looks on my parents' faces clued me in that they were wholly unaware of the spying-on-humans arrangement I made with my uncle.

"This is Theo," Uncle Derrick said, pivoting to the other introduction hanging in the room.

He bowed deeply, and I inhaled. Pure vampire.

I took in his strong build, which was evident even in a three-piece suit. His shoulders seemed too wide for his frame, leading me to believe there were layers of muscles underneath.

When a human becomes a vampire, his or her physique is frozen. Regardless of how many hours a human spent in the gym, when the transition happens, their strength is nearly the same as all other vampires. I suspected that was why egotism was different for humans and vampires — there were only certain things the latter could control, like maintaining their hair throughout the decades.

I eyed Theo's hair cut, which was closely cropped on the sides and a little longer on the top, a recent trend.

My mother led us to the formal sitting room, where glasses of blood sat waiting for us. Theo stared at my mug, and I ignored his gaze as he took it, and me, in.

I watched in moderate interest as my father, my mother, and Philip discussed the distribution network in the region, which ranged from helicopters and private jets to freight trains and trucks. My mother's tentative appointment to the board of directors opened up access to all university hospitals and blood donation centers, which was apparently a big win when tied into the work my father was doing with food and beverage companies.

Everything was always about the blood, the one thing vampires couldn't live without. As the King, my uncle ensured that everyone in the region had access to what they needed to survive, but it wasn't without careful planning. I hadn't even stepped up into the role Uncle Derrick planned for me, and I was already tired of all the back and forth.

I set my mug down. "Uncle, may I be excused?" I asked.

Uncle Derrick waved at me in dismissal, not breaking the flow of conversation until I was almost out the door. "Mina, how about you give Theo a tour of the house?"

Theo's eyes pleaded with mine. Clearly he wanted out as much as I did.

"Sure," I agreed.

He followed me through the kitchen and out to the backyard, past the small pond lined with Adirondack chairs, and up the hill that overlooked the entire property. I sank down in the fresh grass, the scent I now associated with Charlie, and ran my fingers through the blades.

The people we purchased this property from made the garden and landscaping a point of pride. I loved to sit out here, but usually I was alone, not with a brooding, recently turned vampire. I zoned my hearing to the rows of flowers and the bees circling them, still holding on to the last bit of warmth for the year. The sound was peaceful, especially with the birds chirping nearby.

"How old were you when Philip turned you?" I asked, breaking the silence between us.

He leaned back on his elbows beside me. "Nineteen."

I nodded, still staring in the distance at the petals. "When?" This was one of the common introductory questions among vampires.

"About a year ago."

"Well, that explains the haircut," I said, turning my head slightly to peer at him.

His eyebrows pulled together.

"The fade," I explained. "Very 'in' now, and I hope it stays that way for a while."

"Oh," he said, smiling slightly, and rubbed a hand over his head.

The wind ruffled my hair, and his nostrils flared slightly, taking in my half-human scent.

He shivered, and in an attempt to compose himself, he pulled his phone out of his pocket and checked for messages. There weren't any. His fingers moved across the screen before he locked it and turned his attention back to me.

"So what's it like?" Theo asked.

He sat up, revealing somewhat of an anxious look on his face. I appreciated how he wasn't afraid to show emotion, but I figured it was only a matter of time until Philip trained him away from that, to be more vampire and less human.

I laughed. "Which part? Being half-human? Going to high school and spending eight hours a day defying my own natural instincts? Having the King for an uncle and an uncle for the King? Feeling the pressure of the future and the responsibilities that come with it?"

It spilled out of my mouth before I could help it, and I regretted the words. I didn't know Theo, didn't trust him or Philip, and didn't want my frustrations to become gossip among the nobles.

"All of it," he breathed.

I smoothed down the front of my dress, contemplating

how to answer any of those questions and which ones would even be appropriate to answer.

"There are so many stories about you, and I'm just wondering how many of them are true."

I shrugged. "Probably none of them. Or all of them. I don't know."

"Except that your mere existence defies nature."

"I think of it as more of a biological experiment," I deflected.

"So you're leaning into your human side these days, right?" Theo asked. "Going to human school and whatnot?"

"Yes."

It was strange to have a simple conversation with a vampire outside my family and Trinity, especially someone who still held onto pieces of humanity. Theo might be the only other vampire in the region who could empathize with my situation, to understand what it was like to be this age at this time with my challenges.

Should I open up to someone I barely knew? I didn't hesitate when it came to Eloise and Charlie, but the reality was that I could never be totally myself with them. I had to hide half of who I was, how I existed, and what my future held just to keep them safe. I could never be my whole self around them, no matter how badly I wanted it.

Theo loosened his tie and unbuttoned the shirt at his neck. Vampires didn't feel discomfort how humans did, and I suspected the motion was more out of habit than anything else.

"You haven't really given being a vampire a shot, though."

"Not true. I spent the first eighteen years of my life almost exclusively with vampires, and I'm just now getting around to exploring humanity."

"Really?" He didn't seem convinced. "Tell me three of your friends' names. Only vampires."

I bit my lip.

He raised an eyebrow. "See? My point is made."

His self-satisfaction was clear, and it made me feel worse.

"Congratulations, Theo, you did a fantastic job of reminding me how lonely and isolated I am."

"That was not my intention, trust me," he insisted.

"And I should listen to you, the expert on vampirism?" I pointedly looked at his neck, and he actually seemed embarrassed to have gotten caught in an undone state. "Turned your back on your humanity completely?"

"I'm just suggesting that you've lived a life even few vampires get to experience, with all the sheltering and whatnot."

I gazed past the flowers and trees, over the well-kept grass, and looked at the fence surrounding the property. Tall, black, and intimidating, keeping everything out and me in, most of the time.

My genuine curiosity won the battle over my pride.

"Is your life as a vampire really that different from mine?"

"Well, instead of going to human school, I do work with Philip, going to different job sites and meetings with humans to push things along, which is probably just as boring as sitting in class during the day. But at night," he paused, glancing around as if he had a secret to tell me, "that's when the fun begins."

At night, most of my time was spent alone, obsessing over things I couldn't control and trying to learn as much as I could on my own. "What fun?"

He tisked and leaned closer. "I'm kind of a show, not tell, type. Join me tonight, and you'll see."

I jerked back, put off by his smugness.

"I'll pass."

"Oh come on, Mina."

He was pressing me, and I barely knew him.

If I learned anything from the situation with Brooklyn, it was to trust my instincts wholly, and they screamed that something was off about Theo. His intentions didn't feel honorable, and I suspected someone put him up to the task of getting close to me. I just wasn't sure if it was his idea, my uncle's, or someone else's.

I immediately stopped trusting him. "No thanks." I walked back to the house, and of course, he quickly followed.

I'd been so unaware, feeding off of his energy and delighting in the attention from someone relatively my age whose blood I didn't want to drain. I promised myself I'd be more careful, especially as my uncle integrated me further into working with the nobles and meeting other vampires.

"What's wrong?" Theo asked, righting the buttons at his neck and putting his tie back into place.

I didn't answer him immediately, trying to stomach the words. "Did someone put you up to this? My parents? One of the nobles?" I demanded, meeting his dark brown eyes.

"Trying to get me pulled back into favoring my vampire side?"

"No," he balked, and he actually seemed to be taken aback that I accused him.

I was so off-kilter that I couldn't decide if he was telling the truth.

"I don't need you to show or tell me what it means to be a vampire," I snapped. "I'm not any lesser than you just because I am half-human."

"Mina, stop," Theo pleaded.

I wrenched open the door, only for him to slam it shut. He was stronger than me, all full vampires were, and it contributed to my fury and unease.

He turned, nearly nose-to-nose with me. If he were human, he'd be severely violating my three-foot rule, and I'd lose all control. My fangs descended at that thought, which only made me angrier.

I stepped backward, pressing myself against the wall of the house. My open palms hit the cool stone, and I exhaled.

Theo took in my frustration, and I swore he looked right through my anger and stared down the insecurity and helplessness buried deep inside my chest. I forced myself to blink, deciding I was reading too much into whatever this was, and it was time to move past it.

"You can go now, Theo." There was a distinct hollowness to my voice that hadn't been there before.

He worked his jaw. "You're not what I expected."

"What did you expect?" I hated myself for asking that question and how desperately I wanted it answered.

Theo squared his shoulders. "Not this," he muttered, then bowed dramatically and excused himself.

10

I didn't want to give Theo any credit, but by two o'clock in the middle of the night, I was fidgeting to get out of the house, very aware of how reclusive I'd become.

An hour later, I stood outside Charlie's dad's house and pulled the strings on my black hoodie, like I was about to commit some sort of bank heist. Trinity provided me with the address when I asked earlier, and now that I'd come all this way, I suddenly felt shame, like it was unfair of me to bring this on Charlie.

Daniel Schenley lived in a small duplex that was about a twenty-minute run from my house when using my full vampire speed. I hunted for a spare key underneath the rugs and potted plants but came up empty. I circled around the outside, trying to decide if I could figure out how to pick a lock, and nearly squealed with delight at the open window on the second floor.

I climbed up the gutter with relative ease, shifting my

weight between my hands and feet. Thankfully, the spotlight aimed at the backyard was tilted in the opposite direction from where I hung, leaving me in darkness. I gripped the gutter, denting it slightly with the pressure from my fingertips, as I kicked my feet across the window sill.

My assumption was that this room was Daniel's bedroom or home office, but when I slid inside, I almost fell back out when my eyes landed on Charlie's sleeping form. He slept soundly, sprawled out on the bed that took up most of the room.

It took ten sets of his breaths to right myself, and I focused on the steady, slow movements of his bare chest, which fascinated me.

His eyes fluttered occasionally, lost in his dreams.

This pinnacle of serenity before me stirred something up, a new emotion I hadn't tapped into yet. I couldn't put a name to it, but I was overwhelmed by the urge to lay down next to him and curl my body into his.

My shins touched the edge of the mattress. I held my breath and leaned down, inhaling his scent and testing myself with the small task of brushing a strand of hair from his forehead, promising myself if I reacted I would sprint straight home.

The skin of my fingertips grazed the warmth of his, and the sensation startled me. I edged against the wall until my hand met the door handle, easing it open before I lost sight of the real reason I had come.

From what I gathered, most humans took their work home with them, a necessary but unfulfilling evil in their professional lives, and I hoped Charlie's dad was one of them. The doors of the other rooms were shut tightly, so I crept down the stairs, cut through the living room and kitchen, and stopped at the makeshift office space that had been set up in the formal dining area.

Before deciding to infiltrate the house, I scoped out the newsroom offices, but when I counted the fifth security camera, I had to change course. Vampires who existed before technology became mainstream had it so much easier.

I sat in one of the uncomfortable wood chairs and got to work using the light from my phone. Most of the papers were grocery lists, bills, and the occasional scribbled notes from source interviews. I tried a few iterations of possible computer passwords but came up unsuccessful. Nothing here helped uncover what he knew about Uncle Derrick, his business, or our secret. I tried to reorganize everything back to the way it had been when I found it, but I also doubted the exact order of the pile was something Daniel Schenley memorized.

As I let myself back out Charlie's window, I debated on staying for the rest of the night to watch him sleep. I shook off the thought, knowing that I had associated myself with that kind of creepy behavior for longer than I should have already, and I made my way home.

The next day, I still felt a little off in Charlie's presence, as if in the daylight, from a desk away, seeing him move, think, and act in total control of his own movements made me feel like I violated some sort of trust.

It was a privilege to see him so vulnerable, but I hadn't earned it. I'd taken it without his knowledge.

While Mr. Berry droned on about the ten leading causes of death, Charlie caught me staring at him a few times. Instead of being put off by it, he met my gaze and smiled. I tried to refocus on the classroom.

"What about vaping?" Tanner asked. "Not as bad as cigarettes, right?"

Mr. Berry frowned. "It's less harmful, but it's still not good for you," he explained, flipping ahead a few slides in the presentation. "I have the data on it somewhere."

Charlie shifted in his seat, grabbing my attention once again, and stretched his leg into the aisle between us.

The thing about the movies is that they usually miss the trivial stuff of falling for someone, skipping toward the big pivotal moments in a person's existence, but if I've learned anything from being human it's that it's the sum of all the small things that makes it all worth it.

Like how Charlie doodled funny dogs in his notebooks with the most serious expression on his face or how his two shoes were laced slightly differently. The little anomalies somehow made him even more endearing to me, especially when compared to the smooth, snake-like words that came from Theo's mouth yesterday. Part of the reason I liked being around Charlie was that he made me feel human.

"But what about the flavored vapes?" Brooklyn's high-pitched voice broke through into my thoughts. "Surely there has to be a difference between marshmallow and POG?"

"What's POG?" Tanner asked.

"Passion Fruit, Orange, Guava."

She continued on an ill-informed tirade, asking Mr.

Berry questions but leaving no time for him to answer, while offering up near-constant hair flips and commanding as much attention as she could. My irritation with her was at an all-time high. Every time I looked at her, my skin felt itchy.

My phone buzzed, and I held it under my desk to read.

So now that I know the truth about your lack of high school experiences, it's ON after school.

I glanced up at Eloise, who nodded at me in encouragement. I typed up a response to her.

Can't. Busy.

She glared at me, knowing I was teasing her. One of the topics we discussed while I did her makeup on Saturday night was my complete lack of social activities, and now, she seemed determined to change that.

Nope. You're getting the true high school experience. I'll pick you up after gym.

She held true on her promise, pouncing on me outside the locker room. Brooklyn, Marissa, and Jamie walked past us and pretended like we were invisible. I returned the favor.

"Okay, so I checked out the flyers, and you have a ton of options," Eloise said, leading me over to the oversized bulletin board by the main gymnasium doors.

I fingered the various posters and scribbled-on pieces of paper that were tacked up.

"Can you sing?" Eloise asked.

"Not very well," I admitted.

"Dance?"

I shrugged. "You have to have rhythm, right?" I was a rigid, half-vampire, and there would be no bopping along to the latest hits in my future, especially if it was in front of crowds of humans.

"How about NHS? Rita would be thrilled to have someone other than Nick to talk to about their meetings and extra projects."

Rita was nice, and she didn't act any different toward me in our English quad after the garlic incident, but I didn't want to force anything with her or make her pick sides.

"Which clubs are you in?" I asked Eloise.

Her gaze dropped to the floor.

"You are forcing me to do this, and you haven't even done it?"

She clamped her mouth shut, suppressing a smile, and gave me a sideways glance.

"Eloise," I repeated, slowly, before both of us broke out into a laugh.

"What's so funny?" Charlie asked, walking down the hallway with his bag slung over his shoulder.

"I'm trying to coach Mina on how to get a true high school experience," Eloise explained. "Being homeschooled means she missed out on the torture of extra curriculars."

"You told me this would be fun," I cut her off, and there was a little hint of a whine to my tone.

Eloise looked as sheepish as I'd ever seen her. "I meant that it would be fun for me to hear about secondhand."

"I'm not doing it unless you are."

Charlie stepped up, eyeing the same pieces of paper I had taken in. "Can you sing?"

Eloise laughed. "She can't sing or dance or be as smart as Rita," she answered for me.

My jaw dropped open in mock anger. I was beginning to understand the camaraderie that teasing built.

"What about this one?" He pointed to the most professional-looking one of them all, typed up and designed with a pretty sophisticated drawing of our school. "Decorating for the homecoming dance, setting up some signage, painting the floats."

"That sounds tolerable," I admitted.

"I think you'd be amazing at that," Eloise said. "It'd be just like doing makeup but with an uglier canvas."

I chuckled. "I'll do it if you do, too."

Eloise pursed her lips and dug in her bag for a pen, writing both our names on the lines provided to sign up. "Done," she said with a note of finality.

Charlie cleared his throat. "So are you going to go to homecoming, Mina?"

Eloise's head bounced between us. "I need to, uh, hit up the vending machine." She scurried off around the corner.

I focused back on him. "I'm not sure," I admitted.

"I think Eloise would support your attendance, in the spirit of getting you the true high school experience. Like in that movie where Molly Ringwald—"

"You watch romantic comedies?" I interrupted him, needing to confirm my amusement.

"My sister loves them," he deflected. "I don't mind them, I guess."

His cheeks darkened a fraction, and I had the urge to press my fingertips on his warm skin, once again, but I stopped myself. At that moment, I realized that I was barely prepared for contact, let alone a crowded gym where I would be expected to touch and move against him.

"I think I'm going to sit this one out."

"What?" Eloise shrieked, jumping out from behind a plaster wall. "No, absolutely not."

"I agree with Eloise," Charlie said. "What's the point of going to high school if you can't get all dressed up and listen to loud music in a sweaty gym?"

"Well when you put it that way…"

He smiled, assuming I was being playful, but really I was panicking. I'd need to come up with an excuse. Because of Saturday night, Eloise was now well aware I rarely had plans. She kept bouncing around on her feet, and the sound distracted me.

"Well, how about we do a practice run?" Charlie suggested. "Try before you buy. No suits or dresses, well, unless you want to wear one. I don't think that I have a figure for a ballgown."

He was rambling, something I'd never witnessed before. The words were in an uneven cadence. It hit me. He was asking me out, and he was nervous about it, and I liked it.

"Charlie," I stopped him, surprised enough to not stop my smile from spreading. "Are you trying to be clever about asking me out on a real date?"

"Is it working?"

He bit his lip, and I smiled.

"Friday night?"

"Friday night," I confirmed.

His phone buzzed in his pocket, and his eyes bugged slightly. "I'm so late for practice," he said. "But I'll talk to you later."

"Bye," I called, watching him scramble to go get ready.

Eloise stalked back over, tapping the top of her pop can, fresh from the vending machine. "He has it so bad for you. Come on, let's go get ice cream or something, so we can obsess over every detail of whatever that was."

11

Classes on Friday dragged by so slowly that I was partially convinced someone had slowed down the seconds on the clock just to mess with me. I tried to internalize my nervousness, but I was fidgety, thinking through all the firsts I was about to experience.

I'd never eaten in a restaurant before, let alone on a date with a human who was driving me there. Very rarely I would sit in an uncrowded coffee shop to observe humans while I nursed an espresso. It was also how I learned the hard way that humans do not like to be sniffed.

Eloise texted me all day, even as we sat across from each other in the library, asking one thousand questions about what clothes I was going to wear and how I was going to do my hair and makeup. She even offered to come over and help me get ready, but I shut down that idea. Trinity was my uncle's most efficient employee, but even I doubted her skills of filling our house with enough furniture and decorations to be up to human standards in mere hours.

She did seem satisfied when I sent her a picture of my ensemble when I got home, a cream sweater dress with knee-high boots. I even took the time to curl my hair in loose waves.

No jacket?

I checked the temperature app. *No. I won't need one.*

Well, if you do get cold… I'm sure Charlie would keep you warm.

My least favorite rom-com cliché was when a man would give a woman his jacket. I understood chivalry, but from my experience, most female humans had enough items in their oversized purses to sustain themselves for days on a stranded island, yet we were expected to believe that they wouldn't have the fortitude to protect themselves from a cool autumn breeze?

Post that photo to social. Tag Charlie in it. Brooklyn would die.

You're petty.

You're boring.

I heard the rumble of Charlie's truck as it passed through the decorative gates at the end of the driveway. Stuffing my phone and lipstick in my purse, I scurried through the house and waited outside the front door when he approached. My parents were gone for the day or I would have insisted meeting Charlie somewhere instead.

He put a finger up when I took a step forward, and he put the car in park, got out, and walked around the side to open the door for me. Eloise would giggle uncontrollably when I told her that detail.

"Hi," he breathed, meeting my eyes before his gaze dropped to the exposed skin of my legs.

I slid in. Charlie shut the door and circled around,

fidgeting with the top button of his black button-down shirt. I caught a whiff of residual lemon cleaning product and noted that his car was nearly spotless, with clean but well-worn fabric interior and wood paneling. If I had to guess, it was manufactured at some point in the eighties or nineties, nearly two decades earlier than all the other cars I'd seen in the school parking lot. It made me like him even more.

Charlie turned on the ignition and rotated his upper body, putting his arm on the back of my headrest to back down the driveway. I'd sucked down an almost uncomfortable amount of blood in preparation for the closeness. As he navigated us through a few winding curves of back roads, I fingered the string of beads and wings hanging from his rear-view mirror.

"Do you have a thing for butterflies?" I asked, rubbing the plastic pink and purple beads between my thumb and pointer finger.

"Emma does. This work of art was my birthday gift a few years ago when she was going through a big bead phase. She started making bracelets and necklaces, and then she started adding other items she picked up at the craft store to them. I think those are hair clips, actually."

"That's adorable."

"It was, until my mom found out she was trying to sell them online. Emma gave out our home address and one of my mom's credit card numbers to a few strangers, and she got all sorts of bogus charges on her card."

"When entrepreneurship goes wrong," I mused. "There are all sorts of inspirational quotes online about how important it is to fail before you succeed. This story might make a great opening to a TED Talk she gives in fifteen years."

He hummed in amusement. "I hope she hires me at whatever company she's running then."

"Won't you be too busy with your professional soccer career?" I teased.

"Yeah, right, in my dreams." When we did our Health assignment, we talked entirely in theoreticals, and I was glad when his tone turned more serious, divulging his actual plans. "I've actually been working on my early decision application to Carnegie Mellon."

"Studying what? Law? Like what you picked for our Health project?"

He chuckled. "No, all that extra school would be too much for me. I've been looking more into electrical and computer engineering."

"I'm sure that degree will be very useful for Emma's future business, especially when it comes to best practices for online safety and security."

He grinned, glancing over at me while we sat at a stoplight. "What about you? What are your plans for next year?"

Humans spend the first eighteen years of their lives building up to what they're going to do the moment they graduate from high school, envisioning grand plans for college or the workforce or whatever else they end up doing, but I, with none of those plans lined up, settled on a response that wasn't an outright lie.

"I'm going straight to work for my uncle. I've been spending more time with him, learning about his various investments and preparing to take it over one day."

"Don't say that when my dad's around," he warned in a light tone and pressed on the gas. "He has apparently been chasing this story about your uncle for years, trying to get an 'in.' When I went over to his place the next day, he drilled me with so many questions, asking everything I knew about you."

I tried not to flinch. "So you split time between two houses? Isn't it frustrating to bring your stuff back and forth between them?"

He shrugged. "We've been doing it for so long that it feels normal now. Emma and I are usually at my dad's every Tuesday and Thursday night, and we alternate weekends and holidays."

He pulled into a parking lot, and I jumped out of the car before he could come around to offer a hand. Shutting the door behind me, I glanced at the restaurant, relieved to breathe in the smell of curry.

"Is this okay?" Charlie asked. "I never asked what you liked, but I figured we'd be safe with Indian food, with you not being able to eat garlic and me being a vegetarian and all."

"It's perfect," I said.

We walked in, and the short woman at the hostess stand greeted Charlie with a hug, something that I'd never experienced at restaurants while picking up to-go orders. He returned her embrace, and she squealed slightly.

"I haven't seen you since August! Have you been too busy to come in and see me since then?"

My mind flashed back to how Deb, the receptionist at school, melted over him. Charlie seemed to endear everyone around him, but middle-aged women seemed particularly charmed.

"I'm sorry, Sam, I've been swamped with school and soccer and college stuff," he explained.

"Are you staying or taking out?" Sam asked.

Charlie tilted his head in my direction.

"Oh, who's this?"

She offered me a genuine smile, and I returned it.

"I'm Mina." I found that if I took a slight step backward and hid my hands, humans picked up on nonverbal cues to not touch me.

"You know each other from school?" Sam asked.

I nodded, and she escorted us to a table in front of the window.

The walls were painted in bright pinks and oranges and decorated with art pieces and artificial flowers that I wanted to study more, but the sun was setting in equally beautiful colors. We had a great vantage point to watch it happen.

"Yep," Charlie said. "We have Health together."

Sam waited for us to both settle in. "Shall we send you over your usual order?"

"Did you want to look at a menu?" Charlie asked, very considerately.

I shook my head. "I'm up to try anything." Well, within reason.

Sam went over to punch in our order on the computer, and I waited until she was out of earshot to pick our conversation back up.

"I didn't know you were a vegetarian."

He pushed the plastic container of sugars around the

table. "My mom has been for as long as I can remember, and I just kind of gradually adopted it as well. When this restaurant first opened, my mom was one of the first customers, and she and Sam have been close friends ever since."

That explained the hugging.

I wondered if Sam would report everything that happened to Charlie's mom, and the more I thought about it, the more pressure I put on myself. I glanced toward the kitchen a few times and noticed some of the staff staring at us on and off.

Sam slyly dropped off two glasses of fizzy drinks in front of us before focusing her attention on seating more guests. The restaurant started to get busy, and I was once again glad I overdid it on blood before Charlie picked me up.

Charlie held up his glass. "Cheers."

We clinked them together, and I took a tentative sip. The bubbles tickled the inside of my nose, sending me into a wheezing fit.

"Are you all right?"

He leaned forward, hands on the table as if he were ready to jump up and save my life.

I nodded my head, scratching my nose with one hand and patting my chest with the other. I reluctantly let out a few more coughs, getting the side eye from some other patrons, before I composed myself.

"That was not what I expected," I explained. "You enjoy this?"

Charlie raised an eyebrow. "Sprite? You've never had it before?"

I shook my head and brought it up to my lips, trying it once more. With the element of surprise gone, the bubbles were actually a little refreshing as they moved over my tongue and down my throat. Charlie watched me with amusement.

"So homeschooled, no garlic, new to pop, what else do I need to know?"

I considered it for a minute. "I'm a night owl. I used to love reading, but I'm ashamed to admit I spend most of my time watching things instead of reading about them. I don't like a lot of music that's popular right now. I listen to old jazz or podcasts, but most of all, I like silence."

Sam placed metal trays of food in front of us, briefly explaining to me what all the ingredients and dishes were. I was overwhelmed, in the best way, with all the colors and smells. I tore a piece of the dosa, scooping up some potatoes with it, and dipped it in the coconut chutney. It was incredible.

"Silence, huh?" Charlie posed. "Does that mean I should shut up?"

"Definitely not." He didn't have to constantly tune things out all day like I did. "I'm not trying to be dramatic about it. I just think humans tend to drown out their thoughts with their phones, or television, or the dozens of other distractions readily available, and sometimes, I like to enjoy the quiet."

"Yeah, that's fair," he admitted. "Although a little challenging for me to do sometimes since I'm usually with the team or an eight-year-old who asks me a new question every second. The only time I get to myself lately is in the car."

"I've always wondered what it'd be like to have a sibling."

"I recommend it most of the time," he said between bites.

He asked me more questions about what I like to do, even asking me to recommend some of my favorite podcast episodes for him to download. He shared funny stories about growing up with a little sister. I drained the entire Sprite and picked at my food, enough so that he wouldn't notice I wasn't really interested in eating more than a few bites.

At the end of the meal, Sam brought out bowls of hot water with lemon slices inside, quickly explaining that they were to rinse my fingers, not to drink.

Charlie insisted on paying, and as we waited for Sam to return his card, I realized how relaxed I was. Being closer to humans became a little more tolerable over time, but something about him, maybe his easygoingness and general interest in me, put me at ease in his presence.

My body felt good, my posture soft, matching the vibe of the other diners around us, who had forgotten about us since my coughing fit ended. A few families dined, but it was mostly couples, sharing similar plates of food to what Charlie and I had.

I became acutely aware of how much space was between us. Some of the other couples sat catty-corner, touching each other while talking or holding hands, and I glanced over at Charlie, who was watching me take in my surroundings.

The temptation to touch his skin surfaced. I stared at the rough texture and clean, neatly trimmed nails on his hands, and I imagined what it would be like to feel them on my skin.

I picked up my hands from my lap, setting my elbows on the table, and I leaned toward him, inching my hands slowly to his. He moved his hands closer to me, on my half of the table. I extended my pointer finger, lightly tracing the deep creases that cut across the surface of his palms.

He squirmed slightly under my light touch and smiled.

"Can you read palms?"

I shook my head. "I can't tell fortunes either," I admitted.

He flipped his hands over to return the favor. Before he could notice the lack of lines on my own palms, I gently closed my fingers over his, holding his hand in mine. It was a pleasant feeling, being intertwined.

"Are you cold?" he asked, running his thumb in circles around mine. "Your hands are freezing."

"I'm fine."

When Sam approached, I moved to pull back, but Charlie held my grasp, thanking Sam and smiling at her. She said goodbye and that she hoped she'd see us again soon.

I thanked Charlie as he signed the check one-handed. While he calculated the tip, I glanced out the window, wondering if this meant the night was over. I'd spent some time in this part of town after-hours, walking around and looking at the shops closed for the day, the bars ramping up for the evening. Maybe Charlie would want to go see—

My attention jerked when my eyes caught a tall figure underneath one of the street lamps, and I had to stop myself from reacting to Philip, who glared at me from across the street.

The slight squint of his eyes reminded me of the promise I made to Uncle Derrick, to dig into what Charlie knew or if I could somehow leverage it with his father. He bowed slightly and moved back into the shadows.

"Ready?" Charlie asked, squeezing my hand to bring me back to his eyes, which were filled with hope.

I led Charlie a few blocks away from the rows of restaurants and inhaled, sussing out if Philip was lurking around. There was no trace of him that I could detect.

Our hands were still connected, and I tried not to focus on how the blood pumped through his, back up to his forearm and toward his heart. He was telling me his version of how he and Eloise became friends, and it wasn't unlike her story enough to hold my attention.

I picked up my pace, and he met it until we hit the entrance of a small green space, complete with a jungle gym, benches, and empty fountain.

He let go of my hand to run and jump on a metal spinner, holding onto one of the large handles as he moved his body to whip it around faster. I grimaced, imagining all the worst-case scenarios of him flying off and breaking his skull on the concrete or becoming impaled on a fence.

Humans were equal parts fragile and reckless, and they seemed unable to reconcile the two.

On impulse, I lurched forward and jumped on. I intended to stop the whirling or attempt to hold him to one of the safety bars, but it was Charlie who pulled me close, holding me firmly against the yellow metal.

The lights blurred as we spun around while the cool

wind whipped in my hair. His arms snaked around my waist, pulling me flush against him. His eyes flickered to my lips, and I swiped my tongue over them, a little self consciously.

It was slightly unnerving to have another being this close to me, let alone a human whose blood I craved.

His hands grazed upward on my back as he leaned down. His pounding heart practically screamed in my ears, and I pressed my hand against his chest, fascinated by the rhythm. I glanced up at him, knowing that I was causing this reaction in him, his own version of fangs and shakes.

We slowed to a stop, but my world still spun. Our lips were so close, and I could push up on my feet to bridge the gap. Mentally, physically, physiologically even, I was not ready for this. I wanted to be, but my body defied me.

My legs started to shake, rolling a tremor upward. I should have brought spare vials of blood. It would have been easy to hide them in my bag and sneak off into the bathroom, downing them like how humans took shots of alcohol. I'd be drunk off that delicious metallic red. I exhaled. I needed to stop thinking about blood.

I ran my tongue across my teeth, not surprised to find a few millimeters of my fangs peeking out. I pressed it against the tips of each fang, alternating back and forth, willing them to go back in.

"Mina," Charlie whispered, even though we were completely alone.

Out of necessity, I held my breath, rendering a response impossible.

Concern etched across his features. "Are you cold? You're shivering."

His hands moved over my back and arms, trying to create warmth with friction. My eyes hadn't started to burn yet, so as long as I kept my mouth shut, he wouldn't know anything was off aside from my involuntary convulsing.

He brushed my hair away from my face with his fingertips, and surprisingly, the gentleness of the motion calmed me. He traced the lines of my cheekbones and my chin. My body loosened with each passing second, and as Charlie's heart slowed to a normal pace, my outward appearance did, too.

Vampires considered being open and unguarded a weakness, but to humans, it was intimacy.

I was unwound, teetering between the two parts of myself, needing to assert my dominance, to control him the way he had unintentionally done to me, while wanting to offer him the same affection he gifted to me, too.

When his touch drifted to my neck, a sudden rush of adrenaline propelled me to close the space between us. I couldn't decide which half of me I was indulging as I launched upward, bringing my lips to his. He stumbled backward, slamming against another metal railing before enveloping me completely in his arms.

It was a curious feeling, like none I'd experienced before, to move together in tempo. He kissed me with such dizzying passion that I forgot I wanted to fight to be the one in charge.

When I deepened the kiss, swiping my tongue across his bottom lip, it only spurred him further. He pressed one hand into my back and tangled the fingers of his other hand in my hair, holding me like that as time brushed past us.

Gently, he pushed me backward. I glanced up into his

dilated pupils, utterly confused. He was completely breathless, and I felt a little shame for not remembering that he, unlike me, needed regular intervals of oxygen to survive.

He dropped a few light kisses on my mouth between breaths.

"I don't have any effect on you?" Charlie asked lightly, the rising and falling of his chest evident between us.

If only he knew the havoc of my insides. Outwardly, I stayed collected, and I smiled and launched myself off toward the swing set.

He composed himself and joined me on the cold metal swings, where we sat and talked for hours.

12

At my insistence, Charlie dropped me off at the end of my driveway, near the street. I told him it was because I didn't want to wake my parents, but in reality, I didn't want my parents to know I'd spent the last six hours alone with a human boy, taking a lot of risks.

It's not that they wouldn't understand. My parents got together when my mother was still human herself, but it was something about the time we spent together that was so precious, I wasn't ready to share it with anyone else. Well, except Eloise, who had been sending me texts at an increasing rate over the progression of my date with Charlie.

HELLO??????

I rolled my eyes. *Shouldn't you be asleep?*

SHOULDN'T YOU BE TELLING ME EVERYTHING?

We had apparently reached the screaming text stage of our friendship.

I will tomorrow.

IT IS TECHNICALLY TOMORROW RIGHT NOW.

If I promise to take you out for breakfast and spill my guts, will you leave me alone?

Her chat bubble started and stopped a few times.

Pick me up at 10.

I sent her a thumbs up and put my phone back in my purse.

Cutting around through the back of the house to the kitchen, I let myself in and grabbed a mug of blood. My parents were in the main room with jazz radio playing softly.

As I walked toward them, the smooth sound of the music came to a halt, quickly replaced by a panicked voice. "Good evening, listeners. Breaking news out of the North Hills tonight as police responded to an anonymous tip that led them to an empty warehouse where five bodies were discovered. We will not be releasing the names until the families have been notified, but this is believed to be connected to the string of missing women. Police are remaining tight-lipped on the details, but they did reveal that the bodies were all heavily bruised and, in some cases, completely drained of blood."

In a very human motion, I dropped the mug, sending shards of ceramic and blood splatters all over the floor, the walls, and myself.

I ignored the scene at my feet and walked into the room. My parents, sitting on two wingback chairs with a chessboard on a table in between them, shot confused expressions in my direction.

"Is that us?" I asked.

They both looked at each other.

"Is that us?" I repeated again, sounding a little more hysterical. "Are vampires responsible for these disappearances and deaths?"

"I'm not completely sure, Mina," my father said calmly. "If it makes you feel better, I'll confer with Derrick on this tomorrow."

They turned back to their match.

I opened and closed my mouth several times, astounded by their nonchalance.

How could they be so flippant about deaths, regardless of the species? These were human girls, more and more missing each week. It wasn't that abnormal for people to go missing, looking at crime statistics, but the fact that they were drained of blood was a telltale sign something was out of the ordinary.

Suddenly, it hit me.

They weren't surprised because they had already likely discussed this with the other noble families, with Uncle Derrick even. I ground my teeth together in irritation, and without a second of hesitation, grabbed my keys and hopped in my Jeep.

As I drove, I went through cycles of anger, confusion, and anguish over the situation. It was my parents' non-reaction that had set me off, but I couldn't even imagine what the parents of those women were going through. Even if we weren't responsible, vampires had the time, money, and resources to help, and we just stood idly by. On this, and so many other things.

I took the back way to my uncle's property, which was more crowded than I'd ever seen it. Cars lined up as far as I could see. As I off-roaded the same way my mom had a few weeks earlier, the noise grew louder.

Every single light appeared to be on, illuminating the expansive structure in a slightly eerie way, but also giving me a view to see that nearly every room was crawling with vampires. I parked and made my way in.

The vampires were extravagantly dressed, and I felt more out of place than normal. Ignoring the gapes and stares at me and my blood-stained dress, I weaved my way from room to room until I found my uncle, sitting on an oversized velvet chair. Vampires surrounded him as they took sips from different glasses.

"This blood is the first out of one of our testing laboratories, where it was infused with a specific enzyme to change the taste," Uncle Derrick explained, taking a sip for himself, then pouring a few drops into the mouth of the male vampire who straddled his lap.

"It's so much richer," a female vampire at his feet nearly gasped when she got her own taste.

The rest of the group asked him when it would be brought to market, what else was in the works, and a number of other questions I tuned out in disgust.

I understood why vampires had such distrust for humans. After witnessing decades of violence within the human race, not to mention understanding the history of how witches were treated in Salem, they did everything to protect themselves. It made sense to me, the need for discretion and secrecy, but after floating on such a high with my human life earlier, this scene was difficult to stomach.

It even put me off from drinking blood.

My uncle hadn't noticed my arrival, so I slipped out, vowing to catch him when he was alone. I smoothed my hair down, wanting to shield my face in fear of recognition.

Trinity walked down one of the hallways and I turned quickly, opening one of the massive wooden doors and sprinting past a few vampires, only to slam the door on the opposite side behind me. Thomas and Margaret, the woman who made it clear she was not my biggest fan at the last monthly gathering, turned a corner into the room with the long table, and I ran for it again, avoiding vampires until I locked myself in Uncle Derrick's cooler, needing a minute to bring myself under control.

I couldn't lose it in a house full of vampires, I reminded myself, ones who were supposed to bow in my presence, not mock me for a public meltdown. I slid down to the floor, finding comfort in the cool temperature, and leaned my back against one of the shelves.

My head was in my hands when the door opened and shut quickly.

"Hello, Mina."

I knew who the deep voice belonged to without looking up.

"Theo," I practically groaned.

He laughed hollowly. "Well, don't hide your excitement."

I glared up at him. "What can I do for you?"

He bowed, then smoothed out the nonexistent wrinkles in his shirt. I forced the air out of my lungs, watching it turn into a steam of cold fog as it left my mouth.

"Half of the nobles are right outside the door," he

explained. "And I'm guessing that's who you're trying to avoid."

"Part of it," I mumbled.

"Hiding is a very human thing to do."

"Well seeing as I am half-human, it makes sense."

I couldn't hide the edge to my voice. I shifted my posture, kicking my legs out in front of me, and Theo hissed.

"What?" I exclaimed before glancing down at the front of my dress. "Oh, that."

He sniffed. "Is that… yours?"

I shook my head and was surprised that he looked slightly relieved. Uncle Derrick was intentionally vague about what traits of mine were human and what traits were vampire, so it was plausible for Theo to believe that I could sustain a gory injury. He set down his half-drained glass of blood on a shelf and joined me, somewhat tentatively, on the floor.

Laughter from outside the door did nothing to improve my mood.

"Is this that you meant when you said I'd have to see it for myself?" I asked.

He shook his head. "This isn't even the half of it. And if I weren't speaking to the niece of the King, I might say that this is actually a little boring."

"Really?"

The rest of the vampires seemed to be having a different experience.

"Don't get me wrong, this is normal socializing for vampires. It's never actually occurred to me before that you've never made your presence known here, being the heir and all, but I guess it makes sense seeing as you're not as strong or—"

"Okay, enough," I said, a little sharply.

He smirked. "But there is much more to the vampire way of existence than meetings and your own family, Mina. Maybe it's time you explored it."

"And you're going to be my guide to all things wonderfully vampire and eye-opening?"

"I'm willing to be," he said smoothly. "If you'll have me."

I rolled my eyes. "No thanks."

He eyed me curiously, and I crossed my arms across my chest.

We sat in silence for a few minutes, listening to the sounds of the others.

"So why are you here then?" Theo posed the question with as much softness as he could muster, and it seemed like a genuine curiosity.

I picked at my nail polish, a very Eloise trait, refusing to meet his gaze. "The missing girls," I explained. "I want answers."

"And you think your uncle has them?"

"That's what I want to know."

Theo stared at the floor in front of him, lost in thought for a second. "You know, I briefly wondered the same thing, but your uncle has been very stern about making sure we get blood from donors and that no humans are harmed. Even in the past when there have been issues with out-of-control vampires, it hasn't made it to the news. Usually it has been cleaned up and dealt with within hours of something happening."

"That's reassuring," I scoffed. "They just announced that the blood was drained from a few of the victims."

He regarded my words carefully and then shook his head. "I don't know, Mina. I just don't know. It wouldn't make sense for it to be us, to have that risk of exposure."

"That's all vampires can think about. How it impacts them, how it should be dealt with, how we can benefit from it, but what about the potential that one of us is taking a daughter away from her parents or a mom away from her children? Why do our priorities matter more than actual human lives?"

"I think it's a natural instinct, regardless of species, to be concerned about how a situation will impact them," he admitted. "How a stock market crash will impact their finances. How traffic will impact their commute. How someone else's success can cause insecurities about their own failures."

I considered it for a moment. "It seems a little bit desperate."

"Everyone's desperate about something, Mina."

Maybe I overreacted when I first met him. I took his confidence for smugness, his manner of speaking for arrogance, his insistence as disingenuous. Frankly, it felt good to talk openly with a vampire, someone who wasn't my parents or Uncle Derrick, someone who understood both worlds I lived in.

I gave him a once-over, trying to see him with fresh eyes, and he caught my stare.

A loud banging sounded from the front of the house, causing me to jump up.

Theo chuckled. "And so begins the next phase of the evening entertainment."

"What does?"

"Now that everyone has had their fill of blood and polite conversation, the fighting begins."

"Fighting," I repeated.

"More like boxing, I suppose, if you're familiar with it," he explained. "I've got money down. You want to watch?"

"I'll pass."

"Another rejection? Mina, you wound me."

I rolled my eyes. "Somehow I think you're going to be just fine."

"On the bright side, everyone should be there now if you want to make a hasty exit."

We both stood up, and he tentatively opened the door, sticking his head out to confirm we were alone before widening it all the way to let me pass. Until we stepped out of the room, I didn't realize how cold I was. I would need to turn on the heat on the ride home.

Before he turned, he bowed. "I'll see you again soon," he promised.

I cocked an eyebrow.

"If you don't take me up on my offer, I'll at least see you on the twentieth." He took in my blank face and added, "Mina, your ritual."

"Right, right," I said dismissively.

When I got back to my parents' house, I treated myself to a bath and soaked everything in.

13

After our date, Charlie and I seemed to have moved into an undefined yet elongated dating phase. He walked me to each class, sent me text messages in the evening, and expected to hang out during our free time.

Not to say that I wasn't fine with it, but it took some additional planning on my part.

I shot back blood vials in the toilet stall midday, needing to restore my energy for all the extra touching and close proximity. I tried to put a little more distance between us, attributing a lack of touching to a total disdain for public displays of affection, but I made up for it by cheering for him loudly at his game on Tuesday, and by Thursday, we had settled into a comfortable groove of how to be around each other on school grounds.

Eloise and I officially started our work on homecoming decorations, and Charlie joined us occasionally if practice ended early, sitting in a metal folding chair beside us to do homework and complain about Eloise's choice of music.

"I just think the skyline needs more, I don't know, something," Eloise said, staring at my work with disapproval.

"It's a skyline, what else does it need? Animals? Shooting stars? Glitter?" Her eyes lit up, and before she could open her mouth, I added, "I'm joking. Everyone knows that glitter is the worst."

She shook her head. "No, it's a great idea. Think of how fantastic it will look in the sunlight!"

"And how awful it will be to clean up," I muttered.

I didn't see the appeal, but when she told my idea to a few others working on the project, they shared her enthusiasm and quickly located a few options. I sighed and dipped my brush in one of the containers they set down in front of me, adding glitter to some sections of wet paint.

"It looks so much better already," Eloise clapped.

Alex, the head of the committee, agreed with Eloise. They talked through a few other improvements that could be made, stressing over whether the buildings needed a touch more gray to them or if the right shade of blue was being used for the sky.

When we finished for the day, I washed out the brushes at the sink. The water ran clear, and I set the brushes to dry and wiped my hands clean. Charlie and Tanner, freshly showered and smelling divine after practice, surveyed the project so far. Alex and some of the others in the club accosted them with questions and conversation.

"Anyway, I'd love it if you two could come by on Saturday," Alex said brightly. "Bring anyone else from the team who wants to come, too."

"To what?" I asked, inserting myself into the conversation.

She smiled warmly at me. "My parents are out of town, and I'm throwing an all-day rager."

"Mina and I have plans," Charlie started. "But we'll—"

"Be there," Eloise interrupted. "Mina, Charlie, and I will be there."

She bugged her eyes behind Charlie's back. It was her way of urging me to agree.

"Tanner will be there, too," Tanner added.

Eloise glared at him. "And hopefully not referring to himself in the third person."

We took down her number and the other details for Saturday, and the four of us walked out toward the parking lot. Charlie insisted on carrying my bag to my car, which was parked right next to his.

"What was that about?" I asked Eloise. "The thing with strong-arming us into going?"

"I have always wanted to go to one of her parties," she explained. "They're apparently wild. She has a huge house with, like, a sauna and stuff."

With Uncle Derrick's gathering still on my mind, I wondered how different this experience could be. "A sauna? Is that a thing you would typically use at a party?"

"Not typically but maybe this is, like, the next evolution of parties," she said, laughing. "We should have had a sleepover at her house instead of Brooklyn's."

Tanner put his arm around Eloise and suggested we make it a double date. She shoved his arm off her shoulders and rolled her eyes. He pretended to be physically wounded, and they started bickering.

I stepped up to walk with Charlie, hoping that would prevent me from getting pulled into their squabble. "Are you okay if we go? I mean, it sounds cool, but I know we had plans to go to the movies."

"I haven't bought tickets yet. Maybe we could catch the midnight showing if you're not too tired?"

Tiredness would never be an issue for me. "Works for me."

Eloise let herself into the passenger side of my car and slammed it shut. Tanner hopped into his sleek black BMW and sped off without a parting word to either of us.

"You free to come over and hang out now?" Charlie asked me.

"Sure, just let me drop Eloise off, and I'll swing by." I would also suck down some blood, but he didn't need to and couldn't know that.

"Cool, I'm at my dad's tonight," he added casually. "I'll see you in a bit."

He dropped a kiss on my lips and completely missed the scowl on my face. It wasn't that I didn't want to hang out with Charlie, but I felt weird about being at his dad's house ever since I snuck in. The promise I made to Uncle Derrick to dig into what Daniel Schenley knew hung over my head like a storm cloud.

Thankfully, his father was nowhere to be found when I arrived at his house. Charlie pulled up his laptop to continue researching information on health insurance options. We had to create a presentation on the different types and what was best for each income and family situation. I added a bonus slide on why the U.S. should move away from employer-sponsored health insurance options.

I closed my laptop once I finished my contribution. "What other homework do you have to do?"

"Just English," Charlie said, putting the final touches on his slides.

"How'd you do on your *Macbeth* quiz?" I helped him prepare for it earlier in the week.

"Ms. Semple said we'd get it back tomorrow, actually. Hey, that reminds me, what were you talking to her about after class today?"

My teacher asked me to stay back to chat after AP English. Charlie lingered out in the hall while I did, and I had to wave him off to go to his next class or he would have been late. She gripped my *Jane Eyre* paper and drilled me with questions about my future, wanting to know all sorts of details, and it caught me off guard.

"...and then she started asking me all sorts of questions about what colleges I'm applying to, wanting names and prospective fields of study," I recalled. "It was quite strange, like an interrogation of some sorts."

Charlie twirled his pen between his fingers. "So let me get this straight. Ms. Semple asked you to stay after class, walked through all of the highlights of the paper you just received a perfect grade on, and then demanded information about your future plans?"

"More or less," I admitted, trying to make sense of it.

"Mina, she wants to help you get into whatever college you want." Charlie seemed confused as to why he had to explain it to me. "She's clearly impressed by your work."

"Well, what do you think she wants from me for it?"

"Wants from you?" Charlie repeated.

"In exchange for her help?"

Charlie laughed. "Nothing. She just wants to support you and help you."

"With no ill intentions?"

"With no ill intentions," he assured me. "I forget that you've never been to a real school before and that this is all new to you."

I shrugged, still puzzled by the altruistic behavior.

Humans could be generous when they wanted to be, but my mixed feelings on Theo began to bleed into my perspective on other people, making me a little more guarded. Perhaps she found out who my uncle was and wanted an introduction or something.

"I thought you weren't planning on college anyway?" Charlie pointed out.

The more I considered it, the more it sounded like a logical next step. Many humans took on internships while they studied at a university. Uncle Derrick and I negotiated one year of high school, but maybe I could get him to budge on a few years of college, seeing what I could pick up that would ultimately benefit him in the long run, anyway.

"I've just been thinking about it," I admitted.

"That's great, Mina," Charlie said, and he meant it. "I have a ton of brochures and stuff in my room at my mom's house if you want me to bring them over for you."

His offer was sweet and well-intended, but I'd already spent all of Wednesday night doing virtual tours of campuses, researching what options were and how feasible it would be for me to attend.

"Thank you, but I've already signed up for a bunch of stuff online and have more than I can go through already," I said as appreciatively as I could.

He opened the fridge and returned with two cans of pop, tapping on the top of both before offering one to me. "Have you thought about what you would want to study?"

"I've been thinking about something in science, maybe research, pharmacy, or pre-medical."

"Well, a doctor's salary certainly helps our budget," he teased, referencing our Health project.

His muscles flexed slightly when he tore open a bag of chips and offered it to me. I reached for one, unsure how I felt about the overwhelming scent of oil and salt. He watched me take the smallest bite I possibly could, which crumbled all over the table. When I rushed to clean it up, I caught Charlie looking at me with the most exasperated expression.

"I've never had this before," I explained.

He burst out laughing. "First time trying Sprite on Friday, and now you're telling me you've never had a potato chip?"

"My parents have really strict dieting rules."

"Okay, okay, we're going about this all wrong," he said, pushing aside our textbooks and pulling out a notebook. "We're making a list of everything you have never tried, and then we're going to work through them."

I indulged his excitement. "Well, in that case, it might be shorter to make a list of food I have tried and go from there."

He laughed and readied his pen.

"Well, about every kind of nut, fruit, grain, and vegetable," I started. "I've tried a few meats but mostly found them repulsive. Let's see, I've had a cheese quesadilla, a blueberry muffin, espresso, cake, a sip of a milkshake, Indian food, waffles. My favorite food is chocolate. Eloise loves to make fun of me for it."

"Oh, so Eloise knows about this?"

"Not exactly," I admitted.

"You're missing a very key food group here."

"Which one?" I ran through the human food pyramid, the one the U.S. government agency recommended, in my head.

He paused for emphasis. "Processed junk food."

In a flash, Charlie raided the cupboard, pulling out almost every single box and bag. He lined them up neatly on the table in front of me. He was very interested in my take on each item I tried, even coming up with a rating system. Highest on the list were Pop-Tarts, but I liked the s'mores flavor better than the brown sugar cinnamon, and powdered donuts. All the lowest scores were all the salty chips, especially the vinegar flavor.

"You're just discriminating against chips now," Charlie insisted, digging through a box of small snacks. "Here, I have a bag of cheese puffs in here somewhere. Although they aren't in the potato chip category directly, I think they toe the line enough."

I glanced out the window when I heard a car door slam. The ease I felt was replaced with a slight tension, not knowing what to expect, as Mr. Schenley walked into the house.

"Charlie, would you mind grabbing the box out of the trunk?" Daniel asked, removing his coat and dress shoes by the door.

"Can it wait until after Mina's gone?"

He sighed. "It has a bunch of work stuff I need, and it's too heavy for my back."

"Got it," Charlie said, eyeing to make sure I was okay. I nodded, and he went to the car.

I turned my attention to his father, ready to make small talk.

"Did you speak to your uncle on my behalf?" Daniel asked.

"I passed along your request. Did he not get in touch with you?" I tried to keep my tone light and breezy. Uncle Derrick wanted details, and I didn't want to come off as heavy-handed toward my uncle's side. Drawing that definitive line on his side wouldn't help me at all.

He frowned. "He did not."

"Maybe there's something I can help you with," I suggested. "What specifically are you interested in learning more about?"

"His hospital dealings."

Of course he cut right to it, the most sensitive of all topics for us. The direct line to our blood supply.

I groaned internally, realizing I stepped on a grenade.

"Oh," I said, purposely raising my voice to appear young and innocent.

Where the hell was Charlie? He needed to swoop in and break this tension.

"I'm afraid I can't help you."

His suspicion was evident.

"The information I'm asking for is public record," he said evenly. "I will get it eventually, but he's just delaying it. He has one week until I turn this into a legal battle, a very public one."

I stared at him, unable to come up with a response.

"And it's going to get ugly," he threatened. "Really ugly for him and his entire family."

My natural instinct when attacked was to defend, but this was Charlie's father, armed with some suspicious information and an intent to do serious damage, so I stayed rooted to my chair, revealing nothing.

"And for the blood supply."

All sound ceased to exist except for a ringing in my ears. I gripped the edge of the table, trying to keep my composure.

He smiled maliciously. "Please feel free to take my information and 'pass it along' once again. Hopefully this time it's heard."

Charlie stepped in, holding a moving box stuffed with computer parts. "You need this to do your work? It looks like it's from twenty years ago."

"Thanks, son." His father smiled and took the box easily enough, despite his insistence that he needed Charlie's help. "You two have fun."

Charlie took his seat across from me and took in my defensive stature. "What happened?" His gaze moved between me and his father.

"I have to go," I mumbled, not bothering to come up with a better lie.

I swiped the end of the table, knocking my books and school supplies into my bag with ease, and I ran out of the house.

"Mina, wait! What's wrong?" He stepped up to my car door, trying to stop me from leaving. "What happened?"

"I'll see you tomorrow at school, Charlie."

I slammed the door, and making sure he was far enough away from the car, peeled out.

Needing some time to figure out how to handle this, how to tell my uncle, I spent the next hour driving around town. The thing was that Uncle Derrick didn't necessarily care about some reporter prying into his business necessarily, but he would certainly not appreciate the threat of exposure — and the tone he took with me.

I continued to stew over it, and Charlie texting me only made me feel worse.

Sorry my dad was weird. He gets intense about his work sometimes.

No worries.

Are you okay? I don't want you to feel uncomfortable. We can always hang out somewhere else, my mom's or maybe yours?

I'd have to come up with another lie to tell him why he couldn't come over to my house, and I was sick of all the deceit going around these days, so I didn't respond.

When I pulled into my driveway, I resigned to take the coward's way out — I called Trinity and had her remind my uncle of what Daniel Schenley wanted. I softened the conversation he and I shared in his kitchen, acting as though I overheard him mentioning it to someone instead of using it to intimidate me. She promised to talk it through with Uncle Derrick as soon as a few nobles from the Southeast region left. I hung up and breathed a sigh of relief.

About an hour later, Charlie texted again.

I still can't believe your first cake was vanilla. You have so much to learn, Mina.

He wasn't wrong.

14

On Saturday night, Eloise made me suffer through the real-life equivalent of a movie montage scene. She insisted on trying almost everything from her closet and demanded a unique opinion for each outfit.

"Do you think this one is too... puffy?"

I glanced up at her from the pages of a months-old fashion magazine I found on her coffee table while she put on outfit number eleven. This dress was a short, green summer dress with accentuated shoulders and sleeves. She ran her fingers along the frays at the bottom.

"I think it's cute, but you'll freeze," I said, glancing at the thin fabric.

She stood on her tip toes and spun, checking her reflection in the bathroom mirror. "So I'll add tights and a long jacket," she decided, crossing back through the living room to her bedroom once again to rifle through her drawers. "It'll be a vibe."

I sighed, tossing the magazine back to its resting place, and heard Eloise groan.

"What's wrong?" I asked, joining her.

"This is my only pair of tights, and there's a run in it."

Frustration made her voice a little choppy.

"We can stop at the store on the way there," I suggested. "I'll get them for—"

She glared at me with red and watery eyes. "Don't even offer," she cut me off. "It'll make me feel worse. God, I hate that I cry when I'm upset. Like, why can't I be one of those stone cold bitches?"

I smiled. "Because you're a human, not a rock."

Eloise moved to pull off the dress to change her outfit again.

"Wait," I stopped her. "I have an idea. Do you have any scissors?"

She tilted her head over to a small set of overflowing drawers in the table, and I dug through it until I found a pair. "Hold still," I warned.

I grabbed the fabric at random places, either cutting a hole or dragging the scissors down to create another run. After a minute or two of this, I stepped back, admiring my handiwork.

"Do you have any boots? Something with a chunky heel?"

She kicked a pair out from under her bed. "They're all scuffed," she said, with a sigh.

"Even better," I promised, encouraging her to put them on.

I touched up her makeup, adding a little more darkness to her eyelids.

"Oh my," she said, admiring her reflection in the mirror. "I'm like a grunge princess."

"I am your humble servant," I laughed with a bow.

She threw her arms around me, and I stopped breathing, patting her gently until she let go.

"Thank you," she breathed.

Eloise insisted on blaring her "Fierce Women" playlist to get us pumped up on the drive over to Alex's house, where Charlie and Tanner waited for us. Well, Charlie was. By the time we arrived, Tanner was already flirting with a few girls around a long table littered with cups. Judging by the free-flowing alcohol, I was in for the challenge of dealing with lax inhibitions. Charlie put his hand on my back, leading me toward the kitchen.

"Can you believe how he's acting?" Eloise bit out.

"Who?" I glanced around to a bunch of familiar faces, all of whom were chugging various drinks, dancing, or laughing.

She sighed. "Tanner."

Charlie rolled his eyes and started unscrewing the caps on various liquors on the counter. He smelled a clear bottle, cringed, and put it back.

"Is he... supposed to be acting differently than he normally does?" I asked cautiously.

I leaned over the kitchen counter and saw Tanner chatting intimately with Alex, who was pulling various records off a shelf for him to look at.

"Ever since Eloise and Tanner hooked up sophomore year," Charlie began, only for Eloise to smack his hand. "Careful, or I'll mess yours up."

He poured Sprite and two pungent alcohols into each cup, eyeing the amounts as he continued.

"Anyway, when they hooked up, Tanner got all into Eloise, and she wasn't interested in him, and then when she decided she was, he wasn't. It keeps going around and around."

"I see," I said. "And now, you're…"

"Just all-around resentful," Eloise admitted.

"Cheers to that," Charlie laughed, dropping a lime wedge and cherry into each cup.

He raised his cup and pushed the other two toward Eloise and me.

"No thank you, I have to drive." I also wasn't sure how alcohol would affect me.

"What do you mean you have to drive?" Eloise demanded, taking a gulp. "We're staying here."

I cocked an eyebrow. "All of these people are going to sleep here?"

She reached into my purse, pulled out my keys, and dropped them in a big bowl on the counter. "It's the rule."

"Who's rule?"

"Everyone's."

"Charlie, what about your curfew?" I asked, hoping to use it as an excuse to go the movie still, but he seemed to have given up on that idea.

"My mom thinks I'm staying at Tanner's tonight," he explained casually. "Tanner's mom thinks he's staying at my house."

Eloise's face contorted as she downed more of her drink. "And my mom thinks I'm at your house," she said, chomping on a piece of ice.

I swirled the liquid in the plastic cup. "Oh."

"Call your parents now," she demanded.

"Mina doesn't have a curfew," Charlie bragged, taking a sip of his drink. "This isn't half bad, actually."

"Lucky," Eloise said under her breath.

A few more people joined us, and Charlie served as the defacto bartender, mixing the same drink over and over again. I stepped around the counter, wedging myself between him and the open back door, until Nick and Rita arrived and insisted we play flip cup.

While they explained the rules, I took a small sip. I separated the flavors easily enough, already knowing what Sprite and the fruits tasted like, but the alcohol was disgusting, overly bitter and stale tasting. I understood why everyone cringed while they drank it.

I snuck out back, dumping the contents into the yard, and instead of playing drinking games, I sat by the bonfire. The scent of the wood turning to ash and radiating heat always calmed me while sitting in front of the fireplace at home, but it felt luxurious to be under the stars while the flames soared up into the night sky.

"Mind if I join you?" Tanner asked, sinking into the cushion beside me before I could answer.

The laughter and cheers of games in the kitchen caught my attention, and Charlie smiled at me, waving me back in. I shook my head and laid back, listening to the crackling. This was the second party in a row where I had unsuccessfully tried to isolate myself.

Beside me, Tanner ripped open a bag of marshmallows with his teeth, lazily putting one large white puff on the end of a metal rod before sticking it in the fire. I watched in fascination as he twirled it in his fingers with one hand and compiled a sandwich of graham crackers and chocolate in the other.

"Tanner, it's on fire." I jumped up.

"Burned marshmallows are the best." He pulled it close to his face and blew out the flame. "No changing my mind."

"That's disgusting," Charlie said, joining us outside. "I'll show you how it's done, Mina."

He repeated the motions, but instead of charring the outside, it turned a light brown, just gooey enough to gush out the sides of the little sandwich as he pressed it all together.

"Here, try it," he offered to me.

I chewed one of the corners slowly, getting the melty chocolate and marshmallow all over my hands in the process, followed by graham cracker crumbs. "Oh, it tastes like the Pop-Tart," I said excitedly.

"You've never had a s'more?" Eloise asked, carrying a full bottle of liquor and a few cans of pop in her arms.

"Mina has been getting an education on junk food," Charlie explained. "Apparently her parents are on a super strict diet."

I nodded, chewing through another small bite.

"Is a graham cracker really a cracker?" I asked, picking up the box to inspect it closer. "Because it's sweet like a cookie and its purpose for existing in this sense falls into the dessert category, but it says cracker in the name."

Eloise considered it while refilling drinks. "I've never thought about it before, but it seems like it's more like a dessert cookie than an appetizer cracker."

"But it's a graham *cracker*," Tanner said, emphasizing the last word.

"You eat it as pie crust or in s'mores, though, not with, like, charcuterie," Eloise argued.

"Charcuterie?" Charlie burst out laughing. "What the hell is charcuterie?"

She rolled her eyes. "It's a big plate with cheese, crackers, olives, and different kinds of meat."

Charlie wrinkled his nose.

"Who says crackers can't be sweet? I would probably eat it with a brie, maybe top it with almonds or pistachios. Drizzle some honey on top." We all looked at Tanner, stunned into silence by his contribution. "What? It'd be pretty good."

I set the box down, a silent sign to end the debate, and they all nursed their now-full drinks.

"So, this party kind of sucks, huh?" Eloise huffed.

"What makes you say that?" I asked.

"Because the four of us are sitting here arguing over the categorization of graham crackers."

I shrugged. "I don't mind it."

Eloise started laughing, and the rest of us joined in.

"Maybe we should rejoin the party," Eloise posed.

"Nah," Tanner said, much to my relief. "This crowd is…"

"Not your norm?" Charlie finished for him.

He shrugged. "Something like that."

"Well, seeing as we're stuck here for the next, I don't know, eight hours or so, what should we do to pass the time?" Eloise asked.

"I heard Alex has a sauna," Tanner suggested.

I glanced at Eloise, expecting her to back it up, but she frowned. "Apparently at her last party a bunch of people smoked weed in there and ruined the filtration system."

Tanner rubbed his hands together in excitement. "How about truth or dare?"

"What are we, twelve?" Charlie asked, tossing his arm around my back.

"What are the rules?" I asked.

"Jesus, Mina, were you raised in a cult or something?" Tanner asked.

Eloise put her hand on his cheek and pushed his face away. "Ignore him, he's untrained. One person starts by picking truth or dare, and then I'll pick what they have to do and they *have* to do it."

"No matter what," Tanner insisted.

I definitely did not want to play this game. "I don't know… sounds kind of intense."

"It's not," Eloise promised. "It's fun."

"How do you win?" I asked, vowing to do so as quickly as possible.

"You don't," she dismissed. "Okay, Charlie, truth or dare."

"Truth." He didn't even take time to mull it over.

Eloise tapped her fingers on the side of her cup. "Tell me the most embarrassing story you have on Tanner."

He smiled maliciously, much to Tanner's chagrin.

"Don't do it, dude," he begged.

Eloise shook her head. "He has to. It's part of the game."

Charlie cleared this throat. "In Biology freshman year,

we were learning about blood and plasma and how the body functions and whatnot."

I gulped, hoping this story wasn't a long one.

"So Mr. Pruitt notices that Tanner was looking a little green, and he tells me to take Tanner to the nurse's office. We walk there, and he's feeling better, but neither of us wants to go back to class, so we walk into the nurse's office, expecting to spend the rest of the period napping or whatever. But when the door opens, there's a kid there, maybe a senior, who had nearly severed his finger in shop class. There was a lot of blood."

Tanner slumped down, looking a little queasy.

"Before I can react, Tanner passes out right as the nurse turns. His face smacked right into her chest, and somehow his limbs got all caught up with hers, and they fell to the ground, with him on top of her." Charlie couldn't hold in his laughter as he told the story. "I'll never forget the sound of her yelling and his confusion while he came to. The guidance counselor stormed in, and it was a whole thing."

I managed to chuckle, while Eloise broke out into a full cackle.

"Yeah, yeah, real funny," Tanner said sourly. "Lots of concern for my health and well-being."

"You're fine," Eloise dismissed. "Charlie, who's next?"

He turned to me slowly. "Mina, truth or dare?"

Without hesitation I said, "Dare."

"Our first dare of the evening," Eloise grinned. "How nice are you going to be, Charlie?"

He let me off easy, sending me off to go collect a random assortment of stuff from Alex's house without getting caught. Once I was out of sight on the second floor, I zoomed around, collecting a family photo, a pair of Alex's socks, candles, whatever her brother was hiding under his mattress — a nude magazine, gross — and as many snacks from their pantry as I could carry. I dumped it all on one of the outside tables, standing proudly over my bounty.

Once we were restocked and settled back in, I dared Tanner to stuff as many marshmallows in his mouth as he could. He fit ten and then promptly spit them in the fire before challenging me to post an unflattering picture of myself on social media. Eloise scrolled through her camera roll and found one where my eyes were closed.

"Eloise, do you really think that a graham cracker is a cookie, or were you saying it just to disagree with Tanner?" I asked when she picked truth.

"Cookie," she said immediately. "No doubt about it."

We went around and around the circle, and I had to admit, I was having a lot of fun. The party continued inside without us, and aside from a few people stopping by to hand out shots, we were mostly left alone.

"Eloise, your turn," Tanner cleared his throat and scratched the side of his face with his knuckle. "Go to homecoming with me."

Charlie and I exchanged surprised looks, waiting for her answer.

"That's not a truth or dare," she stammered.

"Fine," Tanner said coolly. "Truth or dare."

She gave him a loopy smile. "Dare."

"I dare you to go to homecoming with me."

His voice was even, but somehow the tone was challenging. I wondered if he was drunk and going to regret it in the morning, but it was then I noticed all the cups and bottles sat untouched on the table, likely since we started our little game.

A mixture of emotions rolled over her expression, and she stared at him for a minute before answering. "Fine," she chirped.

"Fine."

"Glad you two got this settled, we're now officially less than a month away," Charlie said, checking the date on his lock screen.

"Wait a second, it's on October twentieth?" I asked.

Theo's reminder of the date sprung into the forefront of my mind. The vampire ritual, which I barely knew anything about but was very much dreading, was the same night.

"Yeah," Eloise said, unable to hide her smile. "It's on all the posters we've been hanging up at school, remember?"

I groaned. "I have a thing that day." The semi-secret ritual. "With my uncle. For business."

"But don't you want to see how the float looks?" Eloise asked. "And the other decorations?"

"I do," I assured her. "But I can't."

Charlie looked legitimately disappointed.

"Maybe I can come after?" I suggested, not wanting to let him down.

"Yeah," Eloise encouraged. "We usually do a group thing anyway, so you could just skip pictures and dinner and meet us at the dance?"

He shrugged, and Eloise pivoted the conversation by making me take a shot of pickle juice as a dare. I didn't mind the taste, honestly.

"Eloise, truth or dare."

She sized me up, trying to decide what was in her best interest. "Truth."

"What's the worst thing Brooklyn said about me that you haven't told me?"

It was a question I had been curious about but hadn't found a tactful way to ask.

After taking a large sip of her drink, she said, "That you're a vampire, but you already know that."

"She told me that, too," Charlie admitted with a grin. "She was convinced of it, kept going on about how pale you are and how you never eat and whatnot."

I stiffened. "And what'd you say to that?"

"That I've seen you in the sun and you don't sparkle or catch on fire."

"I can wear crosses just fine, too," I joked.

Eloise laughed. "Okay, next game. I'm going to go steal a deck of cards and more snacks."

Charlie rested his hand on my thigh, squeezing it once. We all stayed outside, playing games and talking, until the sun rose.

15

The weeks and weekends in October blended together. Between homework, the committee after school, spending time with my human friends, and showing my face at Uncle Derrick's while trying to avoid the scrutiny of Charlie's dad, I was delightfully busy. Being around humans for extended periods of time was becoming easier, like I was slowly drinking in and adjusting to the taste of poison.

On the Saturday before homecoming, Charlie insisted on taking me to a bakery, where he presented me a box of donuts, croissants, brownies, and cupcakes. I didn't even hesitate to reach across the table and plant a kiss on the dot of powdered sugar on Charlie's cheek and felt no ill effects.

We shared bits and pieces of the desserts until Charlie declared he was full, and we walked back over to the park where we first kissed.

"Do you want to come over tonight?" Charlie asked. "We could watch a movie or something."

I shrugged, noncommittally, knowing he was spending the weekend at his dad's house.

"My dad's going to be at work until late tonight. The coroner released an autopsy on one of the newly discovered missing girls yesterday, and he's been glued to his computer and phone ever since."

"Oh?"

"Apparently there were visible puncture wounds on this one, close enough to come off as bite marks."

"Bite marks?" I repeated.

"Yeah. I overheard my dad talking about it this morning. The pictures were sent over to some animal specialist to see if there was any connection to the blood being drained." He stopped once he caught a glimpse of my expression. "You look like Tanner when I brought up his passing out incident with the nurse."

"Yeah, I think I'm just feeling a little off from all the sugar," I lied, not-so-smoothly. "The fresh air helps, though."

"Maybe you could call all your vampire friends and see if they had anything to do with it," he teased, keeping up the ruse that Brooklyn tried to slander me with.

I laughed, knowing that he was poking fun at me, but I couldn't drop the feeling of unease.

When Charlie and I parted ways after I feigned a headache, I sped over to Uncle Derrick's house. For once, I was able to use the actual long driveway instead of off-roading, and I pulled up to the front entrance, making my way up the dozen steps and barging in.

"Mina, we weren't expecting you today," Trinity said, closing the door I left wide open.

I ignored her, peeking into various rooms.

"Do you need something?" Her voice was soft, but I wasn't in the mood for pleasantries.

"Where is he?" I asked sharply.

"Library."

I accelerated my pace, swiftly making it up the stairs and over to the opposite side of the house before most humans would blink. The door was open, sparing me from a dramatic entrance. My father and uncle were hovered over a glass chess board, lightly goading each other when I stepped into the room.

"Mina, is everything all right?" Uncle Derrick asked, concern rampant.

I cut to the chase. "What is this I hear about bite marks? Bodies drained of blood?"

My father's gaze flipped between us, taking in the tension. "Where did you hear about these things?"

"Does it matter?"

They looked at each other like my presence was nothing more than an annoyance, something that would only interrupt their heated chess match.

I was so tired of being paraded around by my uncle as a source of pride, with all of the consequences and judgment that came with being his niece and none of the rewards. I wanted to understand what was happening, and I wanted to understand it right away.

"Is this us, Uncle Derrick?" I pressed. "Are we murdering these women? Is someone among us so unable to control their thirst that they have to prey on these innocent humans? Tell me quickly, and tell me now."

He considered my hunched posture, my heated expression, and stayed silent, which only further enraged me. I held still, knowing that any outburst would make me feel even more petulant, and waited for him to explain.

That was the thing about Uncle Derrick. He was always in control.

"So much fire, Mina. Have I taught you nothing about keeping a level head? Of course these aren't us. Bite marks?"

I weighed his response, finding unease in his dismissiveness but unable to discern if he was deceiving me. Vampires weren't usually that sloppy, and the ones that were tended to be young vampires, abandoned by their creators after being turned. In that state, there's no way they'd be able to coordinate hiding bodies in various locations, especially in a warehouse.

"Come join us, Mina," he said, turning back to the game.

I reluctantly did. My father watched me tentatively as I tried to calm my body down. I was feeling all sorts of new emotions these days, and it was hard to let it go once I had built something up.

The worst part about watching them play chess wasn't just the boringness of the game but how they taunted each other, narrating the faults of the other player's moves right after they made them. I tried to imagine them playing truth or dare, and the memory brought a small smile to my face.

"Your father and I have been playing chess for our entire lives, Mina, and I can count the number of times he has beaten me on one hand."

"Because you almost always end in a stalemate," I said, rolling my eyes.

"That doesn't make my point any less true, does it?"

The three of us perked up at the sound and smell of another vampire entering the house.

My uncle inhaled deeply. "It's just Thomas."

"Everyone needs to stop showing up unannounced," Trinity huffed, waving him into the library.

He bowed to the collective three of us. "Excuse me for the intrusion, your majesty."

"What can I help you with, Thomas?"

He glanced at me, eyes narrowed. "At the request of my wife, I bring you this." He extended his hand, revealing a modern, human cell phone.

Derrick cocked an eyebrow, expecting an explanation. "And what will you have me do with this?"

Thomas looked at the phone screen, and after realizing it was dark, unlocked the phone and showed the paused video. He double-checked to make sure he had all our attention and pressed the play button.

The footage was grainy and shaky, clearly taken by someone who did not have the most familiarity with human technology, but I recognized the park immediately. The person holding the camera moved closer to Charlie and me. I couldn't believe I was too preoccupied at the time to pick up on the scent.

I watched, from a different point of view, the conversation we shared an hour ago, talking about the blood and bodies, and finally, his joke about vampirism.

The gleam in Thomas' eye was unmistakable. He took tremendous pleasure in what he thought was catching the King's heir breaking the Code, and he expected it to be dealt with.

Other than a pure hatred of my existence as a half-human, half-vampire, I didn't understand the motive behind this.

My father broke the silence. "Is that a human willingly acknowledging our existence?"

"It is," Thomas answered for me.

"No," I denied.

Thomas moved the phone closer to me. "How do you deny this documented truth?"

I glanced at Uncle Derrick, whose anger was evident in his eyes, but he remained passive, as he always reminded me to do. I checked the human side of myself, which was in near-hysterics, and fell into my rigid vampire nature. It was the only way I would be able to explain the situation without exposing my fangs and screaming at him.

"It is a misunderstanding," I said evenly.

Uncle Derrick folded his hands in his lap. "Elaborate, please."

"A large part of the human friendship dynamic is teasing and having lighthearted conversations. It's a way of building camaraderie, to delicately point out what's unique to each individual and to find the humor in it."

Seeing that the vampires in the room took in my words without objection, I continued, softening the details and Brooklyn's personality a bit.

"A few humans have noticed that I'm not always aware of common culture references, among other things. The combination of my pale skin and disdain for garlic caught the attention of one classmate who, believing the falsities we vampires have perpetuated through various media, made references to me being a vampire. I have proven this not to be true, obviously, by going out into sunlight and digesting human food, and now, it's a bit of a running joke."

"Why is this the first that I'm hearing of it?" Uncle Derrick demanded, getting nonverbal confirmation from my father that he, too, was unaware.

"Why would you need to hear of this?" I countered. "We are at no risk. I have not violated the Code in any manner, and it doesn't impact your business dealings in any way. Frankly, this entire exercise is a waste of your time."

My words settled in the room, most expressions completely unreadable.

"Although, I would be curious to hear from Thomas," I said, mustering as much confidence as I could. "Do you make a regular habit of using human devices to spy on the conversations of fellow vampires?" I was on a roll now. "Have you been recording other conversations? Our monthly meetings, perhaps?"

My accusations continued until Uncle Derrick raised his hand, putting me to a stop. "Thomas, is there anything you would like to say to these questions?"

He stepped backward, nearly running directly into Trinity. "I do not at this time, your majesty."

"Collect your thoughts and prepare statements. This will be a main topic of discussion at our next monthly meeting. Understood?"

"Yes, your majesty." He bowed and ran out of the room.

When Thomas cleared the property, I let everything I'd been holding in bubble over. "You're just going to let him go? How can you trust him? Who knows what else he is trying to do to us?"

Uncle Derrick coughed. First it was slow, like he was clearing his throat, but it soon became more violent, shaking his body as Trinity and my father observed with looks of pity.

The fact that I was the only one reaching for him in panic made me realize that for the second time since I arrived, I'd been left out of something serious. Trinity handed a white cloth handkerchief to my uncle, which he held to his mouth.

With each cough came a little more blood, and not the fresh, thick smell I was used to. It smelled foul, dead even. Everything in me wanted to run away, just like Thomas had, but I was paralyzed, unable to reconcile what I was seeing.

After five minutes of this, he returned to normal, passing two more bloodless coughs before handing over the cloth to Trinity to dispose.

"Shall we resume our game, Max?" Uncle Derrick asked lightly.

I slammed my hand on his wrist, right as he was moving to pick up a pawn. "What is happening to you?"

He turned to me completely, offering a genuine look of pity.

"I've been poisoned."

16

I started and stopped speaking numerous times before I could collect myself.

Poisoned.

"How is that possible?" I sputtered.

My father stared at my hand, which was still on my uncle's wrist. "That is what we have been trying to figure out." He said it with such lightness it seemed like I asked him about the weather.

I sat still simply because I was unable to reconcile the swirls of confusion happening in my mind. They watched me in trepidation, and I tried to pull the questions out one at a time.

"Who knows about this?"

"The people in this room, along with your mother," Uncle Derrick answered.

"That's it?"

"That's it."

Dropping my grip on him, I tugged at the ends of my hair in frustration.

"And it needs to remain so," my father insisted. "It's crucial that we continue on as if nothing is out of the ordinary."

The vampires would handle this ruthlessly, with half of them vowing for vengeance on whoever did this, the others demanding his stepping down. His businesses, well, most of them would be handled just fine by Trinity, who oversaw most of the day-to-day operations at this point, but Uncle Derrick built a lot of relationships over the years that had yet to be taken on by someone else. Namely, he was waiting for me to step up.

He did his best to contain another coughing fit, but the rumble in his lungs practically screamed in the room. "It's in our best interest to do so, not only until we have more information but until after the ritual is complete."

I groaned. The mysterious vampire ritual with an immovable date of next Saturday that was causing me to miss homecoming. Something with the moon or the eclipse or something made it the only date this year to do it. The secrecy around the event combined with the timing of this latest news — the poisoning — only made me want to postpone it even more.

"Is this really the best time for this?" I asked incredulously. "Inviting all of the vampires in the region to gather in one place when one of them could be responsible for this?"

Trinity made an odd noise, almost a low sob. "Mina, I'll be in my office when you're ready," she choked out.

"Ready for what?" I asked, but she had already spun out of the room.

"A fitting for next week, I assume."

"Uncle," I exhaled.

"Max, do you think you could leave us alone for a few moments?"

My father obliged him, closing the heavy door as he left the room. I took his seat across from Uncle Derrick.

His gaze dropped from my waiting expression to the chess board, where he finally set down the piece he'd been holding, easily sweeping off one of the rooks my father left vulnerable to protect the queen. I studied the board. My father was losing badly, falling into all of my uncle's normal traps.

I rarely played, but I watched plenty.

After nudging the other rook two squares to the left with my knuckle, I sat back, crossing my arms across my chest.

"Nice move," Uncle Derrick complimented, staring at the board with a smirk on his face.

He countered my move, and we moved the pieces across the board, occasionally putting each other into check. It was a tedious game of back and forth, and on several occasions, I thought he'd had me, but I took a deep breath and worked through all my options, finding a way out.

"Being a vampire is like playing chess, Mina, even more so when you're the King." He paused to meet my eyes. "Or the Queen."

He sacrificed his knight for my bishop and smothered another cough.

"Uncle Derrick," I said softly. "What do you know about this poisoning?"

"The signs were so slight, I didn't notice it at first. It was Trinity who pointed out that I was taking in more blood than usual, increasing by a liter or two each day. I dismissed it until last week when my throat began to burn so hot that I had to check my reflection to see that I wasn't actually on fire. I thought it was closing in on itself, and I forced the air out of my lungs and blood spewed all over the floor."

I grimaced, mentally picturing the scene as he described it.

"Since then," he continued, "it has been on and off with coughing fits, getting progressively worse."

The anger I'd felt when I arrived had turned to complete helplessness. "If I hadn't been so preoccupied with being a human, then I could have—"

"Figured out what was happening to my own body before I did? Conducted hours of scientific research, backed by your decades of studying the biology of vampires? Back-logged every single move and interaction I had for the past month to figure out the culprit?"

He was trying to make me feel better by patronizing me. It worked slightly, forcing me to channel all my annoyance toward the chess board.

We resumed our back and forth until we each had three pieces remaining.

"Would you believe me if I told you that between Max and me, I had the more difficult time transitioning after I was turned?"

My surprised expression met his.

King William, the vampire who turned Uncle Derrick and my father, had a fascination with vampire lineage. I'd heard the story of how he, essentially, stalked Derrick for months to vet him before deciding to turn him. His calculated selection process hadn't accounted for my father to arrive at the apartment they shared, and decided, in an instant, to have them both.

"You see, I was the one who encouraged Max to come live with me, partially because of the booming job market in this area after the Vietnam War, but also selfishly, because I wanted to be around family. I was the one who purchased him a bus ticket for that Saturday and filled his head with promises and grand ideas.

"For years I felt that all I simply did was get us both killed. I busied myself with learning what I could about being a vampire, about King William, and everything else, but there was a period of time I went off, with the blessing of the Queen of the Mid-Atlantic, to see how she operated her region and proposed trade routes and joint ventures between the two regions, which ultimately grew to be very successful.

"During that time, I clung to my humanity, even going as far as to watch my human parents through the windows at night grieve for the death of their two sons, which William staged as an apartment fire," he stopped suddenly, staring off, lost in the memory.

"Did your human parents ever recover?" I asked.

Uncle Derrick righted himself and moved his king just where I wanted. "They did not," he said soberly. "I tell you all of this, Mina, not to bring up old memories for the sake of doing so, but to remind you that curiosity toward humans is natural, even more so for you than me. After all, we were born as humans and we feed from them. Just because some vampires choose to turn their backs against it, doesn't mean it's right, or how it should be."

I moved my rook forward. "Check," I said lightly. "So what does this have to do with your health?"

He moved his king a space over while mulling over my question. "I left the Queen of the Mid-Atlantic at the request of William, who began to show the final stages of death, which, as you know, is a surge of abilities. Inconceivable strength and speed even faster than I have now."

"Could he fly?" I asked, knowing that usually meant vampires had less than a month to live.

"Yes. He had hidden it from Max and me, which wasn't difficult given that I was in Delaware for months and your father was busy courting Marie, something that was hidden from me until she became pregnant.

"After William's death, something changed in me, a true acceptance of what I'd become and what power I had. I was drunk on it until I held you, screaming and tiny, in my hands just hours after you came into this world. How could I hold something so precious and not appreciate where it came from?"

I smiled slightly, unable to stop myself.

"But not everyone shares my viewpoint, Mina," he reminded me. "In fact, there are some vampires who disagree with the softness I feel toward humans. There are other vampires who have wanted to see me gone for a while, but there are just as many, if not more, who want something different and believed I could take us there."

"And what's that?"

"An unveiling."

My breath caught. "Of vampires to humans?"

"Yes," he confirmed.

I needed a minute to take in his words. "And you think that whoever poisoned you disagrees with you? But doesn't that defeat the purpose if I'm your heir?"

"I cannot pretend to understand a motive at this point, but I'm merely speculating."

"How is it possible to poison you? Or any vampire? You're indestructible."

"The information from the various parties I mentioned earlier believe that I mistakenly ingested dead blood."

It was terrifying to think of the human that blood sources came from, let alone imagining draining blood from a rotting corpse.

He glared at my shiver. "It's your move."

I sighed, double-checking that the move I wanted to make was the right one. He was trapped at the edge of the board with the remaining pieces, including my own king.

"Checkmate," I announced, sliding my pawn forward.

There was no satisfaction in defeating him.

"Well done, Mina." He genuinely seemed pleased at his demise. "Perhaps you are picking up a thing or two from me after all."

Trinity knocked before opening the door. "Your majesty, your meeting downtown begins in thirty minutes," she reminded him.

He stood up to go find my father.

"Did I hear you beat your uncle in chess?"

"Were you eavesdropping?" I couldn't help my smirk.

She feigned innocence. "Me? Never."

When I was younger, I loved to be in her office. It was a large room, but it was crowded, packed with boxes, file cabinets, books, and racks of clothing, which were all terribly fun for me to hide between as a child. Now, she pushed past all my nostalgia and led me over to the pedestal. I stood in front of the full length mirror while she checked her notes to locate the correct clothing rack.

"Are there dresses in there?" I asked, my own eyes bulging at the size of the garment bags.

"Of course."

"For me? Not for an elephant?"

She unzipped one of the bags, pulling out the fluffiest ball gown I'd ever seen. It was straight from a fairytale. The fabric looked exquisite, pure silk covered with a thin top layer of gold gems that reflected all the light in the room. Seeing that I was impressed, she talked me into trying it on.

Trinity dealt with all the hooks and zippers in the back, while I looked at my reflection in the mirror, expecting to see a better version of myself. I was immediately disappointed.

It was a beautiful dress, lighter than I expected, and was even prettier now than it was on a hanger, but the problem was me. I expected an air of regality, but instead, I was drowning as a hollowed out, pale shell of a being who was playing dress-up.

"What did Uncle Derrick and my father wear to their ritual?" I asked Trinity.

"I was still human back then," she reminded me. "But I think I have a picture around here somewhere."

Ignoring my look of confusion, she opened a cabinet

with a few photo albums until she found what she was looking for. "You know how we vampires are weird about documenting things, so you're lucky that there happened to be a photographer taking feature photos of buildings downtown that day."

She handed over the book, which held an old newspaper clipping behind a plastic sheet. Uncle Derrick and my father weren't in focus, and their side profiles were caught on the side of the frame. I brought it up closer to my face to inspect and was surprised that they weren't dressed in outfits or hairstyles of that era. I was hoping for bell bottoms, but it looked like they were about to go off to a speakeasy.

"If I recall correctly, your uncle was very put off by the current suit trends, so they both wore something of King William's, from the early twentieth century, I believe."

My gaze flipped back from the clean lines of their suits, the confidence at which they held themselves, even unknowingly being captured, to the ball gown in the mirror, and I sighed.

17

It's funny what gets prioritized with a change in perspective.

I prepared and rallied for months to go to high school, to understand more about humans, to get some distance from vampires, but the decision to suspend my attendance came quickly and easily after Uncle Derrick's news surfaced.

Even with his roundabout way of encouraging me to go, I just didn't feel right, sitting among humans and pretending to learn new things in class while he suffered with no hope on the horizon.

I told Charlie I still wasn't feeling well and asked him to pass the message on to Eloise. They both relentlessly texted me all week, making sure I was feeling better and that I wasn't secretly kidnapped or something. Charlie offered multiple times to drop off my schoolwork, but Trinity had it all arranged with the administration that I would pick it back up when I felt ready.

Each day with Uncle Derrick was a little different, and each day, he got a little worse.

On Monday and Tuesday, the days were full and long, with meetings in three different cities in the region and conference calls during the long drives. He took great pride in introducing me to some of his human business associates, who asked me all sorts of questions about college and my future plans, and they seemed delighted to hear that I would be stepping into the business at such a young age.

Even with high school on hold, I planned to talk to Uncle Derrick about college classes, where I might actually learn something useful, when he recovered.

A few of the vampires in the region were wary of me upon introductions, even if they did greet me with a bow. I did my best to act as normal and vampire as possible. During a particularly long discussion on agriculture, I cracked a small smile imagining the horrified looks on their faces if I picked up some of the human food they'd brought out as a demonstration and tasted it.

I did a lot of listening, but I also asked questions, which was actually one of the best ways to prove my engaged interest in protecting the best interest of vampires. They humored me, and I pressed them, slowly and surely gaining their respect.

We returned to the mansion in the early hours of Wednesday by helicopter, and my uncle watched me in amusement as I took pictures of the skyline. Between chess matches and updates from Trinity, I showed him how to use my phone, taking more pictures and looking up information online. Trinity usually set up his phone and video calls for him, and he was very interested in how it all worked.

For the rest of the week, we stayed in the library, having much better control over entertaining the occasional visitors, including my parents, around his coughing fits.

On Friday night, after I thought we were finished, Trinity greeted another vampire at the door.

"Were you expecting anyone else?" I asked Uncle Derrick, who pointedly ignored my question and continued reading in front of the fire.

I made my way to the front of the house, mental defenses on alert until I heard a familiar deep and charming voice.

"Theo," I said in greeting before crossing my arms across my chest.

He gave me a once-over, taking in my athleisure clothes I had gotten for Brooklyn's sleepover. "Is that what you're wearing?"

I glanced down. "Yes?" I said, and it sounded like a question.

"Okay then," he said, straightening his tie.

"Why do I get the feeling you're expecting me to be somewhere other than this house tonight?"

He cocked an eyebrow, and Trinity backed away slowly.

"Trinity," I said, grinding my teeth, and she ran upstairs to the library.

I sprinted up with Theo trailing behind.

"Uncle Derrick," I scolded.

"Level head, Mina," he reminded me. "Theo will be taking you out—"

"I don't need you to arrange my dates for me, Uncle Derrick."

"A date?" Theo scoffed. "That's presumptuous."

"As I was saying," Uncle Derrick continued, "Theo has been telling me about some new vampire establishments that are popping up across our region, and I would like you to go in my place to vet them."

"Vet them?"

"Do you need me to define what the word 'vet' means, Mina?"

I rolled my eyes.

The three vampires looked at me expectantly, and I gave in. "Trinity, do you have a rack of clothes hidden somewhere for me?"

Within ten minutes, I changed, reapplied my makeup, fluffed up my hair, and slid in beside Theo.

"Nice car," I commented, noting the neon yellow paint color. "Really blends in."

Theo accelerated away from the mansion without so much as a second glance. "You're so hot and cold, Mina," Theo accused. "I'm really not accustomed to being insulted this often."

"It's the human in me," I said dryly.

"I think vampires would be less tightly wound if they remembered the virtues of sarcasm," Theo said.

"It is funny how quickly vampires seem to forget human things. Before you know it, you'll be hiring a driver and repelling most human inventions."

"Oh definitely not," he grunted. "You spend too much time with older vampires."

I couldn't disagree. "Old vampires, young humans."

"Well, that changes tonight," he promised. "You'll see."

I did see.

We pulled up to a building that looked abandoned from the outside, but as soon as we stepped out of the car, a valet took Theo's keys and sped off, leaving instructions on how to enter. Theo slid open an all-metal door, gesturing me through until I stood toe-to-toe with an enormous vampire.

"Fangs," he demanded in a somewhat bored tone.

Theo stepped forward, opening his mouth and showing off his fangs. A little self-consciously, I did the same thing. We let ourselves in through the gated entrance. It felt like we were stepping into a speakeasy with its exposed Edison bulbs, dark wallpaper, and padded leather booths.

Vampires milled about, sniffing Theo and me as we made our way to a table in the back, where a server soon appeared, asking if we had a preference for blood.

"Female, AB-negative, no additions," he said before I could ask what she meant. "On my tab, please."

She nodded, and in a flash, returned with two full glasses.

"Female, AB-negative, no additions?" I posed once we were alone at our table.

I swore Theo's eyes twinkled. "Trial and error," he quipped.

"So this is what vampires do?"

It didn't seem that different from a human bar or restaurant, other than all the blood and the fact that I didn't feel the need to deny the half of myself that was always trying to make itself known. This was the longest my fangs had been exposed outside of my house for… my entire existence. It was a little thrilling.

"This is how vampires start the night," he explained. "First there's the blood, and then there's the gambling, then dancing, maybe some other activities, and then more blood, with blood in between."

"Right." I swallowed and ran my finger on the stem of the glass.

I wanted to blame my lack of bloodlust on what happened to Uncle Derrick, or rather what was happening to him, but if I was honest with myself, the more time I spent with humans, the less okay I felt about the entire endeavor. The fact that I could look at Charlie, and Eloise, and everyone else I actively tried not to pounce on during the days and consider them both friends and food was something I was still trying to reconcile.

My phone buzzed, and after seeing Charlie's name flash across the screen, I declined the call.

"Your humanity calling you?" The corner of Theo's mouth ticked as he put his elbows on the table, leaning toward me with a challenging expression on his face.

I slipped it back in my purse. "You could say that."

"Teddy!"

Theo's head snapped the direction of a tall, slender vampire, with blonde curly hair, wearing an oversized leopard print jacket.

"Cara," Theo said with a hint of surprise. "What brings you to our region, let alone this particular establishment?"

She bounced over and glided in beside me, nudging me toward the wall.

Without a moment of hesitation, she helped herself to

my glass of blood. "AB-negative," she commented. "Nice taste."

In one smooth motion, she drained the entire glass, which Theo watched with the slightest trepidation.

"Relax, Teddy," she crooned. "I'm just passing through on my way up north. I was hoping to bump into you, actually. It's been way too long."

She accepted another glass from the server then glanced around, as if she just remembered where she was. Cara craned her neck, trying to take in the entirety of the dark space, and inhaled loudly.

"What is that?" She breathed in again. "It's so strange, it's almost—"

"Human," I finished for her.

She eyed me curiously, and Theo explained. "Mina is half-human, half-vampire. I'm on an assignment from the King to vet a few of these new businesses around town tonight, and she has graciously agreed to keep me company."

Cara sighed. "And here I was hoping we could have some fun."

Theo started to shrug her off, but I stopped him. She seemed so much freer than all the other vampires I interacted with, as if she was actually enjoying herself instead of merely existing and drinking blood every few hours.

"What would you propose to do?" I asked her.

"The halfling wants to play," she said, somewhat impressed. "I know a place."

Theo groaned. "Not Staked again, Cara. I vowed to never go there after the last time."

"No, no, this one's new. It's called Cryptic."

Vampires were clever with puns, apparently.

"Mina, I don't think that's the best idea," he said quickly. "I don't think your uncle—"

"Let's get out of here," I interrupted him with a glare.

If I knew Uncle Derrick as well as I thought I did, the intention tonight wasn't really to check out a few different establishments — it was the experience of it. Cara seemed to have the type of adventurous mentality that guaranteed I'd get just that.

Theo tried to talk me out of it while we waited for the valet to bring his car around. I shrugged him off, listening to Cara's tale of how she'd been spending a lot of time in the Southeast region over the summer.

Between sharing a few cringe-worthy but entertaining stories, she murmured directions to Theo as we sped across one of the city's many bridges. I sat back and cracked my window to take in the view, using the whipping wind as my soundtrack to drown out the bickering that erupted between the two of them.

I kept my eyes ahead on the green signs hanging over the stretch of road.

"This exit," she insisted. "If you miss it, we'll have to cross the river again to backtrack, and it's already almost midnight."

He glared at her in the rear-view mirror and begrudgingly took the exit, going along with her every word as we turned into a below-ground parking garage. Theo pulled up so she could punch in the code, and he eased us down once the gate lifted.

After parking, Cara led us over to an elevator, which was guarded by another vampire who required us to show our fangs before he let us in. The elevator ride up to the penthouse was silent, aside from the dings of each floor.

"So serious these days, Teddy," Cara chided him. "Loosen up."

I eyed her sideways. "Telling a vampire to loosen up is like telling a cloud to turn into grass."

She pressed her tongue against her right fang. "I like you."

The doors opened, and we stepped into what I would liken to a typical human club scene. There were about one hundred vampires crammed into the space, moving along to a beat in the dark, and I was surprised to see a full DJ setup like the ones in the movies.

"Stay close to me," Theo insisted.

He grabbed my wrist and led me through the crowd over to a few tall tables in the corner by floor-to-ceiling windows. I jerked back, and he released me. I rubbed my skin, not because of his pressure but because I couldn't remember the last time a vampire touched me willingly.

"Why don't you like this?" I asked.

The atmosphere practically buzzed with life.

He paused and raised his voice to speak over the music. "After I was turned, I spent a lot of time at places like this, and let's just say, there's a reason I don't anymore."

"What reason is that?" I verbally pushed him but physically, I leaned in closer.

Being so close to him, a man close to my age, and not wanting to sink my teeth into his neck was refreshing. To my dismay, he turned away from me, shifting his attention to the crowd of people in front of us. Cara had successfully infiltrated the dance floor with some wild movements.

"Come on, halfling," she yelled.

She waved her arms at me like she was a vampire wind-mill, and I couldn't help but laugh. This was definitely a good choice. Despite Theo's trepidations, I was glad we ran into her.

Cara and I got lost in the crowd and the music. I had no idea what I was doing, so I followed her lead, moving my hips to the beat as best I could. The bass pumped through me, like a heartbeat propelling my limbs into action. I closed my eyes, getting lost in the rhythm, when I felt someone's hands hit my hips. I jerked forward and whipped around, looking up at a vampire I didn't recognize.

I met his eyes and shook my head.

He dropped his chin and pouted, as if that would change my mind, but I sidestepped over to Cara and tried to fall into the music again. I wanted to get carried away again, to move my body outside of myself, but the magic was gone.

I stood up on my tiptoes, looking for a way out. Theo was no longer standing at the table where I'd left him.

"Cara, I'm going to take a break," I screamed into her ear.

She shook her head and gestured for me to follow her back toward the elevator. After checking over her shoulder, she yanked open a door and led me upstairs to the rooftop. As I stepped up, my ears adjusted from the blaring music to the quiet night and the honking of cars on the street. I inhaled the fresh air and smiled, excited to see the view.

The wind picked up as we neared the top, and Cara panicked, smoothing down her hair.

"You're so lucky you can cut and style yours however you please," she groaned.

I shrugged. "One of the few perks of being half-human."

She practically skipped up the final steps. "I hope you're ready for this."

"Ready for…" The words dropped out of my mouth as my foot touched the smooth stone at the top.

I gasped, inhaling the scent of humans far too quickly than I would have normally, and my body betrayed me for it.

Just like I had reacted when thrown into the dance floor, I followed Cara forward on impulse, processing what was in front of me. Humans and vampires were intertwined openly, with fangs and exposed skin and open wounds visible. The humans seemed to be in various degrees of consciousness, some even moaning as fangs broke skin to slowly drain them.

All I could focus on was the blood.

One human was sprawled out on a lounge chair, unbitten but nonplussed by all accounts.

"Ever drank directly from the source?" Cara mused, already shaking with anticipation.

I couldn't form words, so I shook my head.

Cara leaned over the human, who couldn't have been more than twenty. She whispered to him in a volume so low, I couldn't decipher her words. From outside my own body, I watched as she straddled him and encouraged him to touch her legs.

She started with the palm of his hand, raising it up to her mouth to prick the skin, and then she applied pressure.

The droplets hit her tongue one at a time. It was tediously slow, and she enjoyed every minute of it.

When the blood drained from that wound, she hissed and dove forward. Her mouth moved to his chest, breaking the skin and lapping it up with loud, disgusting noises. She was draining him faster than his body could take, but I was rooted to where I stood, unable to move.

The human's head lulled to the side. The look of enjoyment on his features was palpable, and it transfixed me. With his clean hand he brushed his hair off his forehead, a move I'd seen Charlie do hundreds of times, and when the human looked up at me, I buckled over.

I landed hard against the stone floor and shook my head. I blinked rapidly, clearing my vision and nearly yelled in relief that it wasn't actually Charlie in front of me.

It was an instant wake-up, as if I had dived headfirst into ice cold water.

I had to get off the roof. I stood up, a renewed sense of purpose, and sprinted for the stairs. Cara moved faster than I could, and she closed the distance and jumped in front of me before I could make my exit.

She licked the blood from her lips. "What's the problem?"

"I need to find Theo," I blurted out.

"Why?"

I glanced around, making sure he wasn't already on the rooftop, and I stopped moving. One of the male vampires standing off against the edge seemed familiar to me. His long hair and string-like stature stood out. I gasped, recognizing him as the vampire who draped himself across my uncle's lap a few weeks ago.

My emotions were scattered, and my hands shook as I figured out what I was supposed to do next.

"Mina, don't do anything rash." Theo's voice, coming up from the stairs, calmed me momentarily. "Do as you're told for once, and keep a level head."

A different version of myself would have brushed off that remark, but I clung to it, those familiar words keeping me in check.

"That guy, he was with my uncle, and now he's—"

"With whoever he wants to be with," he insisted. "The King doesn't keep suitors around long enough to get attached, so there's nothing happening here for you to get all wound up about."

"Wait, you're the King's niece," Cara said slowly as recognition hit her. "Mina... Byron."

She ran away before the words were even fully formed.

18

We made a quick exit from the rooftop, and I didn't open my mouth again until we were in the safety of his car.

"I should have trusted your judgment," I admitted, sinking back against the stiff leather.

He was kind enough to not respond, letting me beat myself up enough on my own. We sat in silence for a few minutes, another gracious gesture by Theo.

"Does my uncle know about this?" I asked quietly. "Does he know about the things that happen on the roof?"

He toyed with the key in his hand. "More or less. Places like this are common, but that doesn't mean they stay open for long. It doesn't take long for human law enforcement to track down the locations where humans disappear."

"But those humans seemed… willing."

"I didn't intend to imply otherwise. That is how places like this don't break the Code. Humans are lured in, preached the virtues of vampirism, and used as blood bags for a few months until they're turned."

I nodded, unable to form words.

"Oddly enough, this is why the work of your father is so important, to keep our blood supply viable and safe while alternatives are explored, even more so now with what is happening with the King."

"How do you know?" I was too exhausted to be angry.

He bit his lip. "Your father told Philip, Philip told me, you know how things like that go."

I didn't. Gossiping was more of a human activity.

"This is… a lot to process," I admitted.

Theo tentatively reached his hand over to mine, pressing two fingers against the spot he'd grabbed earlier in haste.

"I tried to warn you."

His tone was factual, not cruel, and it comforted me. I rested my head back and allowed the weight of the past week to collapse on my chest.

"It's all too much," I sighed.

"What is?" Theo dragged his fingers up my arm, light as a feather.

My skin tingled where he touched me, distracting me from all complete thought. "The humans… the future… the poison… the pressure… the blood…"

I barely recognized my voice as I shrugged to maintain my composure.

"Why are you whispering?" Theo asked.

He suppressed a smirk, and his thumb moved to my neck and then up again to trace my cheek bones. When his feathery light touch hit my bottom lip, I met his gaze. His hand rested on my collarbone, waiting for me to react.

Every part of me froze. I didn't know how to respond to

his gesture. Was he just trying to comfort me? Did he expect something from me? How did I feel about it?

Sensing my unease, Theo drew his hand back.

He turned the key in the ignition and we drove home in silence, lost in our own thoughts.

I forced out a breath, remembering that I was with a vampire, and his scent wouldn't cause me physical pain.

If anything, he felt good to be around. I could let down my mental and physical barriers and show myself to him, if only I could overcome my own neuroticism. I wavered on his motive when we first met. He seemed too self-righteous to have honorable intentions about spending time with me.

I assumed Uncle Derrick pressured him into befriending me, and judging by the way we were paired up and shipped off tonight, I was right. But, then again, if this experience proved anything, it confirmed that Theo acted on his own accord while still having my best interest in mind.

Theo deserved credit, and I should have given it to him when we sat beside each other in the industrial freezer. He wanted to protect me, to help me. I decided that I could trust him.

By the time I resolved my inner turmoil, we cleared the gates on my uncle's property. I wasn't ready for the night, my time with Theo, to be over just yet. I should have spoken up sooner.

"Theo, we didn't visit all the places my uncle asked us to," I said, finally breaking the silence. "We could turn around?"

He offered me a tight look. "I'm sure when you explain what happened, he'll understand."

The absolute last thing I planned on doing was talking

to Uncle Derrick about what happened, and frankly, I didn't want to share the details with him. He had enough to worry about, and I had less than twelve hours to get myself together, mentally and physically, before I was surrounded by thousands of vampires, taking part in a ritual, about which no one would give me any details.

Theo idled in the driveway with his foot on the brake, and I took him not putting his car in park as a sign that he wanted to flee.

"Theo," I started. "I should be honest with you about how I am feeling—"

"Good night, Mina," he cut me off.

There was a hardness in his expression that hadn't been there when we first got in the car, and he refused to make eye contact. It surprised me.

"Are you angry with me?" I asked.

He shook his head, but his jaw ticked.

"You're defying your nature," I teased. "Vampires are usually very direct in conversation."

"Well, you're only half-vampire, so perhaps the courtesy doesn't extend to you," he bit out.

The edge to his tone caused me to frown.

"Good night, Theo," I said, stepping out and slamming the car door behind me.

I sat in the bathtub all morning, long after the water ran cold, and tried to reconcile the current state of affairs.

My uncle was dying, a true, final death, and all I could think about was how I upset Theo. It took me longer than it should have to realize that I wounded him because he thought I rejected him. It was his ego snapping at me, not his true feelings, or maybe they were tied together.

"Oh, who knows?" I cried out and sank into the water.

I resurfaced, coated in bubbles and with a resolve to focus on Uncle Derrick, the most important person in my life who was dying. His death would set a number of terrifying events into motion, and more importantly, I would be devastated. The only hope was a miraculous scientific discovery by someone on his payroll, and therefore, it was completely out of my control.

As for the person responsible for poisoning him, if I were the gambling type, my money would be on Thomas or Margaret. That opinion was a little naive. Their dislike of me was clear, even going as far as having me followed, but I wasn't sure that translated into poisoning the King, who by all other accounts, they seemed loyal to. In fact, if anything, their dedication went so far as to deem me unfit.

Begrudgingly, I toweled myself off and moved to sit in front of the vanity. I flipped on the lighted mirror. I felt like a different being now than I did two months ago, and I was surprised that, outwardly, it didn't show.

When I imagined what it would be like to interact with humans, to have friends and human experiences, I never thought the line between vampires and humans would be so blurred that it would result in what I saw on the rooftop last night. It was graphic, almost, replaying it in my mind, so I pushed it away.

I opened the social media app and looked at all the photos of the parade I missed out on. Eloise captured a really cute selfie of her and Charlie in front of the skyline I painted. I felt jealous, remorseful, and empty all at once. A glutton for punishment, I scrolled up through mine and Charlie's texts and spent an hour reading through them.

With an hour before sunset, Trinity knocked on my door to deliver my outfit, which had been altered to perfection. I stepped into the flat black shoes and ran my fingers through my loose waves that I just put the final touches on.

As I walked down the stairs to meet Uncle Derrick, his eyes flashed. I thought he was angry at my appearance, but when I hit the final step, a rare smile spread across his face.

"I expected a princess to walk down the stairs, and instead I got—"

"A half-human, half-vampire," I interjected.

He bowed his head and looked at me straight in the eyes. "The future Queen."

Pride bubbled up in my chest, and I glanced down at my outfit, a metallic red, almost crimson, suit. Trinity brought in my uncle's usual tailor, who custom made it so close to my vision that I barely stopped myself from squealing when I put it on. The lines were perfect, cut so closely to my slight curves that it exaggerated my figure.

From the back of the limo, I stared out the window, looking at the blur of buildings, cars, and people, while we sped across town.

"Where are my parents?" I asked, realizing we weren't detouring into that neighborhood.

"They're meeting us at the venue."

In some of Eloise's photos, I saw tons of parents posing with their dolled-up teenagers, and I couldn't help but frown. In my mind, I had decided I would treat tonight as my own vampire version of homecoming. Although instead of plastic cups and after school art, there'd be crystal and gold.

"I insisted, actually," he admitted. "I wanted to set your expectations for the evening."

"I've been asking you for details for weeks, and you decide to tell me thirty minutes before we arrive?"

He straightened his already perfect tie. "There were concerns that you would try to get out of it."

"Concerns?"

"Your mother mentioned a few things. That Schenley boy appeared at their home multiple times this week, banging on the door and demanding to see you."

I blinked. "So that's why you wanted me to go out with Theo last night."

"Partly." A lightness rolled across his face. "I also am aware that I may have sheltered your existence in a way that didn't shed the best light on our kind. It may be too late to reconcile that, but I had to try."

Good intentions, bad execution.

"Uncle, I understand what is expected of me. I always have, and I take it very seriously." I paused, collecting my words. "But I'm always going to be standing in two worlds, torn down the middle of who I should be. Just because I've been leaning into my human side, exploring that truly for once, does not make me any less vampire."

"I'm aware," he said quietly.

"I'm not going to be able to leave that part of me in the future, but my decisions will likely change the way that we exist as vampires."

He inclined his head toward me. "I'm counting on it."

I stared at him, slightly stunned, as he suppressed a cough.

"Now, let me tell you what to expect for the ritual," he said, changing the subject.

He reminded me of all our vampire family history, which I'd heard many times before, but I paid extra special attention to the new details that he wove in related to the ritual.

"When Jonathan and Eliza arrived from Europe in the 1700s as humans, the United States was in disarray. Their preexisting wealth drew the attention of many, but so did Eliza's beauty and ferocity, and a vampire found her. The vampire was aware of her love for Jonathan but hoped turning her into a vampire would change her affection. Obviously, it did not, and it wasn't too long after that she turned Jonathan as well."

"Right, I know all of this," I confirmed.

"But before Eliza turned Jonathan, for reasons I don't wholly understand, she saved some of his blood."

I recoiled. "Excuse me?"

Wordlessly, he reached into the interior chest pocket of his jacket to reveal a small glass bottle. I traced the jagged lines of the olive green glass when he handed it over. It took me about ten seconds to realize that it wasn't my hands that were trembling, it was the liquid inside it.

"Why does it feel like… it's buzzing?"

"Eliza bribed a witch to keep it alive."

I held the bottle up to the light, both fascinated and repulsed.

"At a time when most women were regaled to staying at home and raising children, she was a bit of a rarity, taking charge in nearly every aspect of her life with Jonathan. Especially the way that they conducted business."

"And yet Jonathan was crowned the first King of our region and not her as the Queen?" I posed.

"We live in very different times now," Uncle Derrick reminded me. "From everything I learned about her from William, I imagine she'd be ecstatic about your future." After another glance at me, he added, "And your ensemble. Women never wore pants in those days."

"So what does this have to do with the ritual tonight?" I said the words slowly, already dreading the answer.

"When Eliza turned William, she gave him a few drops of Jonathan's blood in the process. I assume her rationale was that they were creating a child, an heir, and felt they both needed to be a part of it. It wasn't until after William turned your father and me that he discovered the flask in an old safe, and under the advice of one of the witch's descendants, created this ritual."

"But why? Why is this necessary?"

"He believed it carried on our good fortune, linking the lines of family to each other the only way that was possible since we were already turned. He even went as far as to have it added into a part of the Code of Conduct, that the bloodline, so to speak, should continue."

I exhaled all the air in my lungs. "So I have to drink it?"

"Yes," he confirmed.

I cringed and handed the glass back to him for safe keeping.

"The evening will be our entrance, a formal processional, and then we will greet every vampire."

"But aren't thousands expected to be present?"

"Yes, but you will address some in groups, depending on how large the covens are, some are up to three hundred vampires. From what I recall, it's quite tedious, but it's necessary to establish some sort of relationship. This is one of the rare times vampires have a desire to be included."

"And then what happens?"

"Around midnight, the witch will begin the ceremony by candlelight, and that's when you'll drink. There's a lot of chanting and a call and response, with a few smaller rituals until sunrise, and then it will all be over."

The car lurched to a stop, and Trinity stepped up to the tinted window.

"You ready?" Uncle Derrick asked.

"Yes," I said in a small voice.

He paused with his hand on the handle.

I cleared my throat. "Yes," I repeated, this time confidently, and we stepped out into the cool October air.

19

It took three hours until I felt I was making progress. Uncle Derrick accurately described what to expect, including the tediousness of it all, but the endless droves of vampires, who all stepped up to bow and smell me, was more over-whelming than I expected.

At the very least, exchanging pleasantries distracted me from thinking about how I was going to drink centuries-old human blood in front of thousands of vampires.

When Uncle Derrick showed signs of breaking into a coughing fit, Trinity would step up, insisting there was urgent business to be taken care of in the room just off the raised floor to our left.

The faces I greeted began to blend together, all pale and intense, until a large group of vampires collectively bowed, revealing Thomas and Margaret standing next in line. The oldest vampire in the group announced himself, describing the legacy of their coven and the state of affairs in their small town at the southern tip of the region.

As they stepped aside to allow the line to continue, Uncle Derrick leaned over to me slightly. "That coven was wrought with challenges back in the early 1900s when tuberculosis was prevalent," he spoke quietly in my ear. "They found humor in turning humans who were dying of a blood disease into vampires. I'm pleased to see they seemed to have evolved as the older vampires died out since my ritual."

He resumed his straight posture beside me.

"Your majesty," Thomas drawled as he and Margaret bowed deeply.

"Margaret, Thomas," I said evenly.

Margaret glanced at her husband, who gave her a look of reassurance, and she addressed me directly. "Thomas and I would like to apologize for our actions these past few months. We discussed my outburst and his misguided initiative, and we quickly realized the error of our ways."

I suppressed the impulse to let my jaw drop open.

"We hope you will accept our statements as true," Thomas added. "There is much to learn from you."

Uncle Derrick looked at me expectantly, and I knew this was an opportunity I couldn't miss.

"No," I said, registering the flicker of surprise in their eyes. "It's not a one-way street, Thomas. Although I recognize the monarchy's power in our region, and country, it's not in the best interest of our region, for humans or vampires, for me to dictate and you to blindly follow. I will do what I think is best, but I need people who are willing to disagree, in an appropriate manner, and feel comfortable voicing their opinions. It's not you who needs to solely learn from me. It's us from each other."

Thomas and Margaret exchanged looks of acceptance.

"But I will not tolerate acts of disrespect," I warned, making my tone as sharp as I could. "I am giving you a clean slate, and you will not dirty it again. Understood?"

They both bowed, accepting my words, and I turned my attention to the next group.

"Well done," Uncle Derrick complimented.

He stepped back, confident enough to let me take point, and I found courage within that trust.

My uncle groomed me for this my entire life, and I tried to imagine what this scene looked like from his perspective. Continuing with our vampire family legacy, the current monarch would actively hand off responsibility, but I wasn't sure he expected to be coughing himself to a final death in the process.

He hadn't specified if I would be alone with the witch during the ritual, but perhaps I could figure out a way to ask her for help in curing Uncle Derrick. Then again, I didn't have the complete picture of their dynamic, and having never met a witch before, I didn't know if there was a particular reason not to reveal this information. It was bad enough that so many vampires knew. Like Theo, who I'd thought about more than I should have since we parted ways. It was almost difficult to believe that it hadn't even been a full day since everything happened on the rooftop and in his car.

I craned my neck slightly, spotting him and Philip standing near my parents. They were talking animatedly by vampire standards. Theo was actually using his hands while he spoke, poking himself in the chest to drive whatever point he was making across. I couldn't tear my eyes away from him, wondering what words were coming out of his mouth that had him so twisted up.

As if he could sense it, his gaze flicked over to me. He looked devastatingly handsome in his dark blue suit, and I beamed at his open collar. Theo's choice to forgo a tie was a subtle gesture that I hoped was a message for me, given that I mocked him for his tie when we first met. Every other vampire in the expansive room buttoned or covered so modestly that they practically walked around in straight jackets.

I clenched my fists and forced myself to look away from the sliver of his exposed chest.

Uncle Derrick nudged me back to greet the next round of vampires. Engaging in small talk while feeling the weight of Theo's scrutiny on me was exhilarating, and as soon as I could, I turned back, locking eyes with him. I tried to read his expression or have some silent conversation about what had him all out of sorts, but he revealed nothing.

We held each other's gaze as a thunderous bang sounded from my left.

The wall to my right exploded, and the force of it propelled me into the air momentarily. I hit the cold marble floor, a welcome contrast from the heat of the flames, and rolled.

The sound of the explosion was like nothing I ever heard before, as if metal screamed and ignited, but it was nothing compared to the cries of vampires. Hundreds of them, causing a commotion as they all attempted to leave at full speed. The scent of burned hair and clothing hung in the air.

Uncle Derrick yanked me up, dragging me through one of the side exits. He pushed me out into the open air. He and I both promptly broke into coughing fits. My lungs were filled with smoke and debris, his with blood.

I leaned against Theo's car, momentarily grateful for its stand-out, bright yellow color. Sirens grew louder from all directions. The noise deafened my hearing to any approaching danger, so I inhaled and panicked when I picked up on the scent of vampires heading our way. Any number of them could have been responsible for the explosion.

I pulled the handle of Theo's unlocked car and shoved Uncle Derrick as hard as I could into the backseat. I climbed in beside him and slammed the door, tempering the sound of chaos.

My phone buzzed in my pocket.

"Trinity," I breathed.

"Are you okay? Are your lungs... still viable? Where are you?"

"Yes, yes, and Uncle Derrick and I are safe, hiding out."

Uncle Derrick managed to swallow down the coughing and held out his hand, wanting me to hand over the phone. I removed Trinity's voice from my ear and turned on speaker phone.

"Trinity," he said calmly. "What do we know?"

"Marie is taking point on charming the police and firemen while Max is back inside with a few other nobles, trying to take stock of whatever he can before the humans enter the building. Most of the vampires have scattered from the scene. How do you want me to proceed?"

"Get in touch with the witch and see if she had anything to do with it."

"Yes, your majesty. Anything else?"

"That's all."

I ended the call and slid the phone back in my pocket, brushing off some dirt patches from my clothing. It was a miracle I was almost completely unscathed, but the ordeal seemed to irritate the blood in Uncle Derrick's lungs even more.

My hands gripped his shoulders as he coughed up enough blood to soak his handkerchief completely. I could only watch in horror as a particularly nasty set wracked his body, and blood pooled at the corner of his eyes, as if he was trying to cry blood.

Suddenly, he leaned out of my hold and back against the seat. The coughing slowed, and he collected himself just as the driver's side door opened.

Theo jumped in and slammed the door in frustration.

He slammed his palms against the steering wheel, and I caught the look of pure torture across his features. Theo's anger distracted him enough that he was unaware of our presence.

"Theo," I whispered after he turned on the car.

"Shit!"

It was the loudest I'd ever heard a vampire yell.

He jerked and punched the gas. His back-up camera system pinged loudly, reminding him to stop before he hit the car behind us.

"Where the hell have you been?" Theo demanded.

Uncle Derrick cleared his throat, and Theo righted himself. "Your majesty, I didn't—"

"Why would someone do this?" I demanded, turning my attention to Uncle Derrick. I didn't have patience or interest in Theo's pleasantries.

My uncle put his hand on his chest, pressing down in an attempt to keep his lungs under control. He glanced out the window to where humans in uniform rushed into the building.

"Theo, would you be so kind as to provide us a ride back to my home?" he asked.

"Why?" I repeated. "What was the point of that? An explosion wouldn't even kill us."

I didn't miss the flash in Theo's eyes as he weaved through the police cars and accelerated us away. "What is it, Theo?" I growled.

"I can't think of a sensitive way to ask this." He paused and his forehead puckered. "But... you're half-human, Mina. You can be killed, yes?"

"My skin acts as the same impenetrable shield as yours," I snapped, feeling a little defensive from the way our conversation ended the last time I was in his car.

He nodded. "Okay, but what weakness do you have?"

I had never given serious thought to how someone could successfully kill me if they tried. "Um..."

"You need air, correct?" Theo pointed out.

As if to prove a point, I inhaled. "I once went an hour without breathing, just to see if I could do it. Most humans need to breathe twenty times a minute."

"So if someone, say, set off a bomb and moved quickly enough to subdue you, forcing you to inhale toxic air long enough, you could die?" Theo asked.

Uncle Derrick closed his eyes, as if the conversation was

too much for him. "Have you been thinking about ways to kill my niece, Theo?"

I smiled nervously, but Theo responded in complete seriousness.

"The moment that explosion happened, it was the first thing I could think of. By the time I ran over to where I saw her last, she was gone. I panicked. I trailed groups of vampires, asking them if they saw you, but everyone was too busy fleeing and worried about avoiding the police. I ran back as fast as I could and circled the building again, nearly ripping my hair out because I couldn't pick up either of your scents or enter the building since it had already been blocked off."

He stopped himself, realizing that he was ranting slightly.

"So yes, your majesty, it's all I've thought about for the past twenty minutes."

The rest of the ride was awkward and silent, and Theo refused to acknowledge me when I got out of the car. I huffed, recalling that it was Theo himself who once said I was the hot and cold one of the two of us.

When Uncle Derrick and I were back in the library, I finally asked the most pressing question in my mind. "Who do you think was responsible?"

"We will have a better idea when your father, your mother, and Trinity return with more information," he said, wiping a bit of blood from the corner of his mouth.

"You must have some idea, though," I pressed.

He ignored me, staring off into the fire.

"Thomas and Margaret seemed to atone for their

behavior tonight," I continued. "Do you think they're responsible? Maybe they were just trying to throw us off."

"They were likely so agreeable because I started pouring money into their competitors' businesses," Uncle Derrick admitted with a sour tone.

"Oh," I breathed.

I felt slightly betrayed at his admission, as if it cheapened my own efforts at diplomacy, and it left me a little antsy.

Too many vampires and too much drama for one night trapped me.

I wanted to get out of that room, to get some answers, but all I had to do was wait. Wait for my parents or some answers or another coughing fit to remind me that my uncle was dying and that someone might have been trying to kill me, and suddenly, I had the overwhelming sense that I was being suffocated.

My car keys were in my hand before I even registered what I was doing, and my uncle glared at me. "As I said, we need to wait for your father, your mother, and Trinity to return. Don't do anything noble. I told them we'd reconvene here."

"I have somewhere I want to be."

"Mina," he said in forced patience. "The night I have been waiting for since I held you in my arms as a baby was shattered completely by an attempt on your life or to sabotage your rightful claim to my crown. Perhaps your high school dance isn't as important?"

I stared at the keychain in my fingers. "It's not as important," I agreed with him. "But I just need space from all of this. I won't be long, I promise." I left before he could respond, but the echoes of the blood in his airway haunted me the entire way to the school.

20

When I worked on the decorations, even giving it my best artistic effort, I thought they were too over-the-top cheesy, borderline tacky. Vampires are such minimalist creatures when it comes to belongings and design aesthetic, and my preferences usually lean toward those patterns. But when I walked into the gym, with all the hanging lights and backlit paintings and pictures, I was dazzled.

The same nearly indescribable feeling of driving up toward the city skyline at night surfaced, with everyone dressed up and swaying to the slow song that was blasted through the DJ's speakers.

I made my way through the crowd, needing to remind myself that unlike the earlier gathering, these were humans, not vampires. They weren't averse to touching, and I could hear hundreds of hearts pumping blood. I shook it off and refocused.

Charlie, Eloise, and the rest of the group sat on the bleachers, laughing and chatting away happily. Before I slipped through the crowd, I stopped and took a picture on my phone, wanting to capture the stark contrast between this moment of jubilation and the terror I felt almost an hour ago.

Eloise saw me first, and she leapt up from her seat and threw her arms around me. I stiffened at the contact, returning a pat gently, and stayed still until she released me.

"Oh my god, Mina," Eloise shrieked. "You look amazing, like some kind of fashion model in this power suit. How are you feeling? I was so worried when you stopped answering me this week that you were in the hospital or something. Was it mono? I'm so glad you're okay. And that you're here!"

"I started to feel better a few hours ago, and I wanted to surprise you," I said casually. "I didn't want to miss this."

She stepped back to take in my outfit again, and I was well aware I was the only female not wearing some sort of dress or skirt combination. Eloise, however, looked stunning in her short purple dress. She spent hours sewing it herself and told me all about the laborious process of attaching the individual beads.

As Eloise rushed to fill me in about whatever I missed since I last saw her, a tall, blond blur stormed out from behind her. She followed my eye line to Charlie's back and grimaced.

"Yikes," she cringed.

"Think he's mad at me?"

"Probably more hurt than anything. He's been really worried about you." She paused, taking in my expression.

"We've been commiserating together all week. Did you know he went to your house?"

"I didn't until today," I admitted. "I've been staying at my uncle's. Look, I really want to catch up with you but—"

"Go after him," she insisted, giving my hand another squeeze before I set off to find him.

Tanner called my name. I kept walking and turned to wave at him, nearly crashing into Brooklyn, who stepped in front of me before I made it to the gym door.

She glared at me, arms crossed across her chest. "This was the best week of the school year so far," she sneered. "Why do you think that is, Mina?"

I stepped sideways, not wanting to engage her, but she mirrored my movement. She wanted a confrontation, but I wasn't in the mood. I kept my face blank, waiting for her to pounce. My lack of action infuriated her.

"You don't belong here, just look at you," she sputtered, turning to Jamie and Marissa to back her up, but they stayed put.

I chuckled. "There's nothing to gain by putting someone else down, Brooklyn. If this is how you're going to waste your life, that's on you and the people who indulge it."

She scoffed and began hurling words intended to hurt me, and I slammed the door in her face.

"Charlie?" I called.

I followed his scent past the vending machines where he'd first asked me out, through the lunchroom I rarely entered, and down one of the hallways toward a row of classrooms.

The lights were off, and without the bustle of students

getting to class, it was a little eerie. I rounded the corner to see that the door to Mr. Berry's room was slightly ajar, and I let myself in, closing the door behind me.

The sky wasn't completely black yet, so the dark blue hue and street lamp cast somewhat of a serene filter on Charlie's expression. He sat on top of my desk, staring at the window that I clung to for support on that first day of school.

I approached him tentatively. He didn't move when I stopped beside him. His elbows rested on his knees, twisting up his fingers. He swallowed, and I had to tear my eyes away from the movement of his throat.

"It's been a long week, Mina." He said the words so evenly that I couldn't make sense of how he felt. That scared me. "I've had a lot of time to think, and I've..." He trailed off.

I leaned against the window ledge, facing whatever he was about to say head on.

He kept his gaze on the floor as he took three deep breaths, and then when his eyes met mine, my knees almost buckled. His expression was completely raw, his hair disheveled from running his hands through it, and he looked so strikingly handsome that it was almost too much to take in.

"I think I've figured some things out," he said, the strong, confident, and deep tone of his voice surfacing again.

"Oh?"

He chewed on his bottom lip until he spoke again. "It started with Emma, actually. She insists that she's outgrown 'kid shows,' as she says, but occasionally I'll catch her watching cartoons on my phone. Anyway, she was watching some movie, the one where Adam Sandler voices Dracula, and they were talking about how vampires didn't like garlic, and Emma said, 'Just like Mina! Do you think she's a vampire?'"

I gritted my teeth in an attempt to stop myself from a physical reaction.

"I kind of laughed it off the way I did when Brooklyn started spewing that rumor around, too, because, come on, this is real life. Monsters are for movies." He dragged his thumb along his jawline and continued staring straight ahead as he spoke. "I just continued on with making dinner, and you ignored my call for the twentieth time. I think it was the timing of everything, but I got kind of a nagging feeling that I couldn't let go of.

"So then I'm thinking about the little things, you know, the details that were so insignificant at the time, but now, rethinking everything under a microscope... the fasting, the very small list of foods you've tried, the way your skin is so beautifully porcelain, and the fact that I've been talking for nearly five minutes, and you haven't breathed or blinked once."

If I wasn't paralyzed with the reality of the situation, blinking or breathing to prove a point would be so heavy-handed, it would be a dead giveaway.

"I'm not proud of this next thing I'm about to say, Mina, but I have the feeling you're going to cut me some slack on it," he said, finally meeting my eyes. "I broke into your house earlier."

I gripped the windowsill with both hands, and the wood splintered beneath my fingertips.

"I thought that your parents, who are both freakishly young, by the way, didn't approve of you dating or something, given that you didn't have television or junk food, and I don't know, it's kind of stalkerish now, but I genuinely felt bad that you weren't going to be at homecoming, so I wanted to sneak into your window and surprise you, but I realized that I didn't know which room was yours. The back door was unlocked anyway."

He chuckled. "Your house had so little furniture in it, Mina, that I thought you moved or something, and when I opened the fridge to see if you left anything behind, I... well, you can guess what I found." Charlie traced the veins on the back of his hand. "I'm no Tanner, but the sight was... unnerving enough for me to get the hell out of there and sit in my car, alone, until I got myself together enough to spend a few hours distracting myself with my friends."

I released my grip, and chunks of wood hit the floor. He watched it happen, slightly impressed.

He met my eyes once again. "You weren't really sick, were you?"

I couldn't lie to him, but I certainly couldn't tell the truth.

"Mina, you're a—"

I brought my palm up to his mouth, pressing my skin against his lips. I shook my head, pleading for him not to continue.

"Please, Charlie," I begged him. "Please don't."

He grabbed my other hand, understanding the reason why I felt so cold to him, and brought it up to his chest, where his pounding heart was making me feel a little fuzzy.

I stepped back, reclaiming my own limbs, but he stood, closing the distance between us.

Charlie tentatively brought his hands up, pushing my hair behind my shoulders. He touched the top of my arms, and then brought his palms to my neck, both thumbs caressing my skin.

Vampires usually made me feel weak, inadequate even, but somehow, this human teenager had gained the power to hold my entire being in the balance. It was the most fragile I'd ever felt in my lifetime, and one move could break me completely.

He leaned closer, holding my gaze. "Whoever you are, whatever you are, Mina, I'm all in," he whispered before his lips crushed into mine.

I melted into him wholly, kissing him with passion I'd suppressed for so long, I didn't know I was capable of it. Charlie made me feel so alive, and I clung to it. I opened up to him completely, pouring everything human in me, all my flaws and uncertainty and desire into the movements, and he was right there with me.

His arms snaked behind me, and I got lost in the movement between us, the heat from his body, and how good it felt to erase everything around me except him. I pulled him closer, and he grinned, as widely as I'd ever seen him do so, before kissing the side of my mouth, and then my cheek and ear. His warm hands moved over my skin as he kissed my neck. His tongue swiped against my collarbone, and my hands tugged at his hair.

More, more, more. I wanted more.

I took charge, unable to hold back any longer, and turned us both, pressing his back against the wall. He inhaled in surprise at my strength, and I stripped his jacket off, shedding the layers between me and his skin. He was breathing heavily as he undid his tie and began to unbutton his shirt, but it wasn't fast enough.

He was too slow, too human, and I needed to fix it. He marveled as I unbuttoned his cuffs and shirt at a rapid pace as my hands started to shake. I tore his shirt slightly, too impatient for it to be off, and I wanted his skin so much that I trembled everywhere. I wanted to see it all, the muscles I'd felt, the veins. I wanted to press my ear up against his heart to hear it pump blood.

I hissed at the thought and sprang backward, throwing myself toward the opposite side of the room as far away from him as I could.

Crouching behind Mr. Berry's desk, I chided myself for nearly losing control. I groaned, running my tongue along my fully visible fangs, and buttoned my jacket again. I closed my eyes, now fully noticing their burn, and forced myself to think of shoes, cars, and everything else that wasn't him.

"Mina?" Charlie breathed.

"Stay there, Charlie."

He didn't listen. I tried to expedite the process of going back to normal, imagining my body not in a trembly, red state, and it worked, slightly. By the time he stood in front of me, the only thing visible that could give me away was my fangs, and I kept my mouth shut.

Charlie held out his hand, and I accepted it, standing up to face him.

"Let me see," he said, his gaze dropping to my mouth.

I ground my teeth, defying everything natural in my

body that wanted to be exposed. The pain of forcing my fangs to retreat into my gums was excruciating, but I did it. I opened my mouth, and Charlie looked disappointed that I had thirty-two normal human teeth.

We stood there for a moment, trying to comprehend the new reality we both lived in, and my phone, which had managed to stay silent in my pocket for the entire exchange, began to vibrate.

Taking a distraction when I needed one, I read the message from Trinity.

Come back. We're ready now.

I typed quickly, not even bothering to hide my extra speed in front of Charlie. *On my way. Will be there in fifteen.*

"I have to go."

His brow furrowed. "I thought v—"

"Charlie," I warned.

He righted himself, understanding the clear verbal line that he couldn't cross. "I thought you could stay out all night. No curfew and all that."

I didn't even know how to begin to explain any of it. "It's complicated," I muttered, and it was the best I could do. I pressed a quick kiss against his cheek, the only thing I trusted myself to do, and moved toward the door.

"Mina," he said, causing me to turn back for a final glance. "This is the best homecoming... ever."

It was such a quirky human thing to say, but it was somehow just what I needed to hear. "I agree," I laughed before disappearing into the darkness.

21

I sat in the library at the mansion, trying my very best to focus on the conversation happening around me, one that I definitely needed to pay attention to, but my mind was elsewhere. I considered the very real possibility that what happened between Charlie and me was actually just a stress-induced, dream-like phenomenon and that I never left the mansion. Part of me would be okay with that.

Because to accept everything that happened between us, to delight in the exquisiteness of intimacy, I also had to accept that he knew the truth about me, and there were significant consequences to that.

I felt lucid enough to recall the story of my own parents, how my dad managed to hide his vampirism from my mom for almost a year, claiming to have a job that required him to travel often, and he only visited her during the weeks he felt the strongest. Blood wasn't as easy to come by those days, which is why he made it his primary responsibility to oversee the relationships with blood banks and hospitals, and eventually, explore alternatives.

He was the vampire I emulated most growing up. Although his brother was the King of Appalachia, responsible for the well-being of all the vampires in the region, he was somehow the more serious one. Vampires were deliberate creatures by nature, but he was even more calculated. I certainly never saw him smile.

My parents were my parents, but compared to human relationships I observed, they were distant. Perhaps it was their understanding that when I was born, my purpose would turn away from their interests and to the good of the region. At least that was what I told myself in my loneliest of moments, usually when Uncle Derrick was off traveling somewhere.

"Did the witch have a credible alibi?" My father stood rigid near the bay window. "Did you speak to her directly?"

"Yes and yes," Trinity confirmed. "She was still with the werewolves when I arrived and had been for hours. I spoke separately with the pack leader myself to confirm."

My father took in her words, the lines of his face hardening as he spoke. "Perhaps they were all in on it."

"Max, do you really suspect they're involved?" My mother's tone was only slightly irritated. "I already told you that the officers I spoke with were planning on ruling it an electrical accident."

"Everyone should be treated as such until we know more. Do you think your contacts would provide a copy of the incident report?"

"I'll ask," my mother promised.

"Do you trust her?" Uncle Derrick asked Trinity, who

was making notes on her tablet, as usual.

My father jumped in. "Who? The witch or the head of the pack?"

Before Uncle Derrick could answer, Trinity spoke up. "I trust both."

"We currently have no misgivings with the witches and the werewolves, so I am inclined to believe they had no part in this," Derrick said.

"There's one other thing," Trinity said slowly. "The witch still expects to be paid."

"Unbelievable," my father muttered.

I couldn't help myself. "How much does she charge?"

"She deals in favors," he explained. "Usually for business introductions or contracts."

"And what about now?" I asked.

"She's asking for protection."

"Protection?"

"Evaline is gaining notoriety in all circles, all species, and although she has her spellwork and hired human security, she's seeking additional support," Uncle Derrick explained.

That had me curious. "But why now? Doesn't it seem odd to coincide with the explosion?"

"Astute observation, and definitely something to consider."

"What about the werewolves? I thought we had some arguments over territory last spring?"

"Enough questions, Mina," my father asserted. "We need to discuss our own strategy, not bother ourselves with the petty concerns of others."

It seemed to me that it was worth exploring the current

state of both of these groups, but having no experience in dealing with the fallout of this nature, I sat back and watched as they talked through scenarios of how to handle it. They agreed my mother would keep pressing the officers, my father would continue working with the other nobles to see what they could uncover, and Trinity would guide Philip to cover some additional ground with the others.

All it took was one explosion to derail the entire region's focus. I knew that it was a big, notable event, but as Uncle Derrick's attention centered on this, adding to the stress of it all, my concern for him increased. If he wasn't going to make his health top priority, I needed to.

I had to do something.

My thumbs moved, rapid firing a message to Trinity, who glanced at me quizzically when she saw my name on her phone. *Trinity, can you send me Theo's number, please? His personal phone.*

She read the message and sent over his digital contact card, but not before she offered me a sly look.

Around three in the morning, after my parents left, I was back in my room, alone, to change and figure out what to say to Theo. I had a plan, and I wasn't sure if he would be up for it.

I typed, deleted, and retyped the message a few times.

Theo. It's Mina.

That was the best I could do, and he responded immediately.

Mina. It's Theo.

I sighed. *I need your help.*

He responded by calling me, and I swiped the phone,

bringing it up to my ear.

"Are you all right?" His voice was slightly panicked.

I probably shouldn't have been that vague. "I'm fine," I reassured him. "I didn't mean to make you worry. I just… wanted to ask you for a favor."

"A favor, huh?" Theo seemed entertained enough by the concept. "That's more of a surprise than you willingly speaking to me."

I withheld my smile, even though he couldn't see it.

"What do you need, Mina?" Back to serious Theo.

"Do you know Evaline?"

He paused, so I took that as a yes.

"Can you take me to her?"

His sigh was palpable. "It's the middle of the night."

A fair excuse. "Tomorrow then?" I pressed, letting the hopefulness shine in my voice.

"Noon."

"Okay."

"You'll need to run down the driveway. I need to avoid being associated with whatever this is."

"Okay."

"And Mina?"

"Yes?"

"Please don't scare me like that again."

"Okay."

Hours later, Theo and I pulled up to a modern wellness shop a little after noon, and I offered him a confused look. I should have known better than to lean into every single witch cliche and rumor that I'd heard, given that I was half-vampire and well aware of the difference between fiction and reality.

"Expecting all black, cauldrons, and tarot cards?" Theo teased, finally lightening up. "Maybe in New Orleans, but up here, that would bring the wrong kind of attention, don't you think?"

I nodded, admiring the storefront as I stepped up onto the curb.

He held the door open, and the scent of lavender permeated my nostrils, welcoming me inside. Glass bottles in various shapes and sizes lined the shelves, all with the promise of curing some sort of ailment written on the front in a loopy script, along with baskets containing various soaps and scrubs.

Theo watched me take in my surroundings for a few minutes and then, apparently losing patience with my dawdling, pressed the bell on the counter. A tall woman with deep brown eyes and hair graying at the temples stepped out from the back and scanned the room.

"Get the door and blinds, would you?"

She spoke to Theo without even looking at him, zoning in on me. Theo flipped the lock and pressed a button that automatically lowered the blinds, blocking out onlookers and the midday sun.

Evaline stepped forward and reached for my hands, and I was taken aback by the gesture enough to bump up against one of the reclaimed wood tables. She showed me her palms, proving to me that there was nothing amiss in her gesture, and I tentatively placed my hands in hers.

When our skin touched, her eyes closed immediately, and she squeezed my fingers with an impressive amount of strength. She began to hum to herself, and I glanced at Theo, who crossed his arms over his chest.

"I know who you are," she hissed, digging her finger-nails into our grip as she swayed from side to side. "Half-human, half-vampire, and wholly responsible for the future of all creatures in the region, the one who will bring nothing but misery and pain in the duration of her reign, who will set us back centuries."

I gasped and tried to release her, but she held me tight, shaking her head violently back and forth. Her words couldn't be true. Some insane witch prediction didn't give her the right to make such broad accusations.

But what if she was right?

I started to panic, taking in air much faster than I normally did, needing something to do with my body as she continued.

"I know who you are," she repeated in a dreamy voice.

And then she stopped moving altogether, releasing my grip and taking a deep breath before she opened her eyes. "Because Theo called me to tell me that you were coming," she explained, and both of them became lost in hysterics.

I felt a little wobbly, so I put my hands on my knees to focus on my breath. It took me five cycles of my own exhales to come around, even slightly, to the elaborate joke.

"Sorry, Mina," Theo said between chuckles.

"You don't look all that sorry."

He laughed again. "I know. I'm really not. But that was worth it."

Theo embraced Evaline, and she threw her arms around him without hesitation.

"You… trust vampires?" I couldn't help but ask.

"I have spells in place that will subdue any creature

intending me harm," she admitted proudly. "Can't you feel it in the air?"

It was the lavender, I realized. The air was thick with the scent, now that I focused on it, noting that it smelled a little sweeter than it should. To test her words, I tried to release my fangs, but they wouldn't budge.

"This is my Aunt Eva," Theo explained.

"You're related?" I said dumbly, taking in the obvious resemblance between them.

Theo tilted his head to the side. "Isn't that why you called me?"

"No," I admitted. "I had no idea."

He seemed perplexed.

"Does my uncle know?" I asked.

"No. At least, I don't think so. I was worried that they might have connected the pieces, looking into all known associates of the suspects in the explosion."

"You give vampire detective skills too much credit," I admitted as understanding hit me square across the face. "Now I understand why you've been acting so strange."

"Just to clear the air," Evaline jumped in. "I had nothing to do with that explosion, nor did the werewolves I tended to yesterday."

"Understood," I acknowledged. "I will push my uncle away from that theory as best I can."

From behind the counter she pulled out an empty, over-sized, white ceramic bowl. "Now, let's get to the real purpose of your visit, shall we?"

She muttered words in a language I didn't recognize, and with the snap of her fingers, steaming hot water rose up from the bottom and filled the basin to the edge.

"Can you do that?" I asked Theo.

He ignored the question, piquing my curiosity even further.

"My intuition tells me that you're here for an altruistic purpose," Evaline said in low tones. "Am I correct?"

"I'm not sure if it's completely selfless, if I'm being honest, because I can't bear to see my uncle in pain."

"Theo mentioned that he has likely been poisoned."

"Dead blood," I grimaced.

"And you'd like to end his suffering?"

"Very much so."

"I've learned to bewitch magical objects that can turn a vampire into a corpse with enough force, but to give a vampire a true death… is not something I have done myself."

"No," I nearly yelled, and Evaline's eyes went wide. "That's not what I want," I quickly added.

"And what is it that you want?"

"An antidote."

"Ah," she breathed and began pulling various bottles off the shelf, tilting a drop or two of one liquid in, then pulling the top off to smell another and repeat the process. After the twelfth time, I stopped trying to read the labels.

The liquids swirled together. Each drop of green, yellow, purple, and red transformed the contents before she submerged her fingertips, once again murmuring to herself until the liquid turned black. Steam clouded my vision, and when it cleared, the contents of the bowl had boiled down to less than a cup of liquid, which she poured into an empty vial.

"This is it?" I asked, delicately holding the precious

container in my hand.

She frowned. "I'm afraid not. This will ease his coughing, which I assume is getting worse by the day. It should also help stave off his other symptoms."

"Other symptoms?"

"He didn't tell you what dead blood does to a vampire?" She stopped herself. "I suppose I'm not completely surprised. It's very gruesome, by my standards at least. Blood comes out of… everywhere, eventually, and it's very painful. He'll barely be able to take fresh blood, with the dead blood rotting him from the inside—"

"Eva," Theo warned, seeing my entire demeanor nearly crumble.

"So there's nothing that will cure him completely?" I cried.

She produced a spellbook from a drawer at her feet. An oversized cover and tattered spine were littered with words and letters that I guessed were in whatever language she invoked to cull the magic. Her forehead wrinkled as she gingerly turned the pages over until she found the one she was looking for.

"You would have to make a great sacrifice," she explained. "To reverse death is to destroy the balance of nature, and to atone for robbing death, you must exchange it for two lives."

"I would need to kill two vampires—"

"Two humans, one to a vampire death and one to a final death."

"But that doesn't make any sense," I sputtered. "How does that cancel out anything?"

"I do not question the magic, I invoke it."

I considered it, running through all the possibilities to save Uncle Derrick in my head, but as soon as the words left her mouth, I knew that was not an option. She watched me, taking in my turmoil, and as I shook my head, I registered that I had somehow impressed her, even with my outbursts.

"I can't do it," I confirmed aloud. "And I'm sorry for being rude and ungrateful. I'm usually the opposite. I'm just a little desperate at this point."

"Everyone's desperate about something, Mina."

I frowned, flashing back to the conversation that seemed like years ago at this point in my uncle's industrial freezer. "Theo said that to me once, you know."

"The most important lessons usually come full circle," Evaline mused, putting the book and bowl back in their places. "Oh, let me fix that for you."

The vial in my hand turned boiling hot for a brief second before it changed from black to a bright, blood red.

"I want to help, but I also appreciate discretion," Evaline said. "He doesn't need to know how you acquired that. Just sneak a drop in every time he takes blood, and it will stay our secret."

I smiled. "Evaline, I cannot thank you enough for this. How can I pay you? I heard that you exchange help for favors?"

Theo busied himself with unlocking the doors and fiddling with the lights.

"No need, Mina, I would do anything for Theo," she said, and for the first time, her voice was harsh, an insinuation that I was a threat.

I hoped I wasn't one.

22

As the next week passed, my frustration grew.

The vampires around me were singularly focused on who, or what, was responsible for the explosion. I was the only one more concerned with my uncle, whose condition only appeared to be improving because I kept sneaking drops of Evaline's potion into his blood, masking his symptoms. His somewhat miraculous recovery only renewed his focus on other things.

I was so vocal about my disinterest in the explosion that by Wednesday afternoon, Trinity lightly suggested that I consider returning to human school. I flat out refused under the guise of wanting to spend as much time with Uncle Derrick, which was true, but I also needed to keep spiking his blood.

To cement my decision, I withdrew, telling the school administrator that the sickness spooked my parents so much that they wanted me to withdraw and continue homeschooling until I could take the GED.

Eloise and I talked on the phone nearly every day, and she was bummed that she failed to give me the true high school experience but was "totally fine" after Tanner hooked up with Jamie at the homecoming afterparty. I only exchanged texts with Charlie here and there because between soccer playoffs, midterms, and his family duties, he barely had time to sleep. Occasionally I saw Theo among other vampires who were in and out of the mansion, but he never stayed long and always avoided me if he could help it.

On Friday night, I sprawled out on the carpet of my room to work my way through a stack of books. Uncle Derrick insisted that if I wasn't going to human school, I needed to keep my mind sharp and growing, and he selected more than a dozen business and philosophy books with bold promises on the front covers.

I was five chapters into a book on good and evil when Charlie texted me.

Hey. Busy?

Channeling my inner Eloise, I took a picture of me on the floor, surrounded by books, and sent it to him. *Spending quality time with a few new friends.*

He texted again. *Emma and I were wondering if you wanted to come over.*

Before I could respond, he sent a selfie of the two of them. Emma was smiling so fully that her eyes were shut, and there was a bit of flour on her cheek. I pushed away my books and decided that some messy, unpredictable human time was just what I needed.

I changed quickly, pulling on jeans and a cozy sweater. After hitting light traffic, I parked in front of Charlie's mom's house. I knocked on the door, and Charlie seemed surprised to see me.

"Did you not invite me over?" I asked.

He laughed. "You never responded. We thought you ghosted us."

"Ghosted?"

"Disappeared," Emma explained from behind Charlie. "Like a ghost."

"That makes sense," I decided.

Charlie waved me in, and Emma danced behind him, twirling around in her long, fuzzy pajamas. I set my purse down on the table and kicked off my shoes.

"Do ghosts get to enjoy freshly baked cake?" I asked her, picking up on hints of red velvet from the kitchen.

She giggled and shook her head.

"Well then it's a good thing Mina's not a ghost then, isn't it?" Charlie said.

Emma rolled her eyes. "Duh." She skipped through the living room, leading Charlie by hand back to the kitchen. "Charlie said we have to let it cool before we put the frosting on it."

Charlie and I spent the majority of the night being bossed around by an eight-year-old, and I didn't mind it. We colored pictures, watched funny videos, and built a fort in the living room, where Emma ate more of the icing from the container than on the cake. They attempted to teach me how to play video games, but I found the entire ordeal too nerve-wracking to find enjoyment in it.

She managed to stay up two hours past her normal bedtime and was trying to push it back while brushing her teeth, but Charlie didn't budge. She huffed but still insisted that Charlie tuck her in and stay with her until she fell asleep.

While Charlie read a bedtime story, I wandered into his room. The walls, sheets, and pillows were all different shades of blue, and the carpet, which I believed was gray, was covered in an organized chaos of clothing, books, soccer gear, and newspapers. I sat on the edge of his bed, admiring the framed jerseys on his walls, along with some medals and trophies that were scattered on top of his dresser.

The room at his father's house was plain and temporary, but this, it felt like Charlie. It was like stepping into a deeper part of him.

He tapped his knuckles on the half-open door, and my entire body stiffened as his eyes flashed. I stood up, hoping that he knew I wasn't prying. I was simply curious.

"I like your room." I whispered because I knew Emma's door was cracked slightly.

Before going to bed, she explained to me in great detail that it was her preferred way of sleeping, letting the light in from the hall just enough so that she didn't feel alone. Plus, her mother paid her five dollars after she told on Charlie for sneaking out last year, and she was a business woman, after all.

"My room likes you," he said lightly. "And I like you in it."

I couldn't help but smile. "Can I have a tour of the rest of the house? I was slighted the first time I came over."

It was the first thing I could come up with as an excuse to get out of the close proximity of his bed, which seemed far too intimate. I didn't want him to get the wrong idea.

What happened between us in the classroom at homecoming could not happen again. My lack of practice in that kind of physical restraint was a major hurdle, and I refused to put him in danger.

"Sure," he said, reaching for my hand.

He kissed my fingers as he showed me the guest room, where his dad spent a lot of nights before his parents got divorced. He then opened the door to his mother's bedroom, decorated with a delicate floral pattern. We moved back down to the first floor, where I peeked into the office and formal dining room that they only used for holidays and birthdays.

When our tour ended, he asked if I wanted to watch a movie. I half-heartedly agreed. Sitting with him with the lights off only invited further complications. I suddenly wished we had Emma as a distraction because the tension was thick in my throat. I was overanalyzing everything I wanted to say before I said it, to try and be delicate about how we needed to pause a physical relationship, and I was thinking so much that I didn't speak at all.

"Couch or fort?" Charlie asked.

The couch seemed a little dangerous, and the mess of pillows, wrinkled pages from a coloring book, and chairs from the kitchen table seemed harmless enough. The reminder of Emma's presence would probably be a mood killer.

"Fort, definitely."

He grabbed his laptop from the kitchen table and dove on top of the pillows on the floor, pulling up one of the streaming services while I settled in beside him. Tilting the screen toward me, he offered a loopy smile as I realized he only pulled up vampire and supernatural titles.

"So, what would you, having no real interest or expertise in the subject, pick out of these as the most realistic movie? Obviously, I'm talking in complete hypotheticals and am only asking you because maybe you have seen some of these and have a preference?"

I wasn't totally amused, but I was glad he picked up on the unspoken rule, so I answered honestly.

"Well, I don't think it's necessarily one in particular that stands out as realistic because ninety percent of the depictions are laughably unrealistic, but there are bits and pieces of each that I enjoy."

He unsuccessfully tried to stifle a yawn. "Seeing as you totally left me hanging on our Health project, maybe you could give me a list with some pointers to make up for it."

"Maybe," I deflected.

"Mina," he said, his tone serious. "I have a lot of questions that are going to need to be answered."

I rolled over as close as I could without touching him. "Someday."

"Promise?"

Avoiding his unrelenting stare, I brushed his hair back off his forehead, gently dragging my fingers through the ends. When he closed his eyes, I noticed the dark circles beneath them.

"Are you tired?" I asked, pulling one of the blankets up to his chest.

"I don't want to be," he admitted before finally succumbing to a full, long yawn.

"What is it like?"

"To be this exhausted?"

I smiled sadly. "To sleep," I clarified.

"It's peaceful," he explained in a deep, dreamy voice. "Like how when you close your eyes and everything's black, only you slip deeper and deeper into it until your body gives in and your mind eases into a different existence."

"That sounds... magnificent."

He yawned again and pulled me closer. I relaxed, as best as I could, against the crook of his neck. The first movie on the list auto-played, and he tried to focus on it. I watched him fight the droop of his eyes. By the time the opening credits ended, he was breathing heavily.

"Charlie?" I whispered, and he didn't stir.

Accepting that he succumbed to unconsciousness, I closed the screen and slipped out.

It didn't matter how nice his mother was or how much Charlie said she liked me, I was willing to bet she wouldn't be happy if she came home from work to find a teenage girl in her son's fort. I locked all the doors and escaped through the window in the guest bedroom, where a tree with thick branches grew close enough to the house to help me down.

23

I drove to the mansion with all the windows down, needing a jolt of cold air to help me decompress.

Spending time with Charlie, with any human, was much easier now than it was three months ago, but I couldn't help but wonder when, if ever, I would feel completely at ease.

I arrived home to a strangely silent mansion, with no sounds or smells of others in the house, and mulled over all the complications while I poured some blood into a mug. Begrudgingly, I found out that Theo was right about AB-negative being the best. I considered, with no small amount of guilt, what type of blood pumped through Charlie's veins, and as I really thought about it, I cringed.

Charlie had such a wonderfully normal, human life, with so much opportunity and possibility ahead of him, and I knew I had the ability to destroy it all. I wasn't even sure I liked being a vampire, yet here I was, potentially forcing a human into becoming one.

As I trudged up the stairs, I vowed I would do everything in my power, as a vampire and heir to the region, to protect him and his humanity at all costs.

I took comfort in that promise, and I felt one hundred pounds lighter as I pushed open the door to the room I claimed as my own. Uncle Derrick happily gave me the space. The room was nearly double the size of Charlie's, but it felt empty. I frowned at the oversized velvet couch perched in the middle of the room, considering what a bed would look like in its place. I flipped the switch to ignite the fireplace.

Taking a sip of blood, I began to mentally redecorate the space, picturing how I could cover a wall with artwork and maybe even pictures of the city. I didn't have any sports memorabilia, but perhaps I could find an equivalent that matched my taste.

The front door opened, and I perked up, trying to discern the vampire from his or her gait.

"Mina?" Theo called, ruining my guessing game.

"Up here," I yelled back. "In my room."

In a flash, he collapsed on the couch next to me with a thud, taking my mug from my hands for a sip.

"AB-negative," he noted, swirling the contents before draining most of the liquid.

"Where is everyone?" I asked. "I came back ten minutes ago, and the house was empty."

"They're all off chasing a lead about the explosion." He noticed when I rolled my eyes. "Some digging into recent shipments revealed that one of the southern vampire clans recently imported a large quantity of trinitrotoluene."

I nodded, pretending to know what that was.

He glanced at me sideways. "No one told you?"

I shook my head.

"Interesting," he said, handing the mug back to me.

"Why is that interesting?"

"Trying to protect someone by taking away their choice isn't really protecting them, is it? It's pure deception buried in good intentions."

"You know sometimes it's a little scary how poetic you can be."

"I take that as a compliment."

"Is that why you aren't with them?" I asked a little suspiciously. "Because they told you to stay behind?"

"No, I had a choice."

I stretched my legs out toward the fire, enjoying the warm sensation that worked its way up my legs. "Then why are you here?"

His face was amused. "Is that your very blunt way of trying to get rid of me?"

"Nope." I was glad I didn't come across as too eager.

He shifted forward, putting his elbows on his knees. I took in his side profile, his lips pressed together, the sharp lines of his cheekbone and jaw accentuated by the flickering light.

Vampires were self-assured creatures, claiming to need no one and nothing, not even their maker, aside from blood. I supposed those character traits made sense to prove a toughness or some sort of self-righteous bullshit, and it was the reason I immediately distrusted Theo when I first met him, but something was different about him, and I was just seeing it.

His expression looked almost human.

Maybe I picked up on it because it still hadn't been that long since Theo turned, and I grasped onto humanity with both fists, but we both seemed to share a tangible sense of longing, making us kindred spirits. I considered the possibility that he felt as alone and lost as I did.

After all, he willingly sat in an industrial freezer and tried to shield me from Cara, which counted for something.

"Theo," I said, and the way I said his name was almost a confession of guilt. "I just want you to know that I was wrong about you from the very beginning. I judged you too quickly and too harshly when all you have tried to do is help me."

He rewarded my honesty with a look of unfiltered tenderness. "I know."

The heat of the fire began to spread throughout the room, and for the first time all night, I relaxed. I tucked my legs up and leaned my head against the high back cushion.

I genuinely enjoyed being with Theo, and it wasn't because he was the only friend I had where I didn't have to actively fight the urge to sink my teeth into his skin. I was glad he stayed behind and came to see me.

"So what did you do tonight?" I asked. "Any new vampire hangouts with catchy names I should know about?"

A smile tugged at the corner of his mouth, but he shook his head. "Philip sent me over to Eva's to beg for her help on the explosion, even though I already told him that there was nothing she could do. She's a witch, not a detective."

"He knows about her?"

"Not that we're related, just that we know each other from when I was human. But she was in the middle of lecturing me about not overstepping in asking for her help, among other things, when Trinity called to say that they were rushing off to the Southeast and if I wanted to come, I had about ten minutes to get back to the mansion."

"You could have made it if you drove as fast as you usually do," I teased.

"I could have, but as Trinity was filling me in, I just watched Eva interact with customers, chatting about their wants and needs before exchanging money and going on about their simple, human lives." He stopped and traced the handle on my mug, needing a second before he continued. "I realized that I missed it, you know, the little things about being human, and suddenly, everything about being a vampire was so heavy."

I smiled in understanding. "I get it."

"I figured you would," he said. "Which is why I told them that I would rather stay behind to make sure that you're okay."

"So you used me for a little empathy?" I pretended to be gravely offended.

He smirked. "That's one way to put it."

I asked him questions about Eva, about how painful it was to be turned, and what he was working on with Philip. He was very curious about human school and how I managed to keep it together, only slightly mocking me as I told him about the chocolate bar and the state Uncle Derrick found me in after that first day.

We talked long past sunrise, the conversation easy and flowing for hours, interrupted by two chess matches, which I won, and a blood break.

When noon hit, I texted Trinity, asking for an update.

It's taking us longer than expected to track them.

I frowned at my phone, wondering if Uncle Derrick would start showing symptoms again without my regular interference with the potion. Theo flicked the back of it.

"Did you hear what I said?"

"No." I showed him what Trinity texted.

"Well, I need to go run an errand for Eva anyway," Theo said. "Want to come?"

"Yes, with one caveat."

He raised an eyebrow.

"I'll drive."

Theo groaned but obliged me. As a consolation prize, I let him pick the music for the drive down to the Strip District, a cute area near the heart of downtown.

The light, chilly rain deterred the weekend crowds, which meant I could actually explore and enjoy the area instead of watching from afar. We strolled through almost every antique shop, clothing boutique, and food wholesaler, taking in the pungent smells of cheese, fish, wood, and metal.

Theo stopped abruptly in front of one of the old abandoned warehouses that hadn't yet been converted into something modern and industrial chic. "Wait out here for me, would you?"

I blinked, and he rapped on the big steel door, discreetly showing off his fangs through the window before someone allowed him inside. He was too quick for me to ask him what was inside, and when Theo returned, I would question him about it and about the other places where he needed proof-of-vampirism to enter.

"Mina?" Eloise's voice shrieked from the other side of the street.

I jogged over, and she offered me a quick hug and shelter from the sprinkles under her yellow umbrella.

"I thought you'd be hiding out at home or at the soccer game. If I knew you were available for Saturday shopping, I would have forced you along weeks ago."

"My parents offered me a brief reprieve," I lied. "But probably not the best idea to sit with hundreds of people on metal bleachers for two hours."

She wrinkled her nose. "Who wants to do that anyway?"

"What did you get?" I asked, nodding toward the bags in her hand.

"Some vegetables and pepperoni, and my mom wanted me to get her some weird perfume thing." She noticed I was empty handed. "What are you—" She stopped. "Wait," she said, and the tone of her voice dropped slightly as she glanced over my shoulder. "Look at the guy behind you, Mina. Wait, no, don't look. Well, look but don't."

The metal door rolled closed with a final screech, and I had one guess as to who she was checking out.

"He's coming over here," Eloise said with excitement.

She handed me the umbrella so she could smooth her hair.

"Mina, are you ready?" Theo asked, tucking a thick envelope inside his coat.

Eloise's eyes flashed. "You know him?"

"Theo, this is Eloise," I introduced. "Eloise, this is Theo."

My two worlds collided as Eloise smiled widely and stuck out her hand. "Nice to meet you, Theo."

He shook her hand, and his jaw ticked. "Warm," he muttered. I took that as his code for being surprised that I was talking so closely to a human.

"Not for long," I said, collecting big, fat raindrops in my open palm.

"I was just thinking of stopping somewhere for a late lunch," Eloise beamed. "Do you two want to join?"

"Ah, I wish," Theo said, managing to pull off a look of anguish. "But Mina and I have to get back to her uncle's."

"Oh, so you're one of her cousins?"

"Definitely not." He said it with such seriousness that he implied that it would be problematic if we were related.

"Eloise, if you're heading home, I can drop you off on the way," I offered.

"That would be great, actually. I haven't even checked when the next bus is getting here."

As we walked to my car, Eloise drilled him about what work he did for my uncle and how long we'd known each other. He stretched the truth easily enough, and although he indulged her, he kept glancing over at me, needing silent confirmation that he wasn't making a misstep.

We stopped at a crosswalk, and I tried to see Theo objectively from Eloise's eyes. All vampires were alluring. I speculated that something happened in the turning process to make them more appealing with evolution and the food chain and all that. Even outside of that, Theo was handsome in a brutally upfront way.

The lines of his face were sharp, and his eyes had such a

constant intensity that sometimes even made me feel a little powerless. Eloise seemed immune to his severity, though, easily driving the conversation without seeming intimidated.

Theo placed his hand on the small of my back, nudging me across the street. The motion did not go unnoticed by Eloise, but she kept up the chatter through the short drive to drop her off. When I pulled up to the front of her house, she insisted I walk her to the door even though a full-on rainstorm had started.

Once under the small cover of her front porch, she didn't waste any time. "Spill," she demanded.

"There's nothing to spill, Eloise."

There was no way Theo was missing this conversation, so I needed to play it coy.

"So you won't have a problem if I walk right back over and ask him out?"

She moved as if she was going to, and I jolted, making her stop and smile. I told myself I reacted that way because I wanted to protect her from a vampire.

"He's gorgeous... but Charlie." She ran her hand through her hair in exasperation. "You're my friend, Mina, but he is, too. Has he met Theo? Does he know who you're spending time with?"

I chewed on my bottom lip.

"That's what I thought."

She unlocked the front door in jerky movements, her anger evident. Still, she brought me in for a final hug.

"I miss you, but please don't make me hate you."

I held my breath and returned it fully, wishing I could open up and explain everything to her. Instead, I nodded, and she pulled back, closing the door after she entered the house.

After I was certain I was out of her line of sight, I sprinted to the car, shaking off all the droplets before I hopped into the driver's side. It was past midday, but the sky was a dark gray, releasing heavy rain in waves against my windshield. I refused to look at Theo.

"What's in the envelope?" I asked, taking control of the conversation before he could.

He pulled it from his jacket and opened the clip, revealing a bunch of green leaves and small, red fruits.

"What is that?" I coughed. "And why does it smell like that?"

He resealed it and stuffed it back into his pocket. "It's barberry."

"Never heard of it. Is it illegal by human standards?"

"In some states, but not ours. It's just difficult to come by, so Eva had me track down a supplier. She needs it for the werewolves, apparently."

If they had barberry, a rare plant, what else was in that huge building? "I'm guessing that's not all they grow in that warehouse."

"And you would be correct." He stopped me before I could ask my next question. "And trust me, you don't want to know what else is growing in there."

That only made me more curious, but a streak of lightning lit up the sky, distracting me as I drove. Theo counted under his breath until a jolt of thunder sounded.

"Eleven," he whispered.

I turned off the music. "Eleven?"

"When I was a child, my mom said if you count

between the lightning and the thunder and divide by five, that's how many miles away the lightning struck."

"Why would you need to know that?"

"I don't know. I don't even know if it's accurate, but it's just something I've always done."

He cracked the window, and the sweet smell of the fresh, wet air rolled in. The wind whipped through the space, filling my ears with nothing else until I zipped up the driveway toward my uncle's house.

I turned off the car, conscious that Theo hadn't moved even a fraction of an inch in minutes. Lightning struck, followed by a roar of thunder, creating a sense of foreboding that even I couldn't ignore. I knew what was coming, but I wasn't sure how to react when it did.

Theo rubbed his hand on his dark, designer jeans. "Eloise, she said... do you have a human boyfriend, Mina?"

That directness to him was such a vampire trait, and it wasn't that I wanted every conversation to be the muddled, stammering one of humans, but in this case, I would have preferred tiptoeing. But that could have been true for everything I experienced lately, always trying to pull the best out of each world, crafting my own little idyllic state, and just because I wanted it that way, didn't mean it was right or even possible.

"It's complicated," I said, falling back again on an excuse that was shorthand for "I don't want to talk about it."

"Complicated," he repeated, a little bitterly. "I think I can keep up if you explain it, Mina."

I sighed. "I'm just... torn."

"Between what?"

"The two halves of myself."

"So?" Theo challenged.

"That's my explanation."

"It's a terrible one."

"But you kept up with it, apparently."

"I'm waiting for you to elaborate."

"I just feel like I'm swaying between two different worlds, both of which I don't completely belong in."

"Who cares about that?"

"I do," I said, getting very frustrated.

"Well you shouldn't."

I scoffed. "Theo, you asked me to open up and explain, and I'm trying to, but you're being such a vampire."

"I'm not just being a vampire, Mina, I'm trying to help."

Charlie was my most tangible connection to the human side of myself, all messy and warm, and I clung to it. How could I even begin to explain it to Theo, someone who got to experience two decades of human life completely before everything changed for him.

Before I could even try, he jumped out of the car and took off, sprinting at full speed across the front lawn. I took off after him, raindrops pelting me as I increased my speed. He, like all full vampires, was faster than me. He veered through the trees, running down the path that wrapped around the property, and I struggled to keep up with him.

He slowed as he reached the clearing. When I caught up, he was standing in the middle of the gap in the trees with his arms extended.

"What are you doing?" I was three feet away, but I still had to yell over the sound of the storm.

"Look up."

I did, briefly, not amused by this endeavor. I stared at him expectantly, and he stepped toward me, spreading muddy water all over my feet.

"Mina, don't fight it anymore. Let go of who or what you should be, what category that falls in or whose expectations you have to live up to. It's all bullshit anyway, so just give it up and move on."

I took a deep, therapeutic breath.

The sky unleashed the harshest rainfall yet, and still, I looked upward. The clouds didn't care if I stood under them or huddled away inside. In minutes, I was completely soaked through my clothes and hair, but I didn't feel sticky or weighed down. I felt cleansed, like I was given a fresh start.

Perspective, it changed everything.

Theo witnessed the change within me, watching patiently as my vision cleared.

My body demanded something more, something tangible to cement this feeling, this moment, inside of me. I stepped toward him, and he stared at me expectantly, with his arms hanging loosely by his side, as if he was the vulnerable one in this situation.

"Don't fight it," I said, for him or for me, I wasn't sure.

I closed the gap between us, wrapping my arms around his neck, and pulled him in for a kiss that was so electrifying, I should have counted in my head to see when the thunder would strike.

He slid one hand around my waist and wrenched the other in my hair, moving to deepen the movements that made me feel alive all the way down to my toes. I felt everything, and I didn't want to stop. We moved together, equally desperate for the other's touch.

The rhythm of urgency continued. His hands slid down, and gripping the backs of my legs, he pulled me upward. I wrapped my legs around his waist and rolled against him. He trailed kisses down my neck, and I dropped my head back, soaking it all in and feeling unrestrained, even in his arms.

I could have stayed like this for hours, drowning in him completely, and that realization jolted me back to reality. I caught his lips again, deliberately slowing the pace, and he opened his eyes.

Untangling my limbs from his, I dropped back down to the ground. I brought my fingertips to my lips and lingered longer than I should have, staring at his stunned expression.

I used Charlie to feel human, and I thought I used Theo to feel more like a vampire, but the truth was, Theo only encouraged me to feel more… me.

For the first time in my existence, I didn't merely bridge the two worlds, I stood proudly on top of both of them, with everything at my feet. There couldn't be any other excuses or inner combativeness about my identity or where I belonged.

It was time to stop fighting and start living on my own terms.

"I'm sorry," I said hoarsely. "But I have to go."

"Mina, please don't."

Theo held my wrist, but I wrenched out of his hold. I ran away and couldn't bring myself to look back.

24

I had to talk to Charlie.

Mentally calculating the time it took to play a soccer game, take a bus ride home, and drive from school, I figured he'd been home for about an hour by the time I arrived. The house was dark when I pulled up, and I groaned, realizing it was one of the Saturdays he was required to be at his dad's.

As I sped over to the duplex, my apprehension increased. I didn't want to have this conversation with Charlie, and I wanted even less to do with anything involving his father, who had his lawyers drop off an official letter of intent to sue my uncle a few days ago.

I breathed a sigh of relief when Charlie's car was outside. I knocked on the front door, expecting him to greet me with a sly smile and flick of his hair, but Daniel opened the door.

"Mina," he said with slight irritation.

"Hi, Mr. Schenley," I returned the greeting politely. "Is Charlie around?"

"He's not back from his game yet."

I turned back to look at his car.

"His mother drove him over," he explained, following my line of sight. "But why don't you come in and wait?"

"Oh, no, that's fine, I'll—"

"I insist."

Not wanting to be rude, and hoping that Charlie would indeed be home soon, I followed him in, standing awkwardly in the doorway until he waved me into the room he used as a makeshift office. I sat down in one of the hard wooden chairs, and I eyed his computer, wondering if I could lure him into unlocking it so that I could make note of his password.

"I've been hoping to talk to you, one on one, as it were."

I stayed silent.

"You're aware that I've been trying to get in touch with your uncle for a while now, and our paper has officially taken more severe steps, as I indicated the first time we met?" He didn't give me time to answer. "I know his people are going to drag this out for as long as possible just to drive up legal fees and hope that we drop this, but you see, your uncle is interfering with justice and truth here, and I have the public court of opinion at the tip of my pen."

His eyes narrowed.

"From what Charlie tells me, you've dropped out of high school with the intention of going to work for your uncle."

"I will get my GED, but yes, that is the plan," I confirmed.

"What a shame, Mina. You're a smart girl, I can tell, but getting mixed up with his kind… it's not right."

"Excuse me?"

He flipped open his briefcase, rifling through some papers. He licked his thumb, which repulsed me, as he flipped the pages. Without another word, he handed me what appeared to be the draft of a story, leaving me alone to read through it as he brewed a fresh pot of coffee in the kitchen.

I skimmed through it quickly, waiting for the big reveal on exposing vampires, but I didn't catch that word anywhere on the pages, so I started back at the top.

The first part of the article discussed my uncle's various business investments over the years, and in the past decade or so, he began to invest heavily in health care and medical manufacturing, winning government grants for research on artificial blood, citing a worldwide shortage of AB-negative blood and a desire to supplement blood banks.

While reporting on a completely unrelated political story, *Gazette* journalists found a suspicious amount of money donated to a number of key elected officials, including a senator that Uncle Derrick introduced to me while we were taking meetings around the region. They were building a case to connect the dots of corruption and monopolizing the blood market.

Some parts of the story were a little out there, but most of it seemed to be accurate.

I felt so relieved that this was all the story was that I nearly laughed, but when I set the paper down, Daniel was sipping his coffee and looking at me with a gleam in his eyes.

"Break up with my son, or I'll run that story," he demanded. "It'll ruin your uncle, and you'll have no shot at picking up the pieces of whatever you want in the future. Your name will be dragged down as his business is opened to criminal investigations, not to mention the people who will distance themselves from him. I wouldn't be surprised if he went bankrupt."

He was either really desperate for a story or some sort of validation that all that work was going to come to something.

"So you're resorting to blackmailing a teenager?" I asked as calmly as I could, which infuriated him.

He sputtered angrily as the small black speaker on his desk came to life. The voice cut through the static, rattling off a collection of numbers I didn't recognize in between words such as "murder" and "disappearing girls."

With no regard to my presence, Daniel punched in the address on his phone and ran out, heading to the scene announced over the police scanner. I followed him outside, closing the door behind me, and hopped in my car, speeding to the scene of the crime.

TV crews beat Daniel there, and he was on the phone, yelling at some poor photographer who got the directions mixed up, and he rushed to report the story.

I followed him closely, although he seemed to forget that I existed, listening to the questions he asked get ignored, while he attempted to capture the scene on his phone without the flash on.

We weren't too far from Eloise's house and the Strip

District, a realization that terrified me as they began to bring out the body bags. I lost count after a dozen and overheard a police officer tell the television reporter that all the women were drained of blood, some had visible bruising, and one appeared to be about four months pregnant when she died. Their bodies had deteriorated for weeks until someone stumbled across them.

I leaned up against one of the ambulances, staying well behind the caution tape, and spent about an hour watching detectives, medical teams, and, finally, humans from the coroner's office arrive.

The idea of what someone was doing to those girls made me a little dizzy, but nothing made me want to jump out of my own skin more than when they rolled out the first body on a cart. Even with the thick material of the bag and all of the human scents covering the scene, I breathed in the familiar scent of vampire and withheld a scream.

The rain stopped by the time I made it back to the mansion.

My clothes were waterlogged and filthy, but I couldn't bring myself to change. Anything that would bring me comfort was not deserved at this point. I crossed into the library before I collapsed on the floor, trying to reconcile what I discovered at that crime scene.

I was aware that Theo stood over me, his face contorted with concern, but his voice was muffled, and I didn't even try to decipher what he was saying. He lifted me up to one of the chairs in front of the fire, tracking down a blanket in one of the many closets and wrapping me in it after he removed my shoes.

He brought a cup to my lips to get me to drink blood,

but it was the only thing that brought about a reaction. I threw the mug and its contents in the fire, disgusted by everything to do with vampires.

Theo made phone call after phone call, trying to explain my state of existence to whoever was on the other end, but they were running around the region, too distracted to hear about what was happening within twenty miles of our own homes.

It could have been twelve hours or twelve days until they returned. I was too numb to keep track of time, the only indication of its passing was the increasing pain and need for blood. My fangs failed to retract, the result of my bloodlust, and my eyes felt like they were on fire, but I still refused to drink.

"Why are you doing this to yourself, Mina?" Theo demanded, taking my graying hands into his.

I closed my eyes and sat back, burrowing into the blanket. When I opened them again, it was to Uncle Derrick's face.

"Did you call the witch?" Philip asked Theo.

"I even convinced her to come here," he explained. "She said there is nothing physically wrong with her."

Uncle Derrick leaned even closer to me and inhaled. "Mina, what's wrong?"

I sat up, hearing the other vampires walk through the entryway into the house. The voices and scents were mostly familiar, but there was one that reignited my rage. With each step they took toward the library, the more violently I shook.

The combination of blood withdrawal and pure anger gave me an adrenaline boost, and I tore across the room.

My body moved, fueled by my own fury, and I clawed at the material at my father's chest before I wrenched my nails into his neck, choking him as hard as I could. The actions wouldn't cause him pain, but I hoped it would leave a lasting impression of my feelings toward him.

I wasn't as strong as him, or any vampire, who wrenched us apart. Theo's arms locked around my hips, working in tandem with my uncle to pull me away. I thrashed violently, but I couldn't break the hold.

"What is the meaning of this, Mina?" Uncle Derrick demanded.

My father stood tall, composed, as my mother's wide eyes flipped between us.

"Tell them," I spat.

"Tell them what?"

His voice was calm, but mine was sharpened by ferocity.

"The girls," I cried. "The human girls."

"I don't know what you're talking about."

"Was it you?" Uncle Derrick asked.

He stepped forward, squaring off with my father, whose expression was unreadable. Some of the nobles shifted to block the door, Trinity, Philip, and, surprisingly, Thomas included.

I screamed in frustration before my energy depleted, and I crumpled against Theo, who held me upright. My mother, taking in my raggedy appearance, closed her eyes and brought her hands to her face. She backed up against the wall behind her, and Uncle Derrick stepped between my mother and my father.

"Marie," Uncle Derrick urged. "Do you know something?"

One look at her normally composed expression, and I knew she was about to fall apart. "I… suspected something. All the new scents, blamed on new ventures and contacts at the blood donation and…" she trailed off.

"The human police said one of them was four months pregnant," I said, as strong as I could manage, and my mother looked horrified.

"Max, now's the time to speak to your defense."

My father raised his chin.

Uncle Derrick motioned to Philip, who disappeared, leaving us all standing in silent, palpable tension, but he returned quickly, lugging coils of heavy metal chains.

"My grandmother bewitched those," Theo said low in my ear. "I watched her do it when she was alive."

My mother shook in disbelief as she watched Philip and Thomas wrap my father up, securing the metal tightly so that he couldn't break through it. They started to drag him away, to somewhere in the basement I assumed.

It was selfish of me, but I couldn't let him leave without answers.

"Why?" I yelled, standing up out of Theo's grasp.

I was strong enough for this, to stand on my own and hear the truth.

"Why would you prey on humans? For fun? Did you enjoy assaulting them? Did you ignore their screams as you drained them? How could you do this, knowing that I am—"

"An abomination?" He was so level-headed, the perfect vampire that he and Uncle Derrick always wanted me to be.

"How could you not accept me for who I am, half-human, when you accepted my mother before she turned?"

"I did no such thing. I wanted to turn her immediately, but she became pregnant, saying she'd accept a human death if I attempted to turn her before you were born. I couldn't allow that to happen. From the moment you were brought into this world, I've been finding a way to correct it, to make you whole."

"You forced yourself on the women to get them pregnant," Uncle Derrick speculated. "To test out turning the children, if they survived."

"I've been patient for nearly a decade with our research and transfusion lab, but as you began to aggressively groom my daughter to take the crown, I had to act more quickly. I couldn't stand to be ruled by a lesser being."

"So you began conducting experiments of your own?"

"The girls were not satisfactory, at first, all whining and crying all of the time. I had to get rid of them. It was a little sloppier than I preferred, but I found others who seemed more promising."

Derrick nodded, trying to keep my father talking. "Did you have any successes?"

"The woman who managed to carry a child the longest, I was able to, in utero, turn the child. I wanted to do further research on the mother's blood to see if there was anything different with her compared to the others..."

He stopped, realizing he was speaking as his stream of consciousness played out in his head.

"And then what?" Uncle Derrick pressed.

"I'm so sorry, Derrick," my father said. "I am genuinely devastated by how this turned out for you."

"What happened?"

For the first time, my father looked remorseful. "I

collected a sample before our regular meeting, so I stored her samples in your freezer, needing to keep the blood fresh until I could bring them to the lab. They were marked with a special orange label."

Trinity gasped. "Oh," she cried.

"Yes. You mistakenly gave the blood to Derrick."

"I'm not following," Uncle Derrick said.

"The fetus died hours before I drew the blood from the mother."

Uncle Derrick brought his hands to the middle of his chest. "Dead blood."

The nobles gasped, breaking the composure they maintained as this played out. Uncle Derrick tried to reassure them and began filling them in on the research, successful testing, and symptoms.

I, on the other hand, had a singular goal.

Uncle Derrick taught me many things over the years. Some would be useful, others I could disregard. But one recent lesson, after meeting with some of his contacts in the region, was that sometimes, it's the off-hand comments and silent insinuations that provide the most meaningful insight in a conversation.

When Evaline thought I wanted to kill my uncle, she mentioned something offhand.

"I've learned to bewitch magical objects that can turn a vampire into a corpse with enough force, but to give a vampire a true death… is not something I have done myself."

Theo accidentally confirmed that the chain, which buzzed with thick air that was a similar consistency to the lavender scent in Evaline's shop, was what she referenced.

I was about to use that knowledge to my advantage.

While the vampires in the room were trying to reconcile their new reality and the potential true death of the King, I pounced. I gripped the metal, which hissed and burned against my skin, and wrapped it around my father's neck as many times as I could.

Philip hadn't utilized the full effect of the chain, with most of the metal hitting my father's clothing, but the direct contact of his skin began to finish what I had started earlier.

My father gasped, his fangs visible, and I kept going, fighting off the vampires who attempted to stop me.

Suddenly, a heavy blur hit my stomach. The force caused me to let go of the chain as I flew backward. I expected to smack against the ground and braced for it, but I continued moving. I sped through the room, down the hallway, and out one of the open windows and into the night air.

Uncle Derrick held me tightly as we drifted upward. The huge house shrunk in size the higher we went, and I gave in. I pressed my face against his chest, knowing exactly what this action meant.

Sensing my relent, he slowed us to a hover, and I was grateful we were under the cover of darkness.

"You're flying," I murmured.

He smiled sadly. "I can feel the surge, burning through the rest of my existence. It's like nothing I have experienced before. I think I have you to thank for it."

"How?"

"Whatever you have been putting in my blood eased my symptoms enough to recognize what was happening. Otherwise, I think my final death would have come on suddenly, giving me no time to get everything in order and appreciate these feelings and abilities."

His words nearly broke me in half. "I don't want you to die."

"And I want you to live, Mina, but only one of these things is in our control."

"I don't think I can do it any longer," I said. "The blood… not after this."

He pressed me tighter against his chest, and I gripped his clothing, trying to cement the feeling into my memory. I felt weak without drinking blood for… I wasn't sure how long, but the thought of it repulsed me, as if succumbing to my needs as a vampire betrayed humanity as a whole.

"In your life, you're going to make millions of choices," Uncle Derrick started. "You will have the power to do what's right, to change the priorities and way of life for an entire species if you want, but you're going to need blood to do that. You can't let one person's mistakes have a hold on you like that, even if he is responsible for giving you life, Mina. You can't control his actions, but you can control the way you respond and how you make changes to ensure nothing like this ever happens again."

He slowly lowered us to the ground, on the very spot where Theo and I kissed, where I accepted who I was and vowed to not fight anymore, dropping the back and forth of tearing myself in half. I leaned into that resolve and renewed my sense of purpose.

My father's actions were despicable, and he needed to be dealt with, but Uncle Derrick was right. I couldn't punish myself for his mistakes and misguided beliefs. I need to do better than that, than him, for all of the vampires and humans I would soon be responsible for in our region.

Uncle Derrick still held me in his arms as he tore up the front lawn, but when we approached the front doors, he helped me stand on my own two feet.

25

Logistically speaking, it made sense to tie the funeral and coronation together.

Vampires didn't usually have funerals, even for the King or Queen, but I insisted. It was one of the things I negotiated with Uncle Derrick before he died. We had just under a month together to make preparations, formally redact the blood ritual, transfer business titles, and prepare for what was ahead.

Thousands of vampires gathered on the expansive lawn to watch my long, slow walk up the driveway in a black gown that Uncle Derrick selected for me. I remembered most of the faces from the ritual, but there were many other vampires taking stock of me as I moved toward the house. Uncle Derrick's sleek, black casket sat center on a small platform in the ballroom, and the sight of it renewed my confidence under the scrutiny.

I'd relocated my father, still chained, and my mother to one of my uncle's other properties for the time being. He didn't outright violate anything in the Code of Conduct; although, he did rouse suspicion of our kind and accidentally poison the King, and the realization of that disgusted me. I swore to amend it, and to do so, I needed a majority ruling from the six other royals — four queens and two kings — to execute my plan.

With no consort or family, I asked Trinity to stand by my side as the royals circled us, reciting lines regarding honor, duty, and responsibility that were first written in the 1700s by the founders of the regions. An orchestra played music as a small group of nobles entered the room. Each vampire had a hand on the pillow that held Uncle Derrick's crown.

I stood up a fraction straighter when I set my eyes on it. Uncle Derrick modified it without my knowing. When he wore it, it was a simple headpiece accented with diamonds, but now, it was completely covered in jewels, with large, red tear-drop rubies jutting off the top.

Trinity winked at me as I turned and kneeled on the cushion, facing outward at the crowd of vampires.

The royals and nobles stepped closer, and as the music hit a crescendo, Trinity placed the crown on top of my head.

As planned, when the music slowed to a stop, I stood with my chin held high.

"To the Queen, in life and in death," Trinity beamed.

Every vampire on the property said it. The sound echoed in my ears, with one voice standing out among them. I craned my neck as the vampires broke out into cheers and celebration, with glasses of blood flowing freely, and locked eyes with Theo.

Isabella, the Queen of the Mid-Atlantic, caught my attention first.

"Mina, you're a vision." Her voice was pure velvet, matching her dark red gown.

"I could say the same for you, Isabella."

Her crown was ostentatious, more like an extravagant work of art than a small symbol of status and power. Uncle Derrick was quite fond of her, and they had a very amicable business relationship that crossed between regions, so I gave her the benefit of the doubt.

"It is wonderful to finally meet you," I added.

"I wish it were under different circumstances," she said, and I was surprised to hear the sadness in her voice. "But I heard so much about you from your uncle and have to admit I have been eager to meet you. I assume he prepared you on what to expect with the other... personalities?"

I nodded. According to Uncle Derrick, Isabella was my top ally and would back my plans without hesitation, but the other vampires would need some convincing.

"Well, then let me get you formally introduced. But be mindful that as you were walking up here in all of your radiance, the Queen of Cascadia and the Queen of Plains renewed their decades-long argument over territory."

"Really?" I balked.

"Apparently they both want Idaho."

She introduced me to Quinn and Mary, of the Cascadia and Plains regions respectively, and seeing I was holding my own, went off to rally the others. We all surrounded the coffin and spoke comfortably enough. They seemed intrigued by my existence and wanted to know more about my human side.

I indulged a few questions but eventually interrupted Isaiah, the King of the Southwest, who was in the middle of a long spiel about the time he tried to do human drugs as a newly turned vampire.

"Excuse me, Isaiah," I interjected politely as Trinity motioned for me to join her. "I need to step out for a moment."

He nodded. "Not to worry. You will be joining us later, of course?"

"Possibly," I said, not wanting to make any promises I couldn't keep. "But I am looking forward to reconvening tomorrow at noon."

"Yes," Isabella agreed. "We have much to discuss. I believe my secretary sent over a list of the cumulative talking points to everyone?"

The other royals murmured in agreement.

"There are two things I wanted to add." I placed my hand on Uncle Derrick's casket as Isabella called her secretary over to officially make note of it. "An addition to the Code on how to handle vampire-on-human harm."

"I have long thought a declaration of that nature in the Code was necessary," Isaiah agreed. "Perhaps I can contribute the draft of what I previously have written up on the subject?"

"I would be grateful for it," I said, and I meant it.

"What is the second agenda item you would like to add, your majesty?" Isabella's secretary asked me.

I paused, making sure I had everyone's attention. "We need to discuss when, notice I say when, not if, we will reveal ourselves to humans. A true unveiling of our kind."

Another tactic I learned from Uncle Derrick was to

inform and then back off temporarily. It was why he tended to give vampires time between their wrongdoings and the monthly meetings to digest his words, acknowledge their mistakes, educate themselves, and make amends. It prevented vampires from reacting violently out of instinct, perpetuating this ideal state of levelheadedness.

Each royal held still, squaring up with my gaze, and I didn't dare to move as the words settled between us.

"Is it added to the record?" Isabella asked her secretary.

She finished typing and nodded in confirmation.

"Good." Isabella turned to the vampire at her right. "Now, Isaiah, what were you saying about those human drugs?"

I stepped away from the conversation, silently sending my gratitude to Isabella. She eyed me as I retreated toward Trinity.

"I'll report back to you," Trinity said into her earpiece.

She ended the call and turned to face me.

"What is it, Trinity?"

"There's a human waiting for you at the front gate," Trinity explained with a little bit of trepidation in her voice. "The attendant wouldn't let him in, and for his own safety reasons, I would encourage you to persuade him to leave as soon as possible."

I tried to make my way through the crowd but quickly aborted that direction, as many vampires called for my attention. I slipped out a side door, sprinted down the hallways, and out toward the front gate, avoiding as many vampires as I could.

They would likely mill around the mansion until after midnight, which was when I arranged for Trinity to cut off the blood supply. Uncle Derrick warned me that he learned the hard way how quickly a party can turn into a weeklong binge.

"Mina," Charlie yelled, gripping the bars of the gate. "I've been trying to get in."

I waved off the attendant and stepped up, making no move to remove the barrier between us. How we stood, close but with a temporarily divided line, felt poetic, but it also reminded me of that first soccer game I attended.

Charlie's forehead creased when I crossed my arms across my chest, and his eyes raked over my appearance, lingering on the crown.

"What are you doing here, Charlie?"

"I, uh, wanted to see you," he sputtered. "Make sure you're okay."

"I am." I hated the formality of my own tone, but it was better for him if I didn't soften toward any illusions he might have for us.

He swallowed loudly. "You completely disappeared after that night at my house. At first, I was really mad at you for it, especially when Eloise said that she saw you and you seemed fine, and that gutted me because I was not fine. We'd only known each other for a short time, but I felt like we were starting something real."

Charlie adjusted his collar upward then shoved his hands in his pockets.

"I went through cycles of resenting you and missing you desperately, but I couldn't bring myself to hate you. It wasn't until a few days ago that I was in my dad's office when I stumbled across the research he did on your uncle. When I confronted him, he copped to everything. At least, I hope it was everything, but even if it wasn't, I now understand why you disappeared after he threatened you."

I could see the air from his lungs expelling from his mouth as he talked.

"When I called one of the numbers my dad had on file, the receptionist told me the news that your uncle passed away after a late-stage cancer diagnosis. Mina, I'm so sorry for your loss. I wish I could have been there for you, but now I understand everything and we can move past it."

He sounded so hopeful toward the end, as if him getting the news that his father was abrasive toward me solved everything.

I pulled back and adjusted my crown, not quite used to the weight and feel of it yet.

"That's not it, Charlie."

"What's not?"

"I haven't been distancing myself because of your father and my uncle."

"Is it because of..." He gestured to my crown.

"Partly," I admitted.

"You promised me in the fort you would explain everything to me," Charlie reminded me. "I am ready for it. Explain how you—"

"Charlie," I said, slowly drawing out the syllables of his name. "You might think you are ready for it, but I can assure you that you are not. More importantly, I am not. I very much enjoyed our time together, but we will not be spending time together for the foreseeable future."

He stepped back, seeing me in a new light. "So that's it?" Charlie was bitter, an emotion I never expected to see in him.

To his credit, he didn't argue with me, but he didn't appear to truly accept what I was saying. I appreciated his attempt at self-preservation, something I was very familiar with.

"I brought you this." He handed over the morning edition of the *Gazette* through the fence, and I grasped it in my hands. "My dad deleted all of his research on your uncle and the drafts of the story. Even the back-ups. I checked."

The front page had various photos of my uncle and a polite eulogy. I was mentioned as his next of kin and heir to his fortune, but other than that, it was pretty cut-and-dry. Still, I appreciated the gesture.

"Thank you for this, Charlie. And for everything else."

Charlie helped me in ways that he likely would never truly understand, and I hoped someday, in the not-so-distant future, I could uphold that promise I made to him in the fort.

A few weeks ago, the thought of giving Charlie up devastated me. I wanted to cling to him and his humanity, taking everything I could from him. I was willing to leech off his humanity, but opening myself up to him, to my world, would set a future for him that he hadn't even begun to understand.

Ironically, it was Theo who once tried to steer me away from that thinking. "Trying to protect someone by taking away their choice isn't really protecting them, is it? It's pure deception buried in good intentions," he said to me that night in my room.

At the time, I shrugged it off, but now, it took on another meaning entirely.

My entire existence had been sheltered, with my future

set as soundly as the crown on my head, but instead of forcing my hand and taking away my choice, my uncle encouraged me. He gave me the leeway to explore both sides of myself, and in turn, I realized that I didn't belong with vampires or humans — I belonged to myself, in a category of my own. I was better for it.

"Oh, and Mina?" Charlie called for my attention one final time as I made my way back to the celebration. "I got an A on our Health project."

I offered Charlie a smile, and he returned it. Not with one of his full Charlie grins, but it was better than nothing.

Once out of his sight, I brought the paper to my nose, inhaling the remnants of Charlie's scent. I unfolded it, looking at more pictures of Uncle Derrick over the years until a headline toward the bottom caught my eye.

"'Investigators Rule Convention Center Fire Accidental,'" I read aloud to myself, and as I continued into the first few paragraphs, I actually managed to chuckle.

The building had just undergone major renovations and updates. Apparently, one of the contractors missed rewiring the section of the building because he thought another was responsible for it. Inspectors missed it during their rounds of checks because it had already been sealed with new drywall. Our event was the first time that particular space had been used, and the decaying wires and supporting hardware exploded.

It was pure human error.

I tucked the paper under my arm and walked up the driveway to the mansion, my home, and pushed away the frustration of how much needless time and energy was spent on something that didn't need to be solved. I needed to focus on what I could influence and positively change, imagining a different future for myself, for the vampires, and for humans.

There was one simple thing I could do to take a step toward changing things in my own life. I unlocked my phone and typed a message to Eloise.

Eloise, I am formally inviting you to a sleepover (just you and me) at my house next weekend. Are you free? I walked slowly around the outside, waiting for her to respond.

What, I'm not good enough for a ridiculously stupid but pretty printed invitation?

I smiled. *Why waste money on that when we could spend it on chocolate?*

What time are you picking me up on Saturday?

There was a lot I had to do before then. Aside from making instrumental changes among vampires, I needed to work with Trinity to furnish and decorate the mansion. I hoped Eloise was the first of many humans who would spend time with me at my home, and I wanted to create a welcoming atmosphere to encourage unity.

As snow began to fall outside, I moved back indoors to play the role of a gracious Queen. A number of vampires were still wary of me, most of them came right out and said it, but they trusted Uncle Derrick implicitly and hoped that I would build positively on the Byron legacy. I would certainly try.

When the sky turned completely black and the snow began to stick to the ground, the vampires left in droves. After final goodbyes and reassurances from Trinity that I was relieved of my duties for the evening, I went upstairs to my room. I placed the crown on the newly fashioned vanity, one of the many pieces of furniture I had Trinity begin to fill the rooms with, before I slipped out of my dress and into the holey jeans that Uncle Derrick hated and a soft, long-sleeved shirt.

Feeling a little jittery from the hours of conversation and greetings, I skipped down the stairs with the intention of shooting back some AB-negative, but I gasped at the bare room. The cleaners Trinity hired already cleaned, swept, mopped, and bleached.

Uncle Derrick's coffin was gone, lifted right off the pedestal.

I slipped on a pair of boots and dashed outside, following Theo's scent to the clearing. It seemed like a lifetime ago that we kissed in the rain. I exhaled, my breath visible in the moonlight, until I saw the outline of his form.

He fought against the frozen ground, carving out a grave by hand with a shovel. The thoughtfulness of the gesture made me want to burst with emotion, but I stayed calm as I approached.

I was certain that he heard me trudge through the snow, but he stayed on task, determined to lay my uncle to rest, as I should have thought to do earlier.

While he dug deeper, I traced the smooth, dark wood that housed my uncle's body. The final part of our negotiation was, on his insistence, that I didn't dwell on his death. He was adamant that once his soul, or whatever vampires were dealt, left his body, everything good about him existed within me.

If it was possible for me to cry, I think I would have at that moment.

Theo finished and watched me, waiting for me to collect my thoughts.

I stepped back, curious as to how the two of us could lower the coffin into the grave. Even with our combined strength, it would be an odd angle. There was a reason humans used a machine and belts for this.

He jumped out of the ground, tossing the shovel aside, and just as I was about to open my mouth, he began to mutter in the same language and intonation that Evaline used. I marveled as the snow swirled up around us.

The spiral started within the entirety of the clearing before it folded in on itself, gently brushing snowflakes across my cheek, carrying the coffin to its eternal resting place in the ground. Next, the dirt Theo unpacked moments before reversed course and poured on top of the coffin until the hole no longer existed.

It wasn't lost on me that he could have used his magic from the beginning, but he wanted to feel the dirt and motion of his own strength, to grieve my uncle's passing in his own way, which made me adore Theo even more than I thought possible.

I jumped across the fresh dirt, right into his arms. His body enveloped mine as the snow fell around us. He held me like that, his hands firmly gripping my waist and back as the flakes layered on and around us.

"Should I have called you 'your majesty' and bowed when you approached?"

My nose pressed against his neck, which vibrated as he spoke.

"Please don't ever do that," I said, well aware that he

would have to in a public setting. "At least when we're alone."

"Deal."

I moved toward home and extended my hand. He grabbed it, pulling me back toward him as he began to mutter the words I now associated with witches and spellwork.

The wind picked up around us, swirling the snow in a tornado-like fashion before it came together and transformed into a bouquet of white roses. It landed gently on top of the dirt, marking the grave, and I hummed in appreciation at the gesture.

Before we stepped forward together, into the future and all of its possibilities, he snapped his fingers, transforming the petals into the most beautiful shade of metallic red.

AUTHOR NOTE

This book came together at a very strange time. Personal turbulence aside, as COVID-19 grew into a global pandemic and the consequences of systemic racism became even more apparent, I felt lucky to occasionally retreat into vampires, love, and self-discovery.

It is a privilege to be able to write for a living, and while I'm very grateful (seriously, you're the best! THANK YOU!) you have given time and money to support me, I hope you will also consider what you can do to help make our world a better place for everyone.

Please donate to your local food banks and organizations such as Black Lives Matter, the NAACP Legal Defense Fund, and the ACLU; call out racism, bigotry, homophobia, and misogyny when you see it; support minority-owned businesses; and sign as many petitions as you can to bring about the much-needed change we need in our communities.

Young Adult Romances

Everywhere, Always

Just Play Pretend

Only You in Everything

Perfect Little Flaws

The Extended Summer of Anna and Jeremy

The Stillness Before the Start

Adult Romances

In the Now

Nothing Personal for Breakfast

This Is Your Life

Young at Midnight

"The Islands of Anarchy" Series

New Wave

Rip Current

"The Royally Human Vampire" Series

Metallic Red

Yes, Your Majesty

FREE GIFT FOR YOU!

Want to make your book an autographed copy? Head over to Jennifer's website and get a free bookplate!

https://www.jenniferannshore.com/bookplate

CONNECT WITH JENNIFER

Hi there,

I cannot thank you enough for reading my work. Truly, it means the world to me!

I'd love to connect with you on social media if you're up for it. I'm on all the major social channels, including TikTok (@jenniferannshore) and Instagram (@shorely).

And don't forget to subscribe to my email newsletter (jenniferannshore.com/newsletter) for bonus scenes, new release announcements, giveaways, and more.

All my love! —Jennifer

ACKNOWLEDGMENTS

I'm so thankful for all the love and support from friends, family, readers, other authors, and bloggers who believe in the stories I tell. Your reviews, text messages, phone calls, etc., mean everything to me.

Taylor Starek, my editor and dear friend, who loved Mina as much as I did even before she was a fully formed protagonist. Thank you for your patience, smarts, and kindness, even when you're dealing with an entirely undercooked plot line.

Kelly Lipovich, the genius behind the cover who has been supportive of my fascination with vampires for almost a decade. Thank you for your brilliance and for letting me put those fake fang marks on your arm in college.

Lindsay Hallowell, I'm so grateful for your attention to detail and wizardry in catching those pesky misused commas. (And I'm dropping this in after you proofread, so if there are any typos here, it's all on me!)

A few friends have been dealing with my musings such as "hey, I think I'm going to write a VAMPIRE book next!!" from the start: Kilroy and Frank, who have been incredible best friends and supporters. Christine, who doubles as a savior for my sanity and a huge advocate for my work. Juliette, who makes me cackle and keeps me honest.

My family, thank you for being my biggest cheerleaders from the very beginning! I love you all so very much.

And lastly, but most importantly, to my husband, Grant. Thank you for helping me make this dream a reality. I love you.

ABOUT THE AUTHOR

Jennifer Ann Shore is an award-winning, bestselling author based in Seattle, Washington.

She writes romance stories that go a little deeper than the standard tropes. Her lineup of more than a dozen books includes standalones, a dystopian series, and a vampire series—with titles such as "Perfect Little Flaws," "Young at Midnight," and "Metallic Red."

Prior to publishing, she led an impressive career in New York, first as a journalist and then as a marketing executive, gaining recognition for her work from companies such as Hearst and SIIA.

Be sure to sign up for her newsletter on her website (https://www.jenniferannshore.com) and follow her on Twitter (@JenniferAShore), Instagram (@shorely), and TikTok (@jenniferannshore).